THE SILENCE

THE SILENCE

BARRY K. BRICKEY

To order additional copies of this book, contact:
Xlibris Corporation
1-888-795-4274
www.Xlibris.com
Orders@Xlibris.com
51522

Acknowledgements

Thank you to my family, my parents, my friends, and my band members for giving me the support, love and encouragement to finish this novel. It has been a very long journey, one that I couldn't imagine completing without all of their help and understanding.

The basis for this story began several years ago, during my early teens, when I would visit my friend's speculated haunted house. There were many unexplained paranormal occurrences that happened there, and these incidents later fueled my desire to create *The Silence*.

Special thanks to the following individuals for contributing to make this book a reality: Jon Lamb, Misty Braden, Karie Hammack, Norma Brickey, Rich Richards, Ida Baker McClarin, Penny Baker, Clem Winland, Holly Winland, Karen Almendra, Lynnel Landerito, Susan Noguera, Tim Dillon, Lynn, my Monroe Community College Writing Center savior, and Dean Koontz for his inspiration!

This book is dedicated to the memory of my mother, Helen Caroline Stein Staschke, and my faithful watchdog, Sassy.

Chapter 1

THE AWAKENING

The chilling sound of the scream sent shivers down his spine. Although the noise was distant, it was intense enough to pinpoint.

He found himself on a stairwell looking down into the dimly lit basement. The rails of the stairway were rotted and frail, the wooden steps dried out and decayed.

A second scream pierced the silence, this time becoming more recognizable. From afar, the sound had an innocent resemblance to a trapped animal, but he knew there was more to it; his imagination would not rationalize that simple theory.

A hideous creature lurking below in the depths of the shadows made a lot more sense. After all, don't all monsters dwell in gloomy, damp confinements, waiting to pull young children underground to be mauled, ripped apart, and then eaten?

Once again the voice cried out, shaking him out of the trance.

It was time. The only way to satisfy his curiosity would be to walk down the stairs to look fear in the face. Yes, sir. Demon or no demon, this was not a time for the weak at heart.

As he made his way down the old stairs, a creaking board noisily announced his presence—like a firecracker set off during church mass.

A small light emanated from the bottom of the stairs. The air was damp and cold; a musty scent penetrated his senses, like the rotted smell of an animal decaying on the side of the road.

Holding his breath and creeping forward like a cat, he came upon a doorway covered by a white, translucent curtain—a curtain that concealed light from behind it, but also provided a glimpse of what awaited inside the small furnace room. It was here his fate awaited.

The room appeared to be empty and harmless. The only objects in the area were a furnace, some shelving, and a four-foot circular brick wishing well. Drawing the curtain back, he entered the room. The pungent odor grew stronger and was clearly coming from inside the well.

He stood there frozen, contemplating his next move. He wanted to run. He wanted to close his eyes and tell whatever lurked deep in the well to go away. He wanted to believe that his imagination had once again gotten the best of him. He was just a young boy. And boys always had over-active imaginations; so he was told on several occasions.

Was it a demon: some kind of blood-thirsting beast? Or was it possibly just a poor animal that had fallen in there by mistake and injured itself.

It had to be the latter. No monsters exist. No monsters live in this well.

He was going to look and prove himself right.

The eyes of the thing staring back up were completely white and bulging, as if focusing so intensely they would explode. Its head was deformed: large, bumpy and misshapen upon the top and gaunt and sunken around the sides. A few strands of white hairs dangled from the top of its head and down around the sides of its ears. A menacing grimace revealed stubs of decayed yellow teeth.

The thing looked half-human and half-devil as it stretched and sliced its claws through the air in a feeble effort to try and pull the boy inside.

Looking down at this horrific thing just about cut off the air in his throat. Nauseated, he stumbled back awkwardly, afraid to relinquish his gaze from the beast.

He tried to cry, scream out—for God's sake anything! There were only gulps of dead air.

The thing began whimpering in anguished pain. With every stab through the air it attempted, a muffled murmur arose as it tried to speak a translatable word.

The boy began to shake violently, and knew that if he stayed put another second it would surely get to him and kill him. Quickly spinning around, about to run, he turned face-to-face with another creature. It was lightning fast and leapt upon the startled boy, knocking him backward over the rim's edge and down to the beast waiting in the well.

Chapter 2

The heavy sound of thunder jolted Kelly Adkins from deep sleep. Though he was awake and alert, the impact of the vivid dream left his heart racing and his mind in complete shock.

His forehead glistened with sweat and his clothes were damp with perspiration. Quickly wiping away sweat from his brow, he darted his eyes back and forth from his mother and sister to ensure that his nightmare went by undetected inside of the car.

Kelly wasn't afraid of his mother sensing his fear; it was more the fact that the dream was the fourth in a week's time. He told her of the first, but decided to bottle up the others. Her reasoning for the vivid dream was that the move out of state affected his emotions about their old home in Coral Springs, Florida. It would take some time to resolve his feelings about leaving old friends and the house—whatever that meant. She always talked about things that his ten-year-old mind couldn't understand. He would just smile, nod his head in agreement, and go about his way.

Raindrops splattered against the passenger window.

Kelly tried to imagine what type of things he would encounter when they finally got to the new town. *Would he find somebody like Andy, his best friend of ten years?*

Andy was the best. No one could catch snakes or hit a baseball like Andy could. No way. Not like Andy could, not ever!

Susan Adkins stared hazily out at the deserted highway; deserted, just as her life was now. She was a thirty-six year old mother of two, driving up-country to try and rectify her life. Rectify it or run from it—she wasn't sure which. She had always gotten into shitty situations and needed the help of others to bail her ass out.

Pregnant by age twenty, she was forced into marrying John Adkins, a guy she hardly knew except for a couple of dull dates at a movie theater and a few romps in the back seat of a Mustang.

She wasn't sorry that she had gotten pregnant with Samantha—God no! Sam was a blessing upon her miserable life. The girl gave her purpose and focus. A chance to mature.

The first year of marriage went well. They were both young, and the baby brought on a challenge both welcomed. John seemed to beam with pride, showcasing his new wife and baby girl. But, as time wore on, he spent more and more hours at the office.

Working as an advertising salesman, he succumbed to the pressure of deadlines. At home, he drank excessively and became abusive.

He was a cruel bastard, both physically and mentally—sharp with a tongue as well as strong with a fist.

In their sixth year of marriage, things turned very bleak. Susan believed the only way to salvage their marriage was to have another child.

Having Kelly brightened up the relationship, but it was too little, too late. John's rendezvous with a young secretary in his office put the final stake through Susan's heart; after sixteen years of prison, her shackles were finally removed. Her brother, Richard, a doctor at a hospital in Caseville, Michigan, persuaded her to move away and pursue a job in nursing. It was something she dreamed of: a chance to control her own life and destiny once again.

Just outside Caseville, as early morning traffic approached, Susan pulled off an exit ramp and headed for a diner.

The blue Chevy Blazer turned left onto a deserted, paved road called Elkwood. Giant oak trees stood lean and tall, expressing a serene backdrop. The area was quiet and deserted. A town gas station and a local party store stood kitty-corner to one another. About a hundred yards down the road, a small cafe displayed a sign: "COUNTRY KITCHEN" above it.

Susan pulled the Blazer into the entrance. The only companionship the cafe parking lot had to offer was a Ford Tempo, an old, rusted Dodge pickup truck, and a Harley Davidson street bike. This suited Susan fine—the least amount of distraction the better.

Kelly was the first to race out of the car. No sooner did Susan turn off the ignition key than the boy was out of sight.

Samantha slowly got out of the vehicle; her long, slender frame stiff from travel. Though she was sixteen years of age, her features had already begun to develop. She had smooth complexion and skin that was golden brown from extensive tanning. Her lips were full and broad, covering a perfect set of aligned, white teeth. Body development came at an early age for her, with a sudden growth spurt to a towering height of five-foot-nine and ample breast increase during her first teen year.

Stretching her arms into the air, she took in the scenery of the deserted lot and primped her straight, shoulder length, jet-black hair. The long trip had gotten the best of her nerves. They had driven straight through, only to stop for fast food or emergency bathroom breaks.

God, she thought. *If I have to spend another minute in the car with that kid, I'm gonna' scream.*

Turning towards her mom, she squinted her face as though swallowing a prune. "This place is nasty! Why can't we just stop at a fast-food joint or something?"

"Sam, I'm getting tired of driving all night long. I wanna sit down and get a cup of coffee, clear my head, and enjoy a good meal, okay? We're almost there. Another twenty minutes or so, I'd say, and we should be into Caseville."

"Mom! Come get a look at this bike!" Kelly hollered, sitting on top of the Harley, admiring every detail.

Susan walked over to the bike and pulled the young boy off.

"Kelly, you can't just jump on some stranger's bike!"

"Do you think it belongs to some gang man?" he asked excitedly.

"Yeah, and he's gonna come out here and wrap a chain around your ankles and drag you around in circles through the parking lot if he catches you on his bike," Samantha chirped.

"Please, Sam. Don't tell him stories like that. He already has enough trouble sleeping. Let's go in and get some grub, guys," she suggested, flashing a disgusted look to her daughter.

The decor of the inside exactly reflected the title of the establishment. Intimate small, round, wooden tables with checkered orange and white tablecloths upon them occupied the center of the room; side booths systematically aligned against the wall catered to larger groups or families. A flower in a vase, four menus, and an ashtray were the only objects upon them. A hand-painted wooden Amish village adorned the front bay window ledge. Three large ceiling fans rotated and hummed noisily, but the room was still exceedingly warm.

A tall, slender man wearing a John Deere hat sat at the counter by the register. His face was drawn and tired, the result of an all-nighter at the local bar. He wore a dusty leather jacket, with Levi jeans and black cowboy boots.

Noticing the doorbell jingle as the front door opened, he turned toward them briefly, then returned his gaze ahead.

They made their way over to a corner table by the window and sat down. The view of the car allowed Susan to keep a close eye on the family's possessions.

Besides the occasional clanging of a spoon stirring a coffee cup, the room was silent.

Susan stared at the man; then, remembering the story Sam had concocted for Kelly, wondered how he would really react to the situation. *Violently? Would he be able to control his drunken temper, or would he be a deranged man with a short fuse?*

Once again, she was letting her imagination run wild, afraid something was going to naturally go wrong. *Not all men are drunken, abusive assholes,* she assured herself.

A middle aged woman appeared with a pad and pencil. "How you folks doing this mornin'? Out kinda early traveling?"

"Yeah, we just left Florida. We're headed for Caseville."

"Well, you're not too far off. You should love it there. Neighbors are really friendly, and it's always quiet."

"Is that guy in a motorcycle gang?" Kelly asked.

"No, hon. That's ol' Skeeter. He's just a normal outcast. Don't worry about him, he's harmless. Have you all decided what you want yet?"

Kelly decided on scrambled eggs, bacon, toast and a glass of chocolate milk.

Samantha wasn't much of a breakfast eater, so she decided on a glass of Coke.

Susan was famished. After driving straight through for the last four hours, she had developed quite a large appetite.

She continued to mull over the menu.

"I'll take the morning sunrise." A breakfast consisting of two over-easy eggs, three strips of bacon and two pieces of toast.

"Would you like some coffee, ma'am?"

"Yes, please," Susan smiled.

The man at the counter continued to gaze forward.

"All right then. I'll be right back with your orders."

The waitress walked by four empty booths, an old man picking up his check, and a handsome man dressed casually in a black Detroit Hard Rock Cafe T-shirt and a pair of jeans.

His boyish face immediately caught Susan's attention: bright blue eyes, blond hair and a radiant smile, which he flashed as the waitress passed. Though his face looked like that of a clear complexioned young man, his strong physical appearance left no doubt that he was not a child.

The waitress walked up to the counter and exchanged a brief conversation with the drunken man, who shifted his head up to the smiling woman, mumbled, then looked back down to a plate of runny eggs.

"Kelly, how are you feeling? You okay?" Susan asked.

"Fine," he replied, looking down, playing with his silverware.

"Did you have another bad dream, sweetie?"

She was worried about him. He had told her of the bad dream a while back and it still concerned her. Though he had only referred to one dream, she believed there were probably more. He was constantly up during the night, whether to get a drink of water or just to watch television.

Probably doesn't want to worry me, she concluded. *But why on earth would I get worried? Isn't that what I'm here for? To confide to, fend off bad dreams and make chicken noodle soup when he's sick?*

"Did you have a nightmare in the car this morning? I noticed you were tossing and turning a lot. Did you see that bad thing again, baby?" she asked.

He had described it as some kind of terrible monster, a beast, or whatever the hell it was. All he kept calling it was: the "BAD thing."

How could a kid create such a hideous thing with his imagination? It couldn't have stemmed from television. She monitored his viewing carefully.

His imagination was very sharp and creative, though. He had a natural ability to create his own little fantasy world, either making up space aliens, or playing a warrior fighting against dragons and wizards. He was also an articulate child, teaching himself how to draw at an early age—the last few years learning the task quite well. It was his favorite thing to do. Other kids enjoyed playing outside or sports, but Kelly enjoyed sitting down with a pad of paper, drawing cartoon characters.

She watched the boy's expression as he sat next to her.

He continued to entwine his fork and knife. He was so small, frail, and helpless looking. It tore at her heart to see him keep his fear bottled up inside.

When the question was put forth, he slumped as if all the blood in his little body had been drained.

He hated the question. It made him feel nauseated. But he expected it. She always asked him how he felt and whether he was having any more bad dreams.

At first, he wanted to make up something, but his mind wasn't reacting fast enough, so he thought it would be best to just come out and tell it in all its gory detail. Besides, he was taught that lying was bad, and he hated getting into any kind of trouble.

He looked up to her, his blue eyes meeting hers.

"Mom, it's all right. I'm okay now. I know it can't hurt me. You said so. You told me to remember it's only a dream, and when I wake up, it'll be gone."

"That's right. Dreams are not real. Go ahead and tell me what you've seen, honey," she said reassuringly.

After Kelly told her every last detail, she wanted to cry, to reach out and hold his little hand and hug him. But she didn't want to alarm him. There was no need to make him feel uncomfortable and believe his mom was emotionally shaken. He needed to be reassured that it was a dream, and that things like that don't happen in real life.

She was worried about his fragile mind. *Could the divorce mentally affect him so badly that he was unable to sleep at night?*

The waitress walked around the corner of the counter with their orders; behind her, the man at the counter slowly turned around in his chair. His bloodshot eyes and five o'clock shadow made him look wickedly evil. Flashing a brief smile towards Susan, he nodded his head and turned back around.

Something about the man made her feel uneasy, his ominous presence. Something tragic was looming, and she didn't want to be in his vicinity if and when it did happen.

The waitress arrived with their orders and served them.

"If there's any thing else you folks need, just let me know. Enjoy."

The ceiling fan blades sputtered around and around. The aura of the stranger hung over them like a black cloud over an outdoor picnic.

Kelly doused his scrambled eggs in a sea of ketchup, while Samantha slowly stirred her straw inside the glass of Coke.

While they were finishing their meals, the strange man got up out of his chair and swayed over to the cash register.

Susan's back stiffened. Her mouth became dry. She sat motionless, watching and anticipating his next move.

Her fear heightened as he changed direction and walked toward their table.

*   *   *

Davis Conner had always been a cautious man. Not once did he stumble awkwardly into a situation that he thought he couldn't, or shouldn't, handle.

His father was stern and believed in running a household with an iron fist and keeping a tight ship. He was a cruel bastard, who loved tormenting Davis and his two

15

younger brothers daily, with Davis receiving most of his hatred and malicious venom. A relationship never developed between the two.

One night, after coming home drunk from a strip bar, Davis' father manhandled his wife and forced her to perform a lewd rendition of the Peacock Lounge's main attraction.

Davis recalled walking down those stairs that dreadful night. With big, blue eyes open in amazement, he stuttered, "Please, daddy, don't hurt momma."

With might and anger, his father backhanded Davis, striking him so hard that the blow lifted him off the ground and into a nightstand.

That night, his father left the house and never returned. Davis never received word from him again, not a phone call, letter, or even a message. Davis and his family were left alone to fend for themselves. For years he blamed himself, crying nightly, remembering his untimely arrival upon his father's sick perversion. He couldn't help but feel responsible for driving him away. But as he grew older, Davis realized that his father's demented obsessions had nothing to do with himself; the crazy man was a habitual alcoholic and abusing husband. In actuality, that night's event freed his mother from the hell that she had been continually living through. *It was a goddamn blessing the bastard left us,* Davis thought.

After that revelation, he challenged himself to always be there—for his mother, his brothers, or anyone else significant in his life. He would never leave a loved one abandoned like some poor forgotten sailboat in a maddening sea storm, tossed and torn apart, until the only things left to find were scattered broken pieces.

Sitting at the tiny booth of the Country Kitchen, Davis pushed his plate of eggs and hash browns forward, having lost his appetite. He watched as the intoxicated scum proceeded passed him.

The whiskey-stenched man marched forward towards the young woman and her two children as though his feet were two magnets planted upon steel.

Davis became more attentive.

The mother carefully attended to the youngest child's plate. Her silky, shiny blonde locks draped over her slender shoulders. Soft facial features and a pale complexion complemented her cat-like green eyes. A positive aura surrounded her face as she smiled and laughed, keeping up high spirits in front of the children.

Positive and happy, until now. Davis could tell she was unnerved as the stranger approached; she was threatened by the possibility of the drunk confronting her children.

Davis watched intensely as the man approached. He pictured the tiny boat spinning around in circles on the churning rapids.

Not this time, he thought. *Not again!*

The harsh, distilled smell of the whiskey-drenched man made Susan's stomach queasy. The vile smell of the bum repulsed her.

She kept her glance down and away from his, afraid any slight indication of approval would entice him to stay longer.

He stayed put. She felt him stay put. She could sense him standing there, smug face and all, looking over every inch of her, as if he could control and do any damn thing he pleased.

She trembled.

Finally, after what seemed to be an eternity, he spoke.

"Excuse me, darlin'. But I just couldn't help noticin' you eyein' me."

The voice was a deep, raspy, dry mumble. All of his first words seemed contorted into one long drawn out slur.

"You sure got some kinda pretty face, baby!"

She was disgusted.

"I think you and I should get on outta here and get to know one another better. How 'bout riding over to my house," he asked, oblivious to the two children seated in the booth.

She decided on trying a subtle approach, afraid any slight infraction would send him into a madman-like rage.

"I'm sorry, but my family and I just stopped in to get a quick breakfast after a long drive. Thanks any ways."

She was trembling inside now. She hated confrontations. She hated having to cower just to lighten a mood. Just like she had to with her ex-husband, John, when he became critical and violent towards her. She was always frightened by his sudden mood swings. He would just snap and start slapping the hell out of her for no reason.

Susan was not only worried that this nut might lash out at her, but she was worried for Kelly and Sam's safety. She didn't want him shifting attention towards them, dragging out a scene. The last thing these children needed was a rough transition into a new lifestyle. Great, the first day in their new town and some vagrant propositions their mother for quick sex!

Samantha sat quietly. She had all the confidence in the world that her mom would take care of the jerk. In Florida, there had been a man who had waited at a party store for her and her friends to walk by to and from school.

"Hey girls, you feel like doing a little partying? Feel like getting high with old Darryl?"

The girls had simply stuck their noses up into the air, walked on and ignored him. Later, when she got home, she told her mom of the man. Her mom quickly made a call to the local sheriff's office and explained to an officer of the guy's lewd conduct. The next day the strange man was gone. Some of Samantha's friends later mentioned that the man was a child molester, and that the police had dragged him off to jail. She didn't know if that was true, but she did know that after that day, she never saw or heard about him again.

Samantha looked up at the red-eyed drunk and thought to herself, "no problem, she'll get rid of this creep."

The creep looked at Susan; he was no longer smiling. Her excessive pleasant way of excusing herself from his company was actually her way of saying, *fuck you, asshole!* That harsh thought tasted bitter inside of his mouth.

She probably thinks she's better than me, he mulled. *That has to be it! This dirty bitch just doesn't know me yet. Hell, everyone likes me.*

He looked down at Samantha. "Hey sweetheart, why don't ya swing your pretty little rear over a little bit and let me have a seat next to you."

Stunned, she looked across at her mom for reinforcement.

"Listen, would you please leave us alone. We're just about ready to go," Susan replied sternly.

But the words flew past the man and he pushed his way next to Samantha.

"You ain't doing shit! I said let's get to know one another, damnit! We're all gonna get to know each other . . . real well," he said angrily through clenched teeth, slamming his fist down hard upon the table. "I'm not some piece of trash you can just laugh at. I know you think you're better than me! I'm not dirt!"

Susan's heart raced and her hands began to tremble. She felt weak in the knees and sick to the stomach.

God, why now? Here? Why can't I just get this son of a bitch to leave us alone?

Earlier, when the man was walking towards her table, their waitress had returned to the kitchen. Susan wondered if any of the staff would hear the commotion and stop the maniac.

He smiled sadistically and put his right arm upon the back of the booth.

"Now, why don't we ride down the road to my house and . . ."

"Excuse me, friend, but I believe the lady said no thanks. Do you understand the word no?" A man replied from behind.

The voice came like a lightning bolt out of the blue sky.

Susan hadn't even noticed the strange man approach.

Neither had the creep, who jumped, startled.

Quickly spinning around to face the mysterious voice, his eyes lit up, surprised to see a man half his size challenging his manhood.

Confidence beamed from Skeeter as he looked Davis over from head to toe.

"Friend! You ain't no fuckin' friend to me, half-pint!"

The veins in the drunk's neck bulged outward as he turned tomato red.

Davis knew that he had to act quickly, for the man was ready to fight, regardless of what talk was going on. The matter had to be taken care of as quietly and efficiently as possible.

The lanky man pulled himself up by the back of the booth and stood looking down on Davis, as if ready to pounce at any second. He stood mighty and intimidating at six-foot-four, compared to Davis' five-foot-ten frame.

Davis was a smaller man, but he was in excellent shape. He exercised and lifted weights regularly. Though his arms weren't huge, the muscles were well defined. He developed a washboard stomach from extensive sit-ups, running and swimming. He ran five miles every morning, and jogged at night. He believed a fit body made a sound mind.

Davis stood strong and tall, unwavering like a redwood tree daring a woodsman to chop it down with a minuscule cardboard ax.

18

He repeated, "I believe the lady doesn't want your company."

The tone of Davis' voice was direct and authoritative, and ate through the drunk's skin like acid on paper.

"I'm gonna break your nose. Break it wide open, so that little boy face of yours ain't so pretty. I'm gonna enjoy smashing you to pieces. You don't know who you're dealing with. I ought to . . ."

Davis struck quickly, thrusting his right fist up into the middle of the man's rib cage like a jackhammer into a concrete slab.

The creep doubled over with the fist still lodged firmly into his mid-section and let out a murmur of pain from under his breath.

Davis took a full step back.

The man rose up out of his crouched position. His face was pale and befuddled. Anger soon arose and he swung a wide roundhouse, hitting nothing but air.

The punch was a good six inches from Davis' head. The man's right arm crossed over to his left side, leaving himself tangled in an awkward, twisted position.

Davis wasted no time. Bloodshed was not appropriate in a restaurant, so he decided to go right back to the guy's ribs, while they remained open for the taking.

The second shot was a rapid jab thrown with quick velocity, ripping into the drunk's stomach like a cobra snapping forward on a helpless mouse.

The hit was direct. Crippled by the blow, Skeeter fell breathlessly down to his knees as the wind was taken out of his sail.

Davis never eased up. He snatched the creep by the collar and violently yanked him to his feet. Gripping his left hand around Skeeter's throat—to make sure he had his complete and undivided attention—and placing his right hand on the back of the guy's pants, Davis began dragging the drunk down the aisle, next to the gasping waitress who had just come out to witness the pandemonium, and towards the exit.

Reaching the front door, he slammed the man face first into the glass window of the wooden door. The glass pane rattled, jolting thunderous pain through the wincing man as his red face lay suctioned to it.

Davis pulled the man back slightly, just enough to grab the handle of the door. Once he had a tight enough grip on the doorknob and upon the drunk, he swung the door open and dragged the man with him out into the morning light.

As they traveled across the parking lot, gravel sprayed outward from Skeeter's heels until Davis shoved him hard into an old, beat-up red truck.

"A small bit of advice, Skeeter. Give me your truck keys, walk home and sleep it off. Don't even think about starting any more kind of shit. You'll thank me for it in the morning. I'll leave your keys with the waitress, and you can come back tomorrow and pick them up."

The man held his head down low. He didn't want to look up into the eyes of the man that had just beat the hell out of him. He felt as though he had been crushed in the ribs by a battering ram.

Leaning against his vehicle, Skeeter knew he was inferior to the smaller man. Whether it was a looming hangover or the realization he was overmatched, Skeeter nodded his head in agreement. The smart choice would be take the lumps and get out while he still could. Reaching into his coat pocket, he withdrew and unfastened his truck key and handed them over to Davis. Without another word, he turned and staggered off down the street towards the rising sun like a beaten, aging cowboy.

Davis watched for a few seconds, then headed back into the diner.

Walking away from the truck, a small voice in the back of his head warned, *don't turn your back to him. Don't give him another chance to strike.*

But to Davis the voice was just that—a voice, and nothing more. He walked on, dismissing the thought.

Susan sat anxiously waiting. She watched the front door nervously, expecting the worst. She felt guilty for what had happened, and wanted to run out and help the generous man who had just risked his own well-being to ensure their safety; she also knew the best thing to do was stay put and keep the children safe and calm.

Time ticked by, minute after minute. Her heart pounded with unbridled energy. Finally, Davis walked through the door unaccompanied, relieving Susan's anxiety. Jumping out of her seat, she met him halfway to the door.

He was unmarked, without an ounce of sweat upon his face.

He must have tossed the guy out without a struggle, she thought.

Susan showed a warm smile, but not out of happiness. It was a smile of comfort, relief and ease of a great burden.

He sensed how grateful she was. Her expression embarrassed him, yet flattered him.

She spoke first, but words evaded her a lot faster than she expected they would.

"I want to . . . thank you for everything. I didn't expect, I mean, I didn't know."

"Please, it's all right. There's no need to thank me. People like him just don't seem to have any kind of sense, you know. I just couldn't sit by and watch that guy disrespect you and your kids."

She looked into his eyes. They were bright blue like an ocean. They seemed to flow rhythmically and put her into a hypnotic trance. She felt her insides rolling with a harmony like a tide gently caressing the shoulders of a golden beach.

Those wonderful blue eyes. They seemed to take her to another place, a place safe and warm and peaceful.

"I don't know how I would have handled him. I don't handle confrontations very well. Especially the violent types. I guess I believed I could handle it, but deep down I was afraid and knew I couldn't. He came out of nowhere," she said disappointedly.

"You had every right to react the way you did. People can be unpredictable, especially people with drinking problems. But he's gone now, so don't let that bother you. I guess since you're okay, and there seems to be no more danger lurking around, introductions are in order."

She reddened in embarrassment.

"Davis Conner, ma'am . . . daylight bodyguard at your service," he said, folding his right arm across his stomach, bowing.

His good-natured demeanor charmed her and she laughed with delight.

"Susan Adkins, typical stranded damsel. Pleased to meet you."

Samantha and Kelly approached them to engage in the conversation.

Bright eyed, Kelly exclaimed, "That was cool! How did you do that? I mean, take care of that biker. He was one big, ugly dude."

Davis cracked a wide smile. "That! Oh, that was nothing. You should see me handle a pack of them together. The secret is to show no fear. Those big guys think they can scare us little guys. But you know, when it comes down to it, they're just chicken! Stand right up to them and a yellow line a mile long runs down their backs."

This new outlook obviously pleased Kelly. He quickly reached out his hand and smiled, "Kelly Adkins. Nice to meet you."

Noticing Davis' shift his gaze towards her, Samantha smiled shyly, "Hi, I'm Samantha."

"Davis Conner. Nice to meet you both."

Susan wanted to convey to Davis just how sorry she was for getting him involved. Her docile appearance made her feel vulnerable, and it sickened her. She wanted to let him know that she wasn't the frail daisy that had just shriveled before his very eyes. She wanted to be viewed as a bold, independent woman taking on the world and any other obstacles encountered, if it mattered.

"Samantha, would you please take your brother to the washroom before we leave?"

Samantha looked down at the boy. "Come on, squirt, let's clean up."

Holding his wrist, she pulled him to follow.

"Aw', man!" he protested.

The two scurried off down the aisle between the green padded booths.

Susan watched until she was sure that they were far enough away.

"I'd like to thank you again for your help, but I'm a little embarrassed by my behavior. For God's sake, I'm an adult, and adults are supposed to be composed and fearless, not frightened and intimidated like a child, right?"

"Wrong!" he snapped back, surprising her. He smiled, then began again, more calmly, "Listen, being cautious doesn't mean you're a weak person. It doesn't imply that you're a bad mother, inferior female, or any other crazy notion you've got. If being sensible and calm means that you're a frightened child, then the world could sure use a lot more of you."

"Crazy!" she said with a smirk on her face. "You think I'm crazy?"

"Well, crazy in a cute way."

His innocent expression was too much for her to take. She tried to keep a serious look, but a wide smile streaked across her face.

They stood for a few uninterrupted seconds, gazing into each other's eyes, until he finally broke the spell.

"So, I take it you're out-of-towners?"

"What makes you say that?" she asked quizzically.

"Well, from the children's responses and with their excitement over sitting in a small hick diner," he deduced. "And . . . I also noticed the out of state plates on your car and the luggage jammed inside it."

"Elementary, my dear Watson," she said, placing a thumb against her chin. "We're moving to Caseville from Florida. I bought an old farmhouse on Denton road. Know where that's at?"

"Yeah. I know exactly where that is. I've been down that road quite a few times. Don't panic when you go down that old road, though. It's kinda spooky, especially for someone that's never been down it before. I don't live too far from there, actually. I live just outside of Caseville," he informed her. "You know, Susan, I've lived in this area for a long time, so if you ever need any help, or want some advice, I would be more than happy to help out. It's always nice to have a friend to lean on when you move to a new town. If I give you my number, would you promise to call me?"

"Promise? I don't know if I can keep a promise, but I will give it plenty of thought," she responded.

"Good enough. Take what you can get, I always say."

The kids arrived back from the rest room, laughing about a funny plaque that was hung on the wall inside of the bathroom. It was a wood carving of a cowboy who was lying inside of a bathtub with his legs outstretched around the rim. His cowboy hat was tilted forward and covered his eyes, while his right hand held a bottle of beer.

They laughed out loud about the drunken cowboy, noting the resemblance to poor Skeeter, who probably went home and ended up in the same condition.

"I'll go get a pen to write with," Davis suggested.

Susan and the children walked up to the cash register and paid for their meal, while Davis scribbled his cell number onto the back of an old business card.

"All right, troops, let's head for the wagon," Susan announced.

"I'll walk you out to make sure there's no more trouble."

"Sure. You never know when that mean biker will come back around. He'll probably speed up on his road warrior and throw dirt all over us while doing doughnuts," she laughed.

Davis gave Susan his card, and handed the waitress a ten-dollar bill, motioning to her to keep the change.

Walking out into the parking lot, Susan was dumbfounded to find the Harley bike still sitting there. She was just about to ask Davis, when he walked over to the bike and climbed on, then called back, "I'll see you guys later. Us road warriors have a tough day ahead. You know, with the looting, pillaging and dirt throwing. Don't be afraid to call us, though. We're not *all* bad guys!" he laughed.

Susan smiled. *Not bad at all.*

Chapter 3

The Blazer pulled into the small town of Caseville around eight-thirty in the morning. The town was serene with the arrival of its newest guests.

Though it was the 11th of June, the temperature that morning was relatively cool at 63 degrees.

Caseville was located upon the top thumb area of its mitten-shaped state and a port to the Saginaw Bay shoreline, which was adjoined to Lake Huron, and cold climate changes struck randomly and often.

The day began as a glorious sunrise, electrifying the shimmering glass-like textured water as the sun's rays reflected from it. The mirror effect shone brightly for those who awoke early enough to see its wondrous display. Fishing boats rocked gently upon the docile water, as fishermen sat motionless awaiting the day's first bite.

As Kelly looked out upon the peaceful background, the sun's early rays, magnified through the vehicle's window, warmed his face. He closed his eyes for a brief moment, enjoying the cozy, soothing heat against his cheeks and forehead. It reminded him of back home on the days he was too sick to go to school. A favorite cure he discovered was lying next to the heating register, with the side of his torso close and a wool blanket wrapped around him as he awaited the oncoming heat; a pillow under his head was added for extra comfort—a private sauna, if you will. There he would stay through the morning, or until old TV reruns came on.

He opened his eyes and looked out to the boats on the lake. A slight grin came upon his face. Maybe this was going to be fun. This new town was turning out to be pretty cool indeed.

Two old, brick buildings passed by, one titled "CASEVILLE VIDEO" and the other, "PERRY'S PETS".

"All right!" Kelly shouted. "Mom, let's go get a dog. Can we? Huh? Huh?"

His silver dollar sized eyes revealed his excitement and longing for companionship.

"Honey, after we stop at the house, check out a few things, and unload some items, we'll come back and do some shopping."

Like a balloon pricked in mid-air, he responded solemnly, "Shopping? But what about a puppy?"

"Yes, honey, we'll get a puppy."

"Yes!" he exclaimed, pumping his small fist into the air.

Susan looked in her rearview mirror and saw his face gleaming. His smile put a quick grin across her face. He was happy. It was the first positive outburst she'd noticed from him since the divorce.

She figured they could pick up a dog after shopping at the furniture and grocery stores. She also had to transfer her bank account.

John, her ex-husband, was financially set, so she reasoned, why should she keep any of their old furniture when she could go out and purchase new ones—all on his credit! Plus, the change would enable her to shed old skin: create a fresh start.

The structure and diameter of the town was simplistic. The area stretched no more than seven miles wide and seven miles long, yet was crammed with businesses, such as the local hospital where her brother Richard worked; his specialty was dermatology. She planned on calling him as soon as they unpacked and checked out the town. Richard had suggested moving to Caseville, and he was the one who had spotted and recommended her house.

She chose to come to Michigan because she considered her brother the only true relative left in the family, and she felt the kids needed to spend more time with him.

The realtor promised to have the electricity and water turned on when they arrived, leaving only small details for her to mull over.

The Blazer drove upon the sleepy-eyed streets, passing so quietly and undetected it seemed as though they were visiting a ghost town.

One mile into Caseville, Susan turned down a dirt road that she had highlighted on the map, Denton.

Denton's narrow lane and rough terrain enshrined decades of haphazard travel. Sunken ridges of sculpted tracks led a curvy passageway that had been neglected by the road commission long ago.

A quarter of a mile down the road, a gloomy descent of darkness began to develop. Along the edges of the lane stood row after row of massive oak trees. Large, clustered branches stretched outward over the center of the road, fifteen feet above ground like long outstretched fingers overhead as vehicles passed beneath. The dense leaves shadowed the car and the road, leaving a hauntingly bleak feeling of suffocation upon the smothered travelers.

Finally, seeing daylight once again through the clearing of mass oak, Kelly exhaled in relief. The sudden dark scenery had come without a warning and terrified him immensely. It wasn't the darkness he feared, but what he thought lurked in the darkness. In his mind's eye, he swore he glanced something moving around in the shadows of the trees—some sort of glowing presence. It seemed dumb the more he thought about it, though. There was nothing there, only a tree. He was just being a scardy-cat, as usual.

They traveled around a sharp bend next to a field that had once harvested corn. The ruined and neglected land was evident by decaying stumps of corn stalks, weeds and dead trees.

Susan kept her eyes alert for houses along the way.

Her brother had mentioned a neighboring house two hundred yards across from the house she had purchased.

As she made her way slowly down the road, a small wooden single-storey house came into sight; it's puny diameter made for quaint and confining living for it's occupant. Three puffs of gray smoke wearily filtered out of a brick chimney stack into the clear blue sky.

Approaching closer, Samantha noticed a dirt driveway leading behind and around the house to a deteriorated wooden barn. She studied the barn carefully. It looked as though it had once been used to hold farm equipment, for around the immediate area were scattered remains of tools, parts, and a rusted plow and harness.

One of the barn doors swung open wobbly.

Her eyes fixated on what was about to descend from behind the wooden frame.

A tall, frail, old man shuffled his way from out of the dark confines of the barn and into the morning sun-lit yard, keeping his gaze to the ground.

She wasn't sure if the sun was blinding his vision, or if he was just too feeble to maneuver around.

After two brief steps, he glanced up to their passing car. His eyes seemed dazed, as though he was unbalanced. The wrinkly skin on his face was very dark from tan, a life as a farmer having taken its toll.

Samantha continued to watch him until his motionless gaze became a fragment in sight.

Sitting back into the vinyl seat, she stared forward as the vehicle rocked back and forth upon the trenched road.

"Ma, did you happen to see that old guy?"

Susan turned her head facing Samantha. "No. What guy?"

The girl held her tongue in check for a moment, then continued on.

"He was standing by the barn. Kind of creepy looking, you know. I mean not like he was some sort of perverted serial killer or lunatic. But sorta' just standing there like we were the first car that ever came across his road. He just stared at me with this, 'hello, I'm not with it' look."

"Well, honey, maybe he thought we're with the daily newspaper and that we finally came down his road to deliver. The poor man was probably heartbroken when we drove off past him."

In her best Jimmy Stewart impersonation, she mused, "I say, stop there, missy. Don't you go on by me like that. I've gotta keep up on the times, there, you see?"

The sudden voice of Jimmy Stewart floored Kelly, who was giggling with hysterics.

Samantha, on the other hand, took one look at her mother, then at her brother, and promptly rolled her eyes, "Sheesh, mother, really. Whatever."

The new house stood large and proud, with a look of warmth and comfort, but with an underlying hint of history and mystery to it, and rested on a steep embankment off the main road. A dirt driveway rose back sixty-feet, slanting upward at a thirty degree angle to the house, then evened out and ran alongside the two-storied home. The drive then circled a small island of grass with a healthy birch tree and descended back down to the road.

Behind the house was a small tool shed for garden and lawn supplies.

Its small wooden frame held little for the imagination.

The land that they owned was not meant for plantation, although a small section in back had been dug up to produce a harvest for vegetables, and a fenced in pasture was built for keeping horses.

Five acres of land belonged to them. It was quite a drastic switch from the small, three bedroom, one-storey house with neighbors so close you could hear them scrambling eggs in the morning. Now they were living large in the country.

Trees shadowed the front and sides of the house, shading it from the bright rays of the summer sun.

The recent caretakers had not been kind to the yard, though. The grass was en route to overflow the walls of the house. Surely knowing the sale was completed they could have taken the time to maintain it, Susan thought in disbelief. Oh well, just more items to pick up on the shopping spree.

Turning off the ignition to the car, she sat for a moment in silence.

This moment seemed like it could have never been a reality a year ago. It had seemed like just another farfetched pipe dream.

The air felt fresher. The sky seemed bluer. And the sun seemed brighter now than any period in her life.

She had waited such a long time to break away from despair and depression. Finally, here she was, sitting in the driver's seat to a new wonderful life with the ones she loved, and that meant the world to her.

Susan, Samantha and Kelly stepped out of the Blazer and stood in front of the red brick house. The windows were stained with dirt splatter and dust, and the front door was missing its screen. Minor details, but nonetheless, details that would have to be taken care of.

Standing to the right side of the house, Susan noticed two ground floor windows and two upper floor windows that were facing out at each end of the building.

At the very top left corner, facing the driveway, was a smaller window—the attic.

"Let's walk around and take a look," Susan said, moving through the thick grass around the corner of the house.

They looked up at the front entrance. The door was a massive wooden oddity out of some dungeon movie. Two small windows for viewing decorated the door like a pair of dragon nostrils.

Susan walked toward it and stepped upon a small concrete porch. Raising herself up on tiptoe, she peered through one of the small windows.

Darkness.

"What do you see, Mom? Anything in there?" Kelly inquired, squeezing his body between hers and the door.

"I don't see anything. Nothing. It's too dark inside to tell."

"Try and see if it's open," Samantha inquired.

"It's not going to be. It's supposed to be locked up. Mrs. Sheridan's waiting for me to call her to meet us here."

While the last words were leaving her lips, Kelly's aggressive hand reached for the doorknob. With a click the door opened.

"See, it's open. It's open," he shouted.

Jumping up onto the porch, Samantha pushed her nose to the crack of the door.

"Sweet. Let's go in and check it out."

Before Susan could object, both kids rocketed into the house.

With the front door fully open, the room was cast in large, looming shadows. They stood in the breezeway to the adjoining living room; the small walkway had barely enough room to hold Susan and the children. To the left was an open closet with hangers still hung upon a wooden beam. Above the beam was a shelf for blankets or storage.

Susan gazed around for a light switch.

A switch for the hall light was behind her next to the front door. She lifted the lever, turning on an overhead light that illuminated the large room in front of them.

All three stepped forward onto the cream carpeted living room. It was decent sized, bigger than the living room back in Florida, which could only occupy a couch, love seat and a small television.

The ceiling arched high at twelve feet, and the length ran twenty-three feet from end to end.

A door on the farthest wall was closed, and to the left, an archway opened to a smaller dining area.

"Home, guys. This is our home."

Kelly and Samantha took in the sight of their new domain.

Breathing deeply, then exhaling slowly, Samantha smiled. "Home."

Kelly seconded the notion. "Home sweet home."

Susan turned to their smiling faces. "Do you really like it, guys? I love it. It feels perfect. I think we're gonna be really happy here."

Kelly wrapped his small arms around her waist to reaffirm.

"I think it's great, mom!" he said.

"Why don't you kids go upstairs and pick out which room you want."

With that big decision in mind, Kelly raced ahead with his sister behind on his heels.

Both crashed together at an open doorway leading to the second floor.

Samantha flipped on the upstairs light, and they pushed each other back and forth climbing upward.

Susan could only shake her head, knowing the two would probably kill themselves fighting for the best bedroom.

She glanced toward the closed door. *This has to be the master bedroom,* she thought.

The coldness inside of the room numbed her blood when she walked inside.

She was standing in the middle of the large bedroom, shivering.

How could one room be so comfortably warm and this one be so opposite? Sure it was possible, with the door being closed. But this was beyond just chilly. She could see a mist of her breath upon the air.

Hugging herself, trying to keep warm, she broke down against the icy temperature and fled back out to the heated living room.

She reached the door and stopped abruptly.

She felt something, something tingling down her spine, creeping along her frame. It wasn't the cold; the cold had made her shake involuntarily. This was a creepy chill. Like a beast inside a forest stalking a helpless creature. *Nowhere to run. Nowhere to hide.*

Susan turned slowly to face the bedroom again. The frightened child inside of her began to manifest, afraid of what she might see, or worse yet, what she couldn't see.

Empty room. That's all, she insisted, *just a cold, empty room.*

*   *   *

Kelly peered out the window overlooking the road.

He daydreamed about playing in the yard when the winter brought its first snow. Snow was something new for him, something he looked forward to with the move up north. He had only encountered it once, and that was when he was six and the family had visited his uncle. Wonderful cold snow on his face, furious frenzied flakes dancing in mid-air and powdering to the ground, all great memories stored in his mind to play over and over again if he wanted to.

But now he would feel it again, see it again. He wouldn't have to use his imagination to enjoy it.

He chose the bedroom facing the road. He would spot anyone pulling into the driveway first, and that made him feel important. Besides, Sam wanted the larger room, and Sam always got what she wanted. He could try and put up a fight about it, but what good would it do? She had a great way with words and intimidation.

He lay down upon the thick, navy blue carpet, which comforted him with warm reception. He envisioned having a big party in his room with all of his new friends from school. They would thank him for having such a great time—the best they'd ever had. He had lots of great video and board games, and they could do really cool stuff—stuff that no one else had ever showed them. That put a wide grin upon his face.

Then he started thinking of home again, and the smile slowly faded into a frown as he started remembering his buddy, Andy. They were so close. It broke his heart knowing they would never see each other again.

Andy promised to call all the time, but that's something people always say when they're never going to see one another again. *Even if he did call, it's not the same as being here. Hearing someone and seeing someone are two totally different things.*

He felt alone again, like he always felt when he started thinking. Alone in a strange town—what could be worse?

After lying on the floor for a few minutes, he picked himself up, left the bedroom and wandered out to the hallway. The hallway connected to the library, which was stocked with an assortment of books and magazines. Everything from "Gulliver's Travels" to "National Geographic." At the farthest wall was a small door to a storage compartment. It was just large enough for storing small items, or for hiding small boys, he envisioned.

The storage chamber's wooden door was kept shut by a sliding metal latch to prevent it from drifting open. Across from the library was the bathroom, equipped with toilet, sink and bathtub. Above the small hallway landing was the attic; a rope dangled down from a wooden door hinged to the ceiling.

Kelly tried jumping for the rope aligned above his head, but crashed down to the floor with a dull thud, empty-handed. Discouraged, he attempted again, coming inches away from the snarled string.

Preparing for another lunge, he noticed how dead quiet it was in the house.

Unusual. *Normally, Sam would have screamed for him to stop jumping after his first attempt.*

He walked over to her bedroom. The room was lighted but empty.

She must have gone downstairs while I was looking out the window, he thought.

He left the room, passed the bathroom, and came to the edge of the stairway, where it descended down three steps to a small landing, curved around a bend, and continued down ten more steps into the kitchen and dining room.

About to go down the stairs, he noticed another small room to his right. He had been in such a rush to find his bedroom that he had passed it without noticing it.

Inside the small, narrow room, more books were situated upon shelves.

This previous owner must have been pretty smart, he thought.

Walking over to a small window, he placed one hand on the window ledge and the other on the bookshelf. Sticking his left toe into an open slot, he pulled himself up to look outside. The circular driveway appeared, with the Blazer underneath the large tree.

Leaves on the branches swayed slowly back and forth.

He decided to keep checking around the rest of the house.

He hated being alone with nobody around; it scared him half-to-death.

Jumping down onto his feet, he scampered out of the small room and hurried downstairs, refusing to look back up.

The lights were all on throughout the house. He could see clearly what he was doing. *Better that way. No one to sneak up on you.*

The living room was deserted, though.

He looked to the bedroom. From the angle he had, it appeared as if no one was in there. He was too scared to find out for himself.

"Mom?" he whispered quietly, almost afraid to hear a response. "Hello, anyone there?"

No response.

He turned back and went into the kitchen.

In front of him were a sink, stove, and a refrigerator—nothing else.

He walked to another open room at the back of the house. Peering inside, he noticed lots of windows. It was an enclosed porch. Long, but not very wide.

A door led out to the back yard.

Looking out the window, he could see the little yard shed, but none of his family.

He didn't like this room quite as much as the others. He didn't really understand why. Probably because he was displayed in front of the windows for whatever might be outside to see.

He went back into the kitchen and stood there waiting for any kind of sound.

There was a bathroom that adjoined from the kitchen. He looked inside and found it empty like the other rooms.

Now his heart was in panic. His brain was finally relaying a message, and the message was: "HELP!"

"Mom!" he cried out in terror. "Where are you!"

With that thunderous burst through the calm, he waited for an answer.

"Honey, down here in the basement. We're looking for fuses," she said reassuringly.

His heart eased back into its rhythmic beat, and the world seemed to return back to order.

Happily, he made his way down the wooden steps and into the basement.

When he got to the floor the chilly air nipped on his skin.

Looking around, they were still missing from sight, but he could hear them talking and moving things nearby.

"Where are you guys?" he asked.

"We're in the furnace room, around the other side of the wall."

Kelly walked across the rough concrete floor, passing long metal shelves that had jars filled with thick, dark liquids.

He stepped upon the rocky concrete ground and eased into the dark, dank passage, which was barely a foot and a half wide.

Making his way by feeling along the jagged brick walls, he saw light emitting from ahead.

"Here I come, guys. Don't be scared," he kidded.

When he reached the hallway's end, he saw that the concrete floor dropped off and changed into dirt.

Peering around the corner, he saw Samantha, his mother, and a light bulb that dangled over a four-foot circular brick wishing well.

Chapter 4

"**LOOK, BUT DON'T TOUCH**," the sign above the ferret cage read.

The playful ferrets appeared to pose no threat, but looks could be deceiving. Kelly was all too aware of that. He had the feeling that if it wanted to, a ferret could slash him apart with one quick swipe of its razor sharp claws. It might seem furry and sweet, but he knew better. When he was younger, a playmate's father kept a ferret in their home. Kelly was about to open its cage door when the father warned of the immediate danger he could encounter. The man quickly lifted up his shirtsleeve to reveal a three-inch scar along his forearm.

"Those mean little things strike like a tiger if they feel as though they're trapped, or in any harm or danger."

The father didn't really believe the animal posed a threat to anyone; he was just teaching the child a valuable lesson about not putting his hands into an unfamiliar place without adult supervision.

Ever since then, Kelly handled all animals with delicate care.

But he wasn't there to buy a ferret. He had come strictly for a puppy. A floppy-eared, tongue-wagging puppy.

His mother had told Sam and him to choose one animal each. And he knew exactly which animal that was when he looked into its deep brown eyes.

The chocolate German Shepherd/Collie's head cocked to an angle, not sure what to make of the boy who was staring upon him so affectionately. The moment the puppy realized the boy was interested in possibly taking her home, it began to howl and prance, lifting its head up into he air, while deafening the room with ear-piercing barks. The little dog then dropped into a tight crouch, with its forepaws extended and its butt and tail high into the air. She bellowed a deep growl, and bounced back up playfully.

Kelly was in love. His eyes were glossy from the wonderment of this new friend. Getting a pet was the perfect way to lift his spirits, which had been pretty low since he had seen the well in the basement. He continually worried and wondered if the nightmares he had about the things living in the well were about to come true.

"Wait right here, girl. I'm gonna go tell my sister I found you."

Smiling, he raced off down the aisle looking for Samantha.

After looking down two isles, he finally found her by the kitten kennels.

"Sam, I found the best dog in the whole wide world, and she's all mine! She wants to come home with me."

"Did you? The best in the whole world, huh? Well, if that's so, we won't have to worry about training her how to pee outside," she responded wryly. "I think I've found the one I want, too. Right there," she said, pointing at a white, fluffy Persian kitten. "She's beautiful, isn't she?"

Kelly looked down at the kitten. To him it was just a lazy, good-for-nothing fur ball.

Could it chase a stick, or protect you from burglars? Heck no. All they do is lay around and lick themselves, or sleep. They never kill mice like they're supposed to do. They usually act just like Garfield and watch them run by.

"It's a nice looking cat, Sam," he smiled weakly, trying not to offend her.

While the children were in the pet store, Susan was busy furniture shopping next door. It was a nice luxury having all the stores together in a strip mall.

For the next few days, even weeks, she would be buying and arranging furniture, though she didn't mind that. Shopping was one of her favorite things to do, and she considered herself a pretty good interior decorator.

After signing the last of the paperwork regarding delivery, she set off to the pet store. She had plenty to do in the afternoon: get a hold of her brother, call the phone company, do some grocery shopping, wait for load after load of furniture and appliances to come in.

The silver bell on the entrance door jingled as Kelly looked up to see his mom walk into the store. He stood up and went to her.

"Mom, I found a puppy! She's the one I really want," he said, dragging her by the arm towards the kennels. "See, look at her. Isn't she something?"

She bent down to get a better look at the pup, which was scratching one ear with a furiously fast hind leg.

"Well, hello there. So you're the one who's stolen my son's heart."

The pre-occupied dog scratched for a few more seconds, until the dire-itch subsided, then looked up at the woman and piped back with a sharp yap.

"Well!" she contested. "Aren't we sassy?"

"Yeah! That's what I'll call her, mom. Sassy."

The attention pleased the pup, and it began to bark and run around in circles.

"Well, since she acts so sassy, and she certainly likes the name, then that's what we'll name you," she said, pointing a finger at the steel screen.

The two animals were caged in private holding kennels and placed into the back of the Blazer. The rambunctious dog barked and jumped up and down in his cage, trying to get the attention of the new visitor seated beside her; the subdued cat merely blinked, yawned and licked itself.

*   *   *

After placing a call to have phone service turned on at the house, Susan made a call to her brother, Richard, at the hospital. After a few minutes of paging for him, a light, cheerful voice finally answered back.

"Richard Martin, doctor by day, mental case by night. Can I help you?"

"I thought I told you to keep that problem of yours a family secret. You know, locked up in the closet with Auntie Ruth."

"Well, even Auntie Ruth has to get out now and then and stretch, you know," he deadpanned.

They both started laughing.

"How you doin', Susie? It's about time you guys made it up here. The trip turn out okay?"

"Oh, the trip was lovely, just beautiful. Well, except for your local hoodlum at the diner, but I'll save that story for some rainy day. We just finished furniture shopping. We're on our way to the grocery mart. Can you stop by tonight?"

"Sure, I'll clean up and be over around seven, so you'd better have supper ready," he jested. "Something fancy. None of that frozen garbage."

"Fine. I'll cook up some steaks to celebrate our first evening here. If you're nice to me, I might even whip up a dessert. Love ya, see ya, bye," she said, clicking off the cell phone and giving the thumbs up sign to Kelly and Samantha.

Opening up the driver's door, she slid into the cushioned seat, fastened the safety belt, and fired up the engine.

"Guys, let's commence to finding food."

*   *   *

Kelly watched as two Caseville movers unloaded a large U-Haul truck parked in the driveway. One man was huge. His oversized belly hung over undersized tight-fitted Levi pants. He was the leader of the two.

His mate, a younger man in his late teens, had shoulder-length jet-black hair and a long goatee, and wore a faded Van Halen T-shirt. He seemed very confused. Every time he tried to move something, the larger man would start hollering at him.

Kelly could hear him scream all the way up to his room. *"No! No! No! Not like that! Like this! How many times do I have to show you, Peanut."*

The older, fat man would then take out a rag, wipe the top of his brow, then scratch at the top of his balding head, bemused and frustrated. The frantic scene made Kelly think back to an old Laurel and Hardy movie he had watched, where the two characters tried to move a piano down an outside two-storied stairway. The piano slipped from the grasp of the skinny man and descended all the way down to the street, with the fat man riding on top of it.

Kelly stood at the window and watched as they unloaded couches, recliner chairs, lamps, tables, kitchen chairs, dressers, and the item of his fancy—a large, plasma television.

Bored for the moment, he turned around to see Sassy lying down with her head cocked, trying to understand what in the world her master found so engaging.

Kelly jumped a quick foot at the dog in an attempt to try and scare it. The befuddled animal jumped up onto all fours and backpedaled as hard as it could, flipping its contorted frame over in the process. Scuffling to its feet, the dog ran out into the hallway for safety. A few seconds later, the little pup's head appeared around the doorway, looking into the bedroom to check if the coast was clear.

Kelly smiled at the confused dog. Bending down onto his knees, he called it back into the room to offer his sincerest apologies.

"Come on, girl, you don't have to be afraid of me. I was just kidding. Look, I don't have anything in my hands," he replied, with palms upward. "See?"

The dog entered the bedroom cautiously, keeping an eye on the boy's hand, expecting some mischievous prank. Getting close enough, she nuzzled sheepishly at Kelly's leg.

Kelly picked up the dog in both arms and hugged it, squeezing lovingly.

"Don't worry, Sassy. I'll never let anything bad happen to you. Ever! We're buddies. We've got to stick together and look out for each other, okay?"

The dog licked Kelly on the cheek in apparent agreement.

He placed the dog next to him in front of the window.

"Look at all the new furniture, Sass. See those funny looking guys taking it out of the truck? Mom says more trucks will be coming all day. I can't wait to get my own bed, girl; then we can sleep on it, huh?"

Sassy woofed in agreement.

"I think we'll like it here, don't you?"

This time the dog didn't respond back immediately, nor did it look at Kelly; it just stared out the window and proceeded to growl.

*　　*　　*

Friday evening, Kelly sat at the dinner table raking his fork across a heaping pile of mashed potatoes. Normally, the sweet, fluffy spuds would have delighted him, but tonight, sitting across from his Uncle Richard and the rest of his family, he sat slumped and expressionless.

"Kelly, don't you feel like eating?" his uncle asked. "You've barely touched your meat, and those taters don't seem to be much of a fancy to ya. How come, pal; not feeling well?"

Kelly shrugged. "I'm okay, I guess."

His lifeless demeanor troubled Richard.

"Kell, I had a patient stop by today that you would have loved. He had a bad reaction to some funky chicken that he ate. You should have seen his face. Ghastly! Man, was he looking bad," he replied, wrinkling his nose. "His face was blue, his eyes were swelled up like baseballs, and his cheeks were all puffed up like a chipmunk's."

Kelly looked up in surprise. "No foolin'? What did you do then, Uncle Rich?"

"Well, naturally I had to pop them with a needle. BANG! It sounded like a big balloon being popped," he shouted.

"Richard, don't tease him like that," Susan piped in. "God knows he has a wild enough imagination, just like yours. He doesn't need any coaxing to enhance it."

He began chuckling. "No, little buddy. I gave him some antibiotics that cleared it all up. He only went home with a blue face."

"Noooo!" Kelly exclaimed. "You're fooling with my marbles."

"Yeah, I'm fooling with your marbles," his uncle agreed.

*   *   *

After dinner, Susan and Samantha cleared off the table and started washing dishes. Richard hooked up the television set and connected a DVD player to it, while Kelly went upstairs with Sassy to unpack some of his belongings.

He ran upstairs, skipping every other step as he went upward. Coming around the corner leading to his room, he noticed the library door open. He decided to put off cleaning his bedroom for a while, opting to scan for any good books.

One side of the library held a large four-shelf oak bookcase, while the other three walls were bare. Kelly started at the front end of the lowest shelf and continued across, touching the new and old spines along the way.

Some were ragged with loose binding, as though they had been read over and over. Others were in mint condition, with covers firm and unscathed, either for lack of interest or because of the owners' care.

He pulled out a thick book entitled *Great Expectations*. He was familiar with the author, Charles Dickens, because of the Christmas special on TV last year: "A Christmas Carol," featuring old man Scrooge and Tiny Tim. He liked that one; it was fantasy, complete with ghosts and funny characters.

He decided to take the book for reading. He wasn't the best reader in the world, but he thought he was fairly advanced for a kid of his age. Back at the old school, he won second place in a class spelling bee, an honor he prized highly. He enjoyed reading because it took him to other places to escape reality, especially at times when his mom and dad were yelling at each other, which seemed like most of the time. When he hid in his room and read, it helped distract him from all the horrible screaming in the house. He could be a pirate on a ship at sea, or an astronaut on the moon, or a cowboy. Whatever he wanted to believe, he believed.

The fantasy-styled books shaped his growing imagination over the last few years. He began to be quite clever. Once, he played a prank on his sister with the telephone. He called his home phone from a friend's cell phone. Recording his voice onto a tape recorder, he then transferred that tape to another recorder, but added low batteries to the first recorder to slow the tape down; thus, leaving a menacing, deep voice. Then, in his best Freddy Krueger imitation, he scared the willies out of her—for a couple of days that is, until his mom caught him in the act. The punishment was severe, but he figured great memories like that are hard to come by. Sometimes you have to take the heat for a little bit of fun.

He continued down the shelf until the last book. Suddenly his attention shifted to the small storage room on the bottom of the wall to his right. It was held shut with a sliding latch.

Whatever what was inside of the little room, or wherever the space led to, excited and enticed him. He envisioned some magical portal that led to forbidden places.

With that in mind, he quickly went to the door, slid the latch and opened the door.

Darkness consumed every crack and crevice.

He was now confronted with a choice: should he proceed and discover the treasures that awaited him, or should he leave well enough alone and shut the door, to be safe rather than sorry.

To Kelly, the choice was obvious. Nothing could stop him from going on a frontier journey into the wild unknown, especially when something nice might await him at the end.

Taking a deep breath, he set the book down, entered the hole and began feeling his way inside. The frame of the door allowed just enough room for his shoulders to fit through; he barely fit, scratching the sides of his ribs. Casting a hand outward to understand the distance ahead, he immediately touched the back wall. He then ran a hand to the right, tracing over the wall's angles. There was no opening, which meant the passage led to the left.

With his left hand reaching out, he swiped into the air to the left side of the cubbyhole. Just as he thought, no wall.

He crawled in further, revealing only ankles and feet outside of the doorway.

Suddenly he was stricken with panic, and his body tensed up as he realized the dangerous situation he could be facing.

RATS! What if this storage area was infested with red-eyed, razor-fanged rodents?

The thought of the hairy animals scurrying around in the darkness made his stomach churn with nausea.

Could they sense his presence? Maybe they were hiding against the side of the wall, ready to snap their teeth into his tender skin? Or what if he stumbled upon them mistakenly, bumping face first? Startled, they would be forced to attack him.

Kelly's eyes were open and alert with fear. Any second now, his blood may be spilling upon the floor.

His initial reaction was to retreat as fast as he could. Backtracking, he swung his hands in front of his face to ward off any oncoming rush; thankfully, he hit nothing but air.

Suddenly, his body was caught in the doorway. His back was jammed against the top of the wall.

His breathing intensified as he sucked air in quick spurts. In his mind's eye he could see the beady, red eyes approaching closer through the darkness, inching closer, while his body shook with despair.

He slashed a hand outward again, this time with more force. Back and forth, desperately trying to fend off an attack.

His heartbeat quickened as he touched upon a hairy object.

The size was far larger than what he believed he would encounter. He had heard stories about rats that dwell in sewers and grow to huge sizes, but this was no sewer, and there was no food in here to make it grow to such a size.

Here he was, face to face with something the size of his arm.

He shrieked out in terror.

He was trapped and there was nowhere to go.

In a last attempt to either scare the animal away or injure it, he swung again.

Strange. It didn't feel like animal hair. It was soft fabric and a round, plastic button.

He sat motionless, listening to the beat of his heart pound inside of his eardrums.

Gathering courage, he felt again.

It definitely wasn't a rat, and it wasn't alive—it was hard and motionless.

Unlocking his leg from against the corner of the wall, he slid out through the doorway. In a matter of seconds, he appeared in the lighted area holding a porcelain doll in his hand.

He sat against the wall staring at the new discovery. Its pale, white-powdered, life-like angelic face was fragile, but beautiful. Long curly locks of blond hair spiraled down over her shoulders.

As he looked into the doll's blue eyes, he began to see more than just a lifeless shape. It was a piece of history that had been hidden away by somebody. Maybe it belonged to a little girl from years ago?

A tattered, hand-stitched, maroon Victorian-styled dress draped elegantly down its slender body. Thin, red lips, blushed cheekbones and baby blue eyes had been carefully hand-painted on.

As he looked it over, he realized the porcelain doll was more than just a toy. He didn't know exactly what was so special about it, but he knew something was vastly different.

*   *   *

Samantha tossed and turned during sleep. An ever-present force smothered her like a thick blanket all night. Lying upon her side, she stared across the room at the alarm clock on top of her dresser.

2:52 a.m.

What in the world am I still doing up at this hour? Great, I have to be up in about three hours for school. I'm gonna look like a zombie, she frowned.

A gentle breeze blew inside of her opened bedroom window, lifting the curtains effortlessly like clouds through the sky. Warm air eased over her exposed arms and legs, tickling her skin like a bird's feather.

Sighing with delight, she rolled onto her stomach and tried to force herself to sleep. It was useless, though; she was wide-awake. Venturing off her queen sized bed, she went to the window with curiosity. Drawing back the curtains, she peered out into the moonlit night. The ground radiated under the full moon.

She stood silently, dressed in a white cotton shirt and a pair of University of Michigan shorts. Scanning below her window, Samantha could see the entire backyard clearly. Not like most other nights, when it was too dark and full of shadows. This night was different—it was beautiful.

Soaking up the warm air, she glanced farther out towards an old rotted fence in the field, where horses had once been corralled. Following along the fence, from the east towards the west, her sight passed across a large, dark figure. Surprised, she gazed back excitedly, hoping to find a deer wandering. A tall, bearded man cloaked in a long, dark overcoat stared back at her window. His eyes were radiant white, and so fixated on her that she could almost feel him crawl up the wall of the house straight into her bedroom window, slithering into her room like a slimy snake, as his long, cold, hardened fingers closed in around her throat like a noose.

Samantha shuddered and turned her face away from the inhuman clear pupils. Frightened, she dropped down on her knees, below the windowsill. Her heart thumped like a scared rabbit on the run. Squatting upon hands and knees, she slowly lifted upward, barely revealing the top portion of her head.

The wooden fence appeared in her sight, but the mysterious figure was gone.

Rising up higher, she scanned the remainder of the yard.

He had disappeared.

Flabbergasted, she propped up all the way.

The backyard and field beyond was empty. No trace, or even proof, that such a man existed.

Climbing back into bed, she pulled the covers over her head. She wasn't cold, it just felt so much safer to be hidden out of sight.

Chapter 5

The day started off on a great note for Kelly. Not only was there a glorious blue, cloudless sky (the weatherman had predicted a beautiful, clear night), but his Uncle Richard had promised to take him to the Caseville park to watch the traditional fireworks festival.

Kelly loved to watch the rockets scream upward into the starry-sky, explode into millions of tiny colors, and then descend helplessly to the earth, burnt out halfway to their destined landing. The sounds reminded him of a smoke-filled battlefield packed with cannons and tanks firing large artillery shells towards unsuspecting targets during the dead of night. Soon cannonballs and bullets slicing through dense fog became sketched in his mind.

War fascinated him. He loved looking through old history books that showed tanks and aircraft battling over enemy lines. So, naturally, after hearing his first M-80 crack, he became attached to the allure of the holiday.

Slipping on blue jeans, a T-shirt and a pair of socks, he went to see who was awake.

Samantha lie on the couch watching a talk show, one of those adult ones about transvestites and the ones they love.

"Sam, are you going to the park tonight?"

She lifted her head out of the pillow drearily. "For what? To watch a bunch of colorful lights, and get a headache from all the noise? No thanks."

"It's not a bunch of noise," he snapped. "It's about freedom."

"Get real, stupid. It's lame. Nobody cares about freedom, it's all about commercialism."

Commercialism? Kelly didn't know exactly what that meant, but it sure didn't sound very good.

"Sam, you're being dumb! You don't even know what you're talking about."

"Whatever," she shrugged, choosing to ignore his presence.

The last couple of weeks were stressful for her. She had only been out of the house twice, hadn't made any new friends, or even seen any good-looking guys around. *The town was devoid of teens*, she decided. To make matters worse, she was stuck in the house with a ten-year-old twerp who was always hanging around her or getting in her face.

They had been getting on each other's nerves badly lately. It wasn't really his fault for her agitated state. After all, he was stuck friendless in the house as well. Still, she was a maturing woman of sixteen and he was merely a kid: a child who could amuse himself with toys or the dog. She had to go out and see the sights, go where all the teenage kids were hanging out. Soon she would be getting her license; it would be in her best interest to know the territory that she would be driving in.

Susan was carrying a basket of clothes upstairs from the laundry room when she heard the bickering start again.

She had grown quite accustomed to the bantering in the household lately, and several attempts at separating the two hadn't helped. She had to find the children some sort of activity that would enable them to break the tension of their seclusion. School would be starting in 2 months, which she believed would solve the problem in the long run, but for now she would have to find another option.

Walking into the living room, she came face-to-face with the dispute. "Sam, I don't want you to speak to your brother in that kind of tone. He's having just as hard a time adjusting as you are. So it would be fair, young lady, to cut him a little slack."

"But God, Mom, he's always in my face. Every day I have to hear him whine about something. It's not fair! I can't take it any more."

Afraid his side of the argument wasn't being defended, Kelly shot back. "All I did was ask her if she was going to watch the fireworks tonight! It's not like I was asking her to clean up my room or something."

"I have an idea," Susan announced. "After I get the clothes all folded, let's spend the day up in town. Samantha, I could drop you off either at the Coffeehouse or the arcade."

The thought of sitting alone drinking coffee and looking pathetic didn't really appeal to Samantha, although she really wanted to check out the Caseville Coffeehouse. Her uncle had mentioned that it was where all the action was with the kids her age. It was the kind of establishment that appealed to a younger crowd because of its set up: part coffeehouse, pizza parlor, and dance club. Coffee drinking and socializing had become quite an addiction and event for the Generation Y2K group; it replaced the need to find a good high on the streets with a steady controlled environment where they could enjoy themselves without being hassled.

The dance club was developed to keep the community clean of underage drinking. A large open-spaced hall, adjoined to a parlor room, was filled with laser light shows, strobe lights, neon flashing signs, and a state of the art sound system to accompany the latest hip-hop crazed songs. Every evening the local youths gathered, either to talk about the daily gossip or just to mingle with the opposite sex. The freedom of having a private hangout of their own kept them content and obedient.

After contemplating the idea, Samantha thought it would be good if she got out on her own for a change and saw what all the so-called "rave" was about.

"You can drop me off at the Coffeehouse," she responded, trying not to sound overly excited.

"Good. Then that's that."

Susan then turned to Kelly. "Honey, any place special that you'd like to go?"

The arcade was exactly where he wanted to go. The chance to play "Alien Assault" any time was always a welcomed relief.

"I wanna shoot down some mutants from Mars at the arcade," he said happily.

"You do? What on Earth did those little aliens do to you?" she kidded.

"Mom! I have to save the whole planet from Martian attacks. I've done it before, it's really cool!"

Susan gave him a reassured nod and a smile to let him know how pleased she was to be saved the grief of an outer space invasion.

*　　*　　*

Pulling the Blazer up to the curb of the Coffeehouse, she rested the car in park.

Samantha reached for the handle.

"Sam, I want you to promise me you will not take off with someone you don't know. And if somebody offers you drugs . . ."

"Mother!" she protested. "Oh my gosh, how embarrassing can you be! I'm not a kid. I know all about the dangers of the street. We're not in Detroit."

"And how, may I ask, my mature woman of the world, do you know all of this stuff."

Samantha gave her a sarcastic put-off glance and replied, "You know, from school, and all those stupid talk shows."

"Well, never mind the talk shows. You just be careful and smart, okay?"

"Fine."

Susan pulled out a twenty and presented it. "I expect the change."

Samantha snatched the bill from her fingers. "My pleasure. If there is any, that is."

She opened the car door and climbed out of the vehicle, then turning back, grinned and replied, "Thanks."

When it came time for his turn, Kelly already knew the drill. He was sure she was going to "freak out" when it came time to leave him alone—he being the baby and all. He really didn't mind; he understood that was part of the agreement. If he were going to go out and enjoy himself, he would have to do so on her terms, simple as that.

"Kelly, I'm going to be right next door at the clothing store, so if anything happens, and I mean anything, come right over and get me. Understood?"

"Yes, mom," he responded respectfully.

"I'll give you about a half-hour to yourself and then I'll be back to check on you."

"Sure," he agreed, looking out the window impatiently.

"Okay, then scram."

Kelly got out of the car and proceeded over to the arcade's entrance.

As soon as he arrived at the front door, he heard the animated sounds of bells, blips and beeps inside the game room.

It was packed. Children, teenagers, and even a few adults stood with joystick controllers in hands, eyes mesmerized and focused upon flashing display screens.

Kelly loaded up on quarters, transforming his crisp dollar bills into shiny silver coins. He made sure he was armed with enough quarters so that he wouldn't have to interrupt his concentration with wasted trips to the change maker.

There were motorcycle racing, baseball and football games and shooting galleries. None of them seemed interesting or challenging enough. Anyone could do those. The real game was right in front of him: "Alien Attack." And no one was playing it. Perfect, he thought, placing the first round of quarters into the slot.

Later that afternoon, he was having a record day so far; he had accumulated ten thousand points, gained seven extra lives, and managed to capture two alien leaders.

As he was watching his space agent run through a maze of space ruins, he noticed an unfamiliar glare reflecting off the screen. Someone was standing behind him watching. Strange, he hadn't noticed anyone around him earlier. *How long had this person been standing there? Maybe they were spying on him and trying to learn all of his best moves, trying to rob him of all his secrets.*

A voice interrupted from behind, "You're awesome at this game. Do you play all the time?"

The voice startled him, not because of the question, but because of the tone. He was bracing for some tough, deep voice to challenge him, but instead heard a young, squeaky girl.

Keeping his eyes upon the screen, he answered, "It's all about knowing what to go after and what to leave alone. I mean, if you chase after the wrong aliens, you'll lose all your ship's fuel. If you go after the main guys, you can rack up a bunch of points and still have enough fuel to go around the galaxy."

"Oh," the soft voice responded. "Do you think you could teach me how to play?"

Kelly was floored. *It was bad enough that she was standing over his shoulder watching his every move, but for her, some girl no less, to ask him to teach her the secrets of the game? Craziness! Girls like to play with dolls. They pout and cry when they don't get their way, and they paint their faces up with makeup. They don't know how to play video games. Even if he did try to teach her—and he knew he could—she probably couldn't learn it. They're not very smart.*

"I don't know. This game's really hard. It took me a long time to be great at it," he said, grinning to himself and believing this would end the discussion and send her away.

"Really? Yeah, you're probably right. I am a girl, and it would probably be a lot tougher for me," she responded sarcastically, which went over his head.

Finally, he thought. *That was so easy.*

Turning to get a look at her sad face, and to gloat, he responded, "Yeah, it's probably best if you . . ."

As the words left his mouth he was dumbfounded, and stared blankly at her. She was blue-eyed, red-haired, angel-faced with freckles, and biting on her bottom lip, with the look of a helpless puppy.

His stomach ached. Not that he was feeling queasy or anything, but he felt different. *Why?* His hands were all sweaty and he could barely keep a grip on the control knobs. He felt tingly, like a million firecrackers were going off inside of him, or like he was diving down a steep roller coaster hill.

"Yes?" she responded, still waiting for him to finish his sentence.

His mouth was opening and closing like a fish out of water, but no sound came out. Swallowing, he tried to speak again. This time, the results were mere sputters of the English language.

What in the world was going on, he wondered? *Why can't I speak?*

She looked at him puzzled, not sure if he was having a seizure, or just plain nuts.

"If you wanna' give it a try . . . I've got another quarter and we can play two players," he finally spit out.

"You'll teach me how to play as well as you? That would be really, really sweet of you," she paused, expecting to receive a name.

For a second he stood there dreamily, until he got the drift and bashfully said, "Oh, right. Sorry. It's . . . um, my name . . . my name, it's um, Kelly! Kelly."

"Thanks, Kelly Kelly. I'm Julie Baker.

*   *   *

After several intense lessons of "Alien Attack" and a brief soda pop break—compliments of him—Kelly spotted his mom across the room.

If she sees me hanging around with a girl what will she say? This could be bad.

"Julie, I have to go. I just remembered I have to be somewhere."

"You do? Where?"

"I think . . . it's somewhere, um . . . my uncle's house. Yeah, my uncle wants me to come over, and you know how it is, I have to spend time with him."

He lost sight of his mom. Panic crept in as he realized she could pop up out of nowhere.

As he was watching his backside, his mom appeared from the front, taking him by surprise.

"Hey honey, how did the alien hunting go?" she inquired.

Trying to appear cool and confident, he smiled. "Okay. You know aliens, kill one and a million more come out. No problem, though. Are you ready, mom?" he quickly edged in. "We have to go see Uncle Rich."

"Sure, honey, if you're all done we can get going. But we don't have to be over there until . . ."

"Oh, but he said don't be late. And I don't think we should be late."

Saved, he thought. *Nice reflexes.*

Julie, standing behind him, exclaimed bubbly, "Are you Kelly's mom?"

Susan turned to look at the smiling young girl.

"Yes, I am. Hi, I'm Susan. Were you playing video games together?"

43

"Yeah, he's been showing me all his secret tricks . . . even though I'm a girl. My name's Julie Baker. It's very nice to meet you," she said.

"That's very chivalrous of him! Kelly, maybe Julie would like to go with us to the fireworks. Julie, do you have any plans tonight?"

"No, ma'am. I'd love to go," she immediately responded cheerfully.

Yikes! Could anything worse happen, he thought? *What next, having her over to the house for dinner? Don't I have any say in this, or am I just invisible,* he wondered?

"Great. Why don't you give Kelly your number and we'll call you before we leave. I'll talk with your folks and make sure it's all right with them if you go. And if you don't have plans after that, you can have dinner with us."

"I'm sure they won't mind, really," Julie contested. "And that would be great."

"Just to be on the safe side, I'm sure your parents would like to meet us first."

Standing between the ladies, Kelly shook his head, befuddled. It was getting worse by the second. First his mom meets her, then she sets him up on a date, and now he has to go and meet her parents. He had the feeling the evening would probably end up disastrously.

* * *

Samantha sat at the counter of the Coffeehouse's parlor. She ordered a French vanilla cappuccino instead of the usual soda. She had never tasted a flavored coffee in Florida, but if that's what kids in Michigan were into, well, she would have to adapt.

The parlor was empty and quiet. Since it wasn't quite noon yet, the joint wouldn't be happening until at least three or four. The dance side wasn't open until six.

The parlor was lit like a carnival. Bright colors erupted from the walls and pillars. Pink and blue stripes slashed across the wall in cheerful fashion from one end of the hall to the other. Samantha actually felt like wearing sunglasses to protect her eyes from the excruciating explosion of light.

Every other floor tile was painted baby blue or white. The room reminded her of one of those cheesy 1950's hamburger shops, where girls wore long, pink hoop skirts with black poodles embroidered on them, and the macho, greasy-haired guys wore leather jackets and jeans.

This wasn't like Florida at all. There she could go to a concert, or hang out at the mall, which had more stores in it than this town had houses. *Where was the nearest concert arena? Did anyone go to concerts, or did they have to drive out of town for a hundred miles to catch the hottest group?*

Although the Coffeehouse was "cheesy" and deserted, something about it appealed to her. Maybe it was the feeling that she was starting a new life in a totally new environment. Silly as it sounded, some kids grow up in big cities and never enjoy simple pleasures. Like going for quiet walks, going to a town fair, or boating and fishing. She was getting a chance to grow up in a small community where people were very neighborly, and knew one another. It wasn't an air-polluted, over-populated, dirty, crime-ridden tourist attraction; it was warm, clean, quiet and refreshing. She could breathe, think and become a better writer. She was definitely accustomed and used to the fast-paced city life, but she also longed for a change in her environment and life.

If only she had someone in this perfect little place to fall in love with.

*   *   *

At eight o'clock, Kelly walked side by side with his mom up Julie Baker's front driveway to her house. He scuffled along the gravel, preparing himself mentally for what he would face. He had spent an unusually long time getting ready for this big fiasco. Normally, he could be dressed and ready to go within a couple of minutes; but today, strangely enough, he found himself taking extra care and attention to his grooming. Hair alone took a great deal of time to perfect. What normally consisted of a quick brushing took precision and repetition.

Once he got his hairstyle to a somewhat self-satisfactory look, he sought out his mom for another opinion. The baggy clothes he normally wore were discarded for a more color-coordinated, handsomer look.

As he walked the walk of the damned, his mind raced for the proper introductions that would have to be made: *Thank you, sir, for letting Julie go with us.* Nope, too nice. *Sir, what a nice house you have here.* Way too fake. *I'm new here, so please don't kill me.* No! No! No!

It was hopeless. He would ruin it for everybody. Julie would hate him, his mom would hate him, and poor Mr. and Mrs. Baker, they don't even know him yet, and they'll probably hate him as well.

"Kelly, you be sure to thank the Bakers now, okay?"

Great, here it comes now.

"Yes, mom," he spoke back unenthusiastically.

Susan knocked on the door; the stillness of the night, with the exception of a few crickets around the bushes, heightened the anxiety in his mind. *What if some huge, cigar smoking, angry guy appears at the door?* Kelly could hear the guy's voice now, talking with some tough New York mobster accent: "You here to see who? Get outta here. You some kinda' wise-guy or somethin'?"

Cable television wasn't helping his imagination for the better.

Kelly cringed at the thought. Nervously, he looked back at the car. His uncle sat in the front passenger seat, while Samantha sat reluctantly in the back.

The front door of the single-storey, white home cracked open, and inside Julie stood, smiling brightly as a diamond in the sun.

With a great burden lifted off his shoulders, he sighed with relief.

She opened the door fully to let them in.

"Hi, Kelly! You look really nice. Hello, ma'am," she smiled at Susan.

"Don't you look adorable, Julie," Susan answered back.

Julie had also put a lot of thought into her appearance. She wore a pink blouse and jean shorts. Her long, red hair was pulled back into a ponytail.

Julie escorted the two into the living room, where her father and mother rose to meet the new guests.

Her father was a large man with a clean-shaven, rosy-cheeked, bulbous face, but far from intimidating looking. His thin, black hair receded slightly above the temples. He had a jovial demeanor and seemed like the type of guy who would be a perfect fit to host a television game show or a cooking show.

He offered an outstretched hand to Susan, and a warm smile.

Mrs. Baker seemed like a pleasant and very attractive woman. She had a long, slender frame, kept a straight, regal posture, and had a long elegant neck that was decorated with a pearl necklace. She shook Kelly and Susan's hand.

"Julie tells us you just moved into town. I hope you'll like it here. We're a very quiet and organized town. You won't find any corruption here. I'm Corina, and this is my husband, Daniel Baker."

"It's a pleasure to meet you both. I'm Susan Adkins, and this, I'm sure you've heard about already, is Kelly. Kelly and Julie really hit it off today at the arcade."

He smiled bashfully.

"Julie is such a sweetheart and a well-mannered young lady. How long have you lived here?"

Susan could tell who wore the pants in their family by the woman's immediate control of the conversation.

"Yes, she's our only child. She's a blessing. I'm sure we spoil her a little too much with certain freedoms, but she's a wonderful student and is never a problem. Well, let me see. We've lived here close to twenty years, and I can't recall any trouble in our neighborhood, either. Can you, Daniel?"

He opened his mouth to speak but was cut off by his wife.

"No, I don't think we have. You'll love it here, Susan. If you need anything, Daniel and I will be more than happy to help make your transition here smooth. Isn't that right, dear?

Her husband contemplated speaking, then nodded in agreement.

"Susan, do you have other family in Caseville?" Corina asked.

"Yes, I also have a daughter, Samantha. She's out in the car with my brother, Richard. When I divorced my husband in Florida, I decided to move to Michigan to be closer to him."

"Well, if there's anything that our family can do, let us know; we would be glad to help. Isn't that right, Julie?"

"Definitely," she said, grinning at Kelly.

"Corina, we'll have her back right after the fireworks. Maybe, if it's all right with you, we'll take her out to eat afterwards."

"Sure, go out and have a nice time."

They walked to the front door where Mrs. Baker gave Julie a warm hug. She turned to Kelly. "It was very nice meeting you, young man. You'll have to join us for dinner sometime."

Kelly nodded. "I'd like that very much, thank you. I love to eat."

* * *

The evening went perfectly for Kelly and Julie. The fireworks display was better than he had ever imagined. Julie explained to him all about the traditional Caseville Fourth of July festival, how almost every year she and her parents would head out to the park, sometimes packing a picnic, and sit back and enjoy the marvel of the light show.

This year, the park was packed with spectators. Some enthusiastic kids even brought super-soaker water guns, Frisbees and footballs to throw around. It was a wild time for all, and not one person seemed to go home disappointed. Even Sam, who had sworn to the heavens that she would not partake in any festivities, found herself engaged in conversation with an older boy who had offered his services as tour guide for the night.

The weather was a warm eighty-two degrees, and just as the weatherman had predicted, there was not a cloud in the sky. Glittering stars in the Milky Way provided a fantastic backdrop for the glow of red, white and blue explosions.

Kelly sat all night without a care in the world. He had finally found a friend who was just like himself: someone who liked to laugh about silly things, play practical jokes, read adventure stories, and was pretty good—for a beginner—at "Alien Attack." It didn't matter that she was girl; she was just like one of the guys.

They sat side by side watching the final rapid-fire, big hurrah of the night. It was a memory to cherish for a long, long, time. A friendship and trust was forged on this special night, one that would be everlasting.

When Kelly got home that night, he wasn't feeling very tired. In fact, he felt rejuvenated, like an energized battery. How could he sleep after having the time of his life? He wondered whether Julie felt as he did. *Was she thinking about him, as he was of her, at that very moment?*

Although he believed he could go on daydreaming all night long about the festival and Julie, his mom put things back in perspective and made it perfectly clear that bedtime had arrived.

After he brushed his teeth, kissed his mother goodnight and said prayers, Kelly shut off the light switch and climbed into bed.

He lay in darkness for the moment, dwelling again on the exciting day. He was determined to have good dreams this night, and his terrible nightmares would not get the best of him.

This night *was* different.

He dreamt about Julie, how her face lit up every time he told a joke, and how he always seemed in a happy mood whenever he looked at her. He envisioned himself chasing after her inside of a cornfield, playfully slapping at the long stalks as he ran at full speed. She would search for a place to hide and he would attempt to find her.

He was running with all of his might, as row after row of corn stalks flashed by. His heart was pounding and felt like a ticking time bomb that was ready to explode.

He finally spotted her in a clearing, as the sun shone down upon her. She stood there smiling, ready to greet him.

He reached out with both arms to tag her, but instead, tackled her playfully, as they fell to the ground laughing. There were no normal outside noises: no birds, automobiles, planes passing overhead, or spoken words.

But strangely, there was one sound throughout most of the dream: a constant tapping noise, like a record skipping.

He focused intently on the sound.

It wasn't familiar. It was ringing from his ears—louder and louder, increasing in volume the longer he listened.

With total concentration upon the sound, his vision became blurred.

Julie's happy face faded to black, as the noise in the background drummed on.

Kelly was suddenly awake in bed, staring ahead into the darkness of the bedroom.

CREEK . . . CREEK . . . CREEK.

The sound echoed from the corner of the room by his door.

His body stiffened underneath the covers, as his mind raced to remember what objects were within the area of the mysterious noise.

He could envision his closet there, along with a study desk and a wastebasket, nothing else except . . . a rocking chair.

He lay upon the bed on his stomach, face buried into the pillow, sweat beading upon his forehead.

Light from the moon shone through his window and illuminated a corner of his room by the chair.

He cursed under his breath for being so stupid and not bringing Sassy upstairs with him when he went to bed, like he had on other occasions. He had been so engrossed by the evening's events that he had totally forgotten about his faithful watchdog.

CREEK . . . CREEK . . . CREEK.

He knew what the mysterious sound was, the rocking chair, but what was causing it to rock? *Someone, or something, was in that chair.*

A chill like a glacier sliding underwater crept over him. Whatever sat in that chair had him pinned against the wall with no escape route out. He was trapped, and not a soul could rescue him before this thing, whatever it was, got to him.

If he pretended not to notice it and just lay still, the thing would eventually take him by surprise in the darkness, and he didn't want that to happen. To be fed upon when you least expected it would be like walking into a lion's den wearing a blindfold and being basted in barbecue sauce.

He had to get to that door; it was the only solution.

CREEK . . . CREEK . . . CREEK

The sound was maddening in his mind. He couldn't take hearing the chilling squeak of the floorboard as the wooden leg of the chair rolled upon it. He couldn't stand not seeing the face behind the force. He had to get a glimpse of whatever sat in that chair!

If he could just peek around the pillow without alerting the thing, maybe then he would know what he was up against.

48

His body was hot. It felt like he would burst into flames at any minute, as the weight of the blankets scorched him alive underneath.

CREEK . . . CREEK . . . CREEK.

The moon reflected silhouettes of tree branches upon the bedroom wall just beyond his feet. The shadows bounced and swayed like a puppet controlled by strings.

He began turning his head slowly in the pillow, keeping his nose buried deep within it to avoid alarming the thing in the chair. As his sight focused off the pillowcase and onto the floor, he followed a trace of a light beam that shone straight towards the chair.

Two gray and blue veined feet appeared.

Startled, but unable to look away, his eyes continued farther upward.

Bony legs draped inside a long, black gown pumped up and down in a rocking motion.

Focusing upon the whole chair now, his mouth opened in ghastly horror.

A withered, old woman with the menacing grin of the Devil sat rocking back and forth.

Her bottom lip protruded, and the corners of her mouth sliced toward her cheeks in a wicked smile. Clear, bulging, white eyes were open and alert like a cobra's, ready to strike quickly. The skin under her neck hung loosely as she rested her head against the back of the chair. Her hands lay motionless upon the chair's arms.

Kelly knew she was aware of his awakening: she had been waiting patiently for him to acknowledge her. Now that he had, she was paralyzing him with a stare so powerful that it made him numb and nauseous inside.

Blackness seemed to roll in around his eyes as he quickly realized he was about to pass out. Any moment now, he would lose consciousness.

She began to tap her fingers slowly upon the armrest, driving each fingernail into the wooden finish. The hollow sound of the long tips cut across his spine.

Looking at him, she laughed. First in a mild amused tone, then into a harder, congested, phlegm forced burst, which made her wheeze with deep breaths afterwards.

She placed her trembling, frail hand into the air.

With one finger erected, she pointed at him and spoke in a voice that sounded as though her vocal chords had been severed in half.

"YOU are the chosen one—and YOU will die!"

She smiled with deep pleasure, squinting as she examined his reaction.

Kelly had heard enough. There was no way he was going to sit still while she carved him up.

He ran as fast as he could, throwing off the sheets in frenzy and speeding past the chair through the doorway. He took the stairs three at a time, almost rolling down the last five steps. When he got to the living room it was dark and empty. Looking up at the clock on the wall, he discovered it was 1 a.m. Everyone was in deep sleep.

Opening the door to his mom's bedroom, he proceeded in.

He shook her repetitively.

"Mom? Mom? Are you up?"

She looked up at him drearily, then snapped alert.

"Hmmm. I am now. What is it, honey? What's wrong?"

"I can't sleep. I had a bad dream again."

He knew it was more than just a bad dream. But if he went on screaming about an old witch in his bedroom after midnight, she would just assume it was a nightmare and tell him to go back to bed. He didn't care what she thought, though. He just wanted to feel safer. And laying next to her, he felt just a little bit more protected.

But how much longer would he be able to remain safe?

*   *   *

The next morning, Kelly prepared for his mother's interrogation.

His mother was the worrying type, and it was just too obvious that she would dig until she received a satisfactory response to her questions.

Ever since he had seen that well downstairs—the same stupid well that haunted him in his dreams—he feared that his nightmares might come true.

But how could he actually see into the future? How could the well be in his dreams one minute, and then be here in real life?

He didn't want to think about what lurked in the well from his dreams, and if it was living for real in the well in his house. But he did, and often. Day and night, he thought about the evil presence that he feared in the basement. He wondered if it was possible to find out if something was really inside of the well, without actually looking in it. But he had no intention of making the same mistake in reality that he had in the dream. He had no intention of meeting those two cold familiar eyes once again. No way, no how!

He sat at the kitchen table eyeing a bowl of soggy corn flakes, occasionally stirring them with a spoon to take the pressure off his mind while he thought of a way to dodge the big sit-down meeting.

Glancing into the kitchen, he watched as his mom poured milk into her coffee cup. She stirred in some sugar and came into the dining room, pulling up a chair as she set her cup down upon the table.

"You wanna' start, or should I?"

Kelly instantly noted the sarcastic tone, and he began the story. "Last night, I saw someone in my room. I was sleeping and I heard my rocking chair squeak on the floor."

"Kelly, what are you talking about?" she asked, frightened. "Why didn't you tell me this last night! There was someone in the house?"

"Yes. She was a wicked, old lady," he blurted out quickly. "She was rocking in my chair, smiling at me. I was really, really scared, mom. She looked like a witch."

"A witch? Oh my God, Kelly. You gave me such a scare! I thought there was a burglar in the house," she said, smiling at him.

Noticing his disappointment over not being taken seriously, she began to reassure him. "Sweetie, there's nothing here in this house that can hurt you; no monsters or witches. It's just your imagination. You're just a little shook up about fitting in a place where you don't know anyone yet. That's all. You're sleeping in a room that's unfamiliar to you. You'll get used to it, though. And soon you'll find some friends here, and you'll adjust to the house. It takes time. I promise, you give it just a little more patience, and before you know it, everything will be fine."

"Mom, she told me that she was gonna kill me!" he cried, bursting into tears. "KILL ME! I'M NOT LYING!"

With that declaration, he ran out of the room and up the stairs.

"Kelly!" Susan called out after him.

Sassy, who had been content lying upon the floor near a heat vent, witnessed the commotion and proceeded to follow the runaway boy.

Kelly lay upon the bed face down. He was sickened at the thought of nobody believing him, and felt as isolated as ever.

He looked up at the chair. Funny, his attempt to run from his problem brought him right back to where the problem began.

It was daylight though. His fears paled in the sanctity of light. At least he couldn't be snuck up on. Whatever wanted to get to him had to materialize from air, which would be even scarier if it did happen, although it seemed highly unlikely.

Susan appeared at the door feeling ashamed, but looked lovingly at him.

Maybe I reacted too quickly, she thought. His imagination could have confused him, and not believing him wasn't helping any.

"Kelly, I'm very sorry. I should have listened to you. It wasn't right for me to jump to any conclusions."

She rubbed the tears off his flushed cheek.

"What does conclusion mean?" he asked sadly.

"Basically, it means that I screwed up. I jumped to one final, firm answer, one that I wanted to believe, honey. I shouldn't have told you that it didn't happen. If you saw something last night, then I believe you."

He flashed a big smile. "Thanks, Mom. I knew you'd believe me."

"I want you to know, Kelly, if anything happens, and I mean anything, don't be afraid to tell me."

"Okay," he assured her.

Reaching over, she hugged him and felt the warmth of his body. It made her feel needed again.

There was a time in her life when the children were younger that they needed her undivided attention and comfort. But once they had reached a stage in life when their hormones and adolescence took over, she felt as though her guidance was discarded.

Now, as Kelly acknowledged her support, she felt as loved and needed as ever before.

Chapter 6

August 29th: Opening Day of School

The golden, warm rays of the sun shined brightly through the bedroom window and onto Kelly's sleeping face. The heat gently massaged his once cool face and gingerly lifted him from deep slumber into a hazy state of brief confusion.

He rubbed across his eyelids with the back of his hand and stretched his arms and legs to ease his tired muscles.

The sun was barely above the horizon, peeking just a third of its massive body over the Earth's soil.

The alarm clock on his dresser read 6:50 a.m. and wasn't due to ring until 7:00 a.m.

The excitement of a new life and friends had kept his adrenaline pumping all night. He had awakened three times during the night, the latter of which he spent pacing around the kitchen searching for a quick snack to ease the restlessness. If he was lucky, he may have gained a good two or maybe three hours of undisturbed sleep during the night; it didn't matter, he could have gone the entire night sleepless and still felt ready to go in the morning.

Lying upon the bed looking at the ceiling, he savored the moment, lavishing the thought of riding the bus for the first day of school. He had never ridden a bus to school before because the family car was always the usual transportation.

Everything seemed in perfect order. The only thing left to do was get out of bed and start the day, yet, he couldn't. He tried. But he couldn't bring himself to move a muscle.

Suddenly, things didn't seem so rosy anymore. He began to panic thinking about the worst things that could happen at school, and suddenly the day now seemed bleak and unsure.

BEEP BEEP BEEP BEEP.

The alarm's bright pitch cut through him sharply, like a knife through shaving cream and he jerked, startled.

BEEP BEEP BEEP BEEP.

Slamming his hand down on the top of the clock, he shut off the alarm in mid-siren.

For a moment he felt paralyzed, not sure whether to jump up enthusiastically, or just simply lay still and hope nobody noticed him in bed.

"Kelly? Time to get ready for school. Are you up?"

He groaned, sliding deeper under his bed sheet. It was time to activate plan #2, which was . . . a big zero. He had no plan #2 developed yet. He was doomed.

Susan's silhouette stood motionless in the doorway for a moment. He contemplated excuse after excuse rapidly through his mind. Each one was worse than the one before it, though.

"Kelly," she coaxed. "It's time to get up, sleepy-head. It's your big day. Come on. Up and at 'em," she said, entering the room.

"Mom, I . . . don't feel like going today. I feel bad."

"What's the matter, honey? Are you sick?"

"Yeah. My stomach feels funny and stuff. I think I got it bad this time," he said, adding as much discomfort to his voice as he could muster up.

She put a hand to his forehead.

"I don't feel any fever. You sure nothing else is bothering you?"

"Noooo," he whined. "I just think I should stay home today . . . until I get all better," he moaned.

Sitting down upon the mattress, she stroked her fingers delicately through his messy, blond hair.

"You know, when I went to my first day of school, I was terrified. I was shaking so badly with fear. I swore to my mother that she would never make me go there, because I hated school that much."

"You did?" he asked, sitting up, taking more notice.

"Yes, I did. I thought that none of the other kids would like me, and that I would be the dumbest student in the whole class."

"What did you do? Did you run away from home."

She giggled out loud. "No, of course not, silly. Something a lot smarter. I reached down deep and found the courage to look my fear in the face, and then I marched right into that school. I knew that if I was going to be afraid of every single thing in life without at least trying to make an effort, that I would never succeed at anything."

"Really?" He gawked in amazement. "How come?"

"Well, I figured if I didn't give myself a chance to prove that all that silly stuff was just in my head, I would have never been able to live with myself. I would have always wondered what school was really like. And I'm glad that I went, because you know why? I had a great time and met a lot of special friends."

"Honest?" he asked.

"Honest," she replied nodding. You can set your mind to do anything, baby. The only thing that's stopping you is yourself. And you can never be a failure if you know you've given it your best try.

"All right, I'll go to school. But I don't think Sassy will like it if I'm gone all day. She gets lonely sometimes."

"I think Sassy will be fine. You just leave that little pup to me and I'll make sure that she's busy enough not to think about it, okay?"

"Okay," he smiled, hugging her around the neck with delight.

*   *   *

While Kelly searched over the back panel of a Cap'n Crunch cereal box for an ad for a yellow, plastic spin-top prize, Samantha was upstairs frantically applying make-up as though she was Michelangelo painting his last great masterpiece.

Every color she applied was too bright and cheerful, or just too dreary. She either caked it on too thick, or barely used enough to be noticed, in her judgment. Her hair wasn't turning out any better than her face was. She wanted to give it just the right curl, but instead wound up with large, uneven rolls. She felt like screaming: it was the most important day of her adolescent life and she was all thumbs. She couldn't do anything right. Worse yet, she hadn't even scanned through her wardrobe to find an outfit. Yesterday, she had discovered something decent to wear, but that was only a backup in case nothing better presented itself in the morning. Now she was afraid to even start looking. She might spend the whole morning locked away in her closet, considering what to wear.

Hopeless. That's what she was, hopeless.

Susan stood behind her at the side of the bed, keenly aware that if she dared to interfere or interject any ideas, her daughter would interpret it as a sign that her mother lacked confidence in her. She didn't want Samantha to feel that she has bad taste or that her decision-makings were questionable, because her self-esteem would be shattered. That would be the last thing Samantha needed in life these days. No, if she wanted her mom's opinion she would ask for it; until then, she would let her daughter make her own decision.

"I look terrible! Can you believe how nasty these pants and shoes look together? I'll die if someone sees me in these," she replied, complaining to herself, instead of her mother.

Reaching into the closet, she pulled out a pair of white ankle boots. Turning back, she wrinkled her nose, frowned and asked skeptically. "What do you think of these, mom?"

"I think those are gorgeous. They'll go perfectly with your jeans and dress top."

"Yeah? Yeah, they are pretty nice. I like 'em, too. Thanks for the help."

"I didn't do anything. You're the one who picked them out in the store, and from out of the closet to go with your ensemble. Thank yourself."

"Yeah, but just the same, thanks."

*   *   *

The morning air was brisk, but not so bad that a jacket was required for Kelly as he waited for the bus in front of the house. He stood armed with a notebook, pen and paper in one hand, and a Peanuts lunch box filled with a sandwich, Jell-O pudding cup, and an apple in the other hand.

Periodically, he would turn around and look up to see his loyal dog perched against his bedroom window, staring back, confused and wondering why her best friend was standing on the corner without him.

He had tried to give Sassy a heart-to-heart talk about his requirement to attend school, but the dog seemed oblivious to any kind of reasoning.

Now, as he watched the dog in the window, he began to feel guilty for abandoning her. *How would Sassy get through the whole day without him? Who would feed her when her supper dish was empty?*

Just as Kelly's sympathetic side began to eat at him, the rumbling of a school bus broke his thoughts.

The bus rocked and bounced slowly down the dirt road, as the driver took her time to avoid potholes on the unpleasant assigned route.

Samantha's bus had arrived an hour earlier, and as usual, she had had to rush outside to catch it before it passed the house.

The yellow bus pulled to a complete stop, causing its hydraulic air-pressured brakes to hiss with the indignity.

The latch to the door swung open noisily and presented a smiling, gray-haired lady. "Good morning," she announced.

Kelly climbed aboard the first step and smiled back bashfully to the woman seated in the high-rise driver's seat.

As he climbed upon the second step, he looked back once more at Sassy, who was still watching affectionately, and boarded the bus.

*   *   *

The day was not going as expected for Kelly. He discovered that his assigned locker was the wrong one, after struggling to open it for ten minutes. The extra time that he spent on the combination made him late for his first class, and when he arrived there, his teacher scolded him because of his tardiness in front of the seated students.

At least one comfort was Julie. Luckily, his seat was right behind hers, and she made him feel a little better by giving him another cheesy grin.

*   *   *

The noon lunch bell rang, bringing instant relief to an already overly long day for Kelly. He walked the crowded hall with Julie towards the cafeteria.

The lunch line for pizza was already forming quickly. They had both brought lunches from home, so they found an open table and sat down.

"How do you like living in Caseville?" Julie asked, pulling a peanut butter sandwich out of a sandwich bag.

"It's not bad. I haven't did much yet. I guess once I've been here a while it'll probably be pretty cool."

"Done. Haven't done much," she corrected.

He shrugged, rolling his eyes with disinterest.

"I think you'll like it here. Everyone's really nice. I'm sure you won't have any trouble making friends," she said confidently.

Reaching into his lunch box, he pulled out a bologna sandwich, smothered in ketchup and mustard, and a pudding cup. Fishing around deeper, he came across an orange-flavored drink box. He promptly pulled apart its fastened straw and forced it into the sealed opening on the top of the box.

As Kelly bit into his sandwich, two kids approached their table.

One was a behemoth, sporting a short, spiked red haircut that highlighted his robust, freckled face. The other boy was tall and gaunt, with long jet-black sheep-dog hair that restricted his vision.

Kelly was well aware of whom they were coming to visit: they were coming over strictly to greet him on his first official day. The only question was whether it was going to be a warm or rough reception that they had in mind.

The heavyset kid stepped next to Kelly, eyeing him thoughtfully for a few seconds before he spoke.

Bending down, so that his nose was touching Kelly's, he smiled.

"Hey there, Wimp. That's your name, isn't it? Wimpy? You sort of look like a little baby whiner. I guess that's how all babies look, like little wimps."

Julie, furious at the rude interruption, scowled back. "Derrick, there isn't a bigger wimp in this whole school than you. So why don't you go back to your kindergarten class and play with your Barbie dolls!"

The black-haired boy chuckled.

"Shut up, butt-head!" Derrick snarled, pushing his friend in the chest with his fist.

"Do you need her to fight your battles for you, cream-puff? Can't you even fight on your own?" Derrick questioned, his face as red as his flared hair.

Suddenly, a knot began to develop in Kelly's stomach. Not only did he want to avoid getting into a fight on his first day of school—especially since he'd never been in one before in his life—but he also was hoping to avoid embarrassment of epic proportions in front of his new friend. Julie's sassy remarks were very heartfelt, but they weren't helping his situation.

Now he was in the awkward position of defending his manhood in front of her. If he backed down to this jerk she would think he was a big sissy, especially after sticking her neck out for him. He would never be able to walk the school halls again without people whispering, 'Hey, there goes cream-puff! He couldn't fight his way out of a wet paper bag.'

As Kelly sat considering his options, the boy in front of him grew more impatient. Deciding to speed up the conversation, he slammed his balled fist down into Kelly's bologna sandwich, imprinting his hand in the bread.

"Cream-puff, I'm talking to you! What's it gonna be? Are we gonna fight or what?"

By this time, students from other tables began to migrate toward the scene.

Kelly's knees began to shake and his stomach churned sickly. He wished that he were anywhere else at that moment—anywhere. Perspiration dampened his forehead and clothes.

The surrounding students watched with eager excitement like seagulls monitoring a fast-food parking lot for unattended French-fries.

Julie looked over at Kelly with great shock after watching his sandwich get destroyed.

He stared ahead nervously at the bully and his voice rose in a squeaky high stutter as he tried to piece together a coherent sentence. "I . . . ddddon't want any . . . ttttroubbble with you. Let's just ffforget the whole thing, okay?"

"Forget the whole thing?" Derrick laughed. "I'll forget the whole thing after I wipe your face around the floor like a mop!" he yelled, grabbing Kelly by the shirt collar.

Just as the bully made his move, Julie jumped from her seat and ran toward him. Nearing him, her gaze turned to the table next to them and she reached for the first thing that caught her eye.

Derrick drew back his fist, but just as he was about to deliver a devastating blow, his face was covered by a slice of saucy pepperoni pizza.

In a wild rage, he spun around to find the perpetrator, but instead was doused in the face by a carton of cold milk.

Coated with milk, tomato paste and cheese, he growled and lunged at Julie, who had thrown the food. As he reached out to get her, she backpedaled out of the way, causing him to slip on a puddle of milk underfoot.

He landed backward on a table with a crash, and yelped out in pain.

Kelly's eyes grew big. He didn't know whether to run for his life or yell "hooray."

Julie, however, took the initiative and taunted Derrick by doing an extravagant victory dance over him.

Two teachers witnessed the commotion and ran over to the scene.

"All right, all right! Break it up. Come on, enough of this,"

An older, dwarfish, balding teacher grabbed Julie by the arm and escorted her and Kelly out of the cafeteria. The other teacher took Derrick, along with his sidekick, and followed suit.

Principal Skeemer had just sat down at his desk with a hot cup of coffee when his door was thrust open and Carl Stein and Ron Fosgate, the school's custodian and English teacher, escorted in four students—one of which looked and reeked of milky pepperoni.

The day was going so well, he thought; *almost made it through it without any disasters.*

Getting up from behind his desk, he spoke unenthusiastically, "What do we have today, Carl?"

"Food fight. These damn kids today have no respect for food or rules. They're all monsters, I tell you. Every one of 'em are animals," he barked.

Kevin Skeemer sighed wearily. He was quite used to Carl's exaggerations.

"I don't think there's much more to it than that," Ron Fosgate surmised. "Just kids clowning around."

Kevin Skeemer stepped in front of Julie and Kelly. "You two have anything to add to the story?"

"No, sir," Julie shook her head. "It was just a stupid food fight. I'm sorry that it happened."

"How about you two," he asked, looking at Derrick. "You seem like you got the worst of the meal. Any thoughts on the matter?"

Biting his lip, Derrick responded with embarrassment, "Nope. It's no big deal."

"Good." he said, noticing the bell for the next class was about to ring.

"Class is about begin. I suggest you kids think about this incident real hard. Don't expect me to be as lenient next time. Julie, I'm very surprised that you would be involved in this. You're too smart and well behaved to be acting this way," he said sternly.

"I'm sorry, Mr. Skeemer. It won't happen again," she said respectfully.

"Now go on, or you're going to be late."

The kids turned and stepped away.

"Oh, and Derrick," Mr. Skeemer called out. "Go to the bathroom and get that cheese off your face, please."

Julie and Kelly walked to class, but before they went inside, Kelly stopped her.

"Thanks for helping me back there."

She smiled at him. "That's okay. I enjoyed it. Derrick's such a major dweeb. I'll mess with him any time I can. You're not a fighter, are you?"

"No, I don't like to fight at all," he responded, looking to the floor, embarrassed.

"Don't worry about it. Not everyone likes to fight. I think it's cool that you don't get involved in stupid stuff like that."

"Really?" he asked, amazed.

"Yeah," she insisted.

*　　*　　*

The knob to the side door of his house remained locked after Kelly tried to jiggle it open for the third time. Growing frustrated, he ran around to the front of the house and tried opening the main door, which was also locked. Suddenly, he remembered that his mom had gone to the hospital for a job interview and was supposed to leave the spare house key under the welcome mat.

Relieved, he ran back to the side of the house, where he retrieved the silver key.

He was thankful not to be stuck outside alone while Samantha was still at school attending to a newspaper project.

Sliding the key into the slot, he turned the lock and entered.

The house was quiet; too quiet, he felt.

He stepped through the foyer and entered the stillness. Closing the door behind him, the pane of glass rattled as the door locked into place. Prying off his tennis shoes on the side door landing, he glanced down each stair, which led into the darkness of the basement: it seemed to swallow the room.

The worst part about silence is the anticipation of a noise, he thought. If he could only hear one little noise, he could deal with that; but there wasn't a sound, only absolute silence.

Kelly knew something was down there in the basement—waiting, watching him up on the landing with keen interest. Something was there, concealed in the darkness, snarling, crawling slowly on the floor towards the stairs to get a closer look at him.

Kelly shivered. His imagination was scaring him senseless once again. He decided to vacate the area, just in case something was down there, lurking.

Leaving his shoes behind, he ran up three short steps that led into the kitchen and then headed for the living room. He turned on the television and increased the volume louder than usual—just in case a stranger was in the house, he hoped that the loud noise would startle and drive them away.

Inspecting the living room, everything seemed fine, but he wasn't absolutely convinced.

Okay, Kelly, you're just scaring yourself, you big baby, he admonished. Just relax and act as though everything's normal. Nothing's going happen to you, he reassured himself.

Even though his nerves were on edge, he was very hungry, so he decided to make a sandwich and grab some chips. At least that would fill time.

He went back into the kitchen and took out a jar of mayonnaise and a bag of Wonder Bread, intent on making his favorite "mayonnaise sandwich."

Reaching into the cupboard above the stove, he took out a bag of corn chips and headed back towards the living room.

Where was his faithful sidekick, he wondered? "Sassy? Come on, girl."

No response.

"Sassy! Where are you?" he yelled.

Going to the opening of the stairs leading up to the second floor, connected from the kitchen, he looked straight up toward the next level.

"Sassy?"

He set the bag of chips on the kitchen counter and went up the stairs. As he rounded the corner of the second landing, he noticed that the attic ladder was pulled down to the floor.

Strange. *Had his mom been sorting through the attic earlier? Maybe she forgot to close the door when she left. What was up there anyway? Probably a bunch of junk or some antiques. Or rats?*

He approached the ladder, keeping his body pressed against the side of the wall as he peered up into the dark chamber.

An object crashed and fell to the attic floor just above him. Startled, he instinctively stepped back away from the sound.

"Sassy? Are you up there? Come on down, it's just me. I'm not . . ."

As the words escaped his lips, an object tumbled out from the attic and rolled down the stairs until it rested upon the last step in front of him.

It was the doll, arms and legs sprawled out and its head resting against the back of the step. Its eyelids seemed to jerk open in sudden awareness and stared at him.

"What the . . . !" Kelly exclaimed, standing there frozen in one spot.

He was too terrified to move a muscle and felt helpless. The doll stayed motionless and appeared to be lifeless, but there was a hypnotizing effect to its gaze.

Sassy darted out of Kelly's bedroom and slid to a stop in front of the doll. Grabbing the rag doll between its jaws, the dog began to shake it back and forth violently.

"No, Sassy! Stop! Put it down!"

The dog released the doll to the carpet, trotted over to Kelly and sat down, expecting to be rewarded for heroic behavior.

"Bad dog!" he reprimanded.

The baffled animal lifted its ears at the harsh tone, then laid down on the floor.

Kelly picked up the doll and inspected its limp body to make sure it was neither damaged, nor alive. He wasn't sure why he had commanded his dog to leave it alone; maybe it was curiosity. Something about the doll frightened him, but also, drew him towards it.

Satisfied that the figure was not going to becoming animated, any time soon, he placed it in his bedroom upon the wooden rocking chair.

Downstairs, the side door of the house slammed shut and his Mom's voice called out, "I'm home. Kelly . . . Samantha?"

Hearing the friendly voice, he raced down the stairs to meet her.

"Hey, honey, how was your first day?" Susan asked.

"Mom, guess what? You won't believe it. When I got home from school the attic door was down and . . ."

"Kelly, you didn't go up in the attic? Baby, I don't want you playing up there," she butted in.

"No, listen. That doll that I found before came rolling down the stairs. I think it's alive. I know it is," he said, horrified.

"Doll? What doll?"

Exasperated that his point wasn't getting across, he took a deep breath.

"A few months ago I found a secret room in the library. I found the doll in there. And now it's moving. I saw it move!"

"Kelly, there's no secret room. It's a storage chamber. And I don't know why the attic door was left open, but maybe the doll just fell out harmlessly."

"No!" he implored. "I didn't put it up there. It was in my room the whole time. How could it get up there by itself? I didn't do it."

Seeing the worry in his eyes, she began to calm him down some and tried reasoning with him.

"Maybe Sammy set it up there to try and scare you. You know, for all the times at the old house that you got her?"

He bit his lip for a second and thought. That made a lot of sense. He could see her doing something sneaky like that.

"But how did it fall down the stairs right in front of me?"

"I'm not sure, honey, but dolls don't move by themselves. There's probably a good explanation. Don't fret about it. Hey, I've got some good news," she smiled. "You know the job that I applied for at the hospital? I got it! I start next week. Isn't that great! I get to work with Uncle Rich."

"You won't be home anymore?" he said, his voice trembling.

"I'll be starting on afternoons for a while, until I can get on days. It'll only be for a little while. Just until I learn the ropes."

"What time will you be home?"

"I'll be working from four-thirty in the afternoon to one in the morning. But I'll have the weekends and some weekdays off. And I'll be able to spend a little time with you when you come home from school, too."

"Does it pay a lot of money?" he asked slyly.

She was happy to see him finally come out of his anxiety.

"It pays pretty good, starting out. Once I'm in there for a while it'll go up even more," she said, bursting with excitement. "Now give me a big hug and promise me you won't worry about that doll, okay?"

He nodded in agreement and threw his arms around her.

That evening during dinner, he told her about the two bullies at lunch and also about his tardiness for class. He spoke fondly of how Julie single-handily put Derrick in his place, and how she introduced Kelly to her friends.

"Over all, it was an okay day," he surmised. "At least I didn't get a black eye, he kidded."

*   *   *

During the night as Kelly and Samantha watched television, Susan went upstairs and closed the attic door. She then checked out the secret room in the library that Kelly had told her about. It didn't alarm her; it was only a small storage compartment, nothing unusual about it.

After searching the library, she went into Kelly's bedroom where the rag doll sat peacefully in the rocker.

Susan picked up the doll and held it out in front of her. She studied its beautifully painted porcelain face.

"So, you're the evil little one behind all this panic," she said with a smirk.

She laid the doll back down and surveyed the room for anything else he might have forgotten to mention. Noticing their old family portrait on his dresser, she reached down and examined it.

God, she was so young when that photo was taken, and the kids were practically babies. It was one of the few times that she and John were actually happy. Funny, back then she thought everything was going to be perfect. *Perfect my ass,* she thought now, and placed the glass frame back down onto the table.

She sighed deeply and left the room. As she walked out into the hallway, the sound of shattering glass resounded from Kelly's bedroom and stopped her cold.

Walking back into his bedroom, she found the picture frame lying upon the floor and its glass encasing spider-webbed.

"Dammit!" she cursed aloud, pissed at herself.

Scooping up the frame and picture, she hand-picked the remaining glass shards until each and every sliver was accounted for, and then discarded them into the waste basket along side the desk.

Turning to the doll in the chair, she deadpanned, "And you . . . shut up!"

The doll looked back at her with the same blank expression that it displayed earlier, except this time, she had the feeling it was mocking her.

*   *   *

After watching a boring episode of "20/20" about health care for the elderly, Samantha went up to bed.

She stopped off in the bathroom to brush her teeth before retiring for the night.

Her day, for the most part, had gone by quietly. Compared to Kelly's, it had been pretty uneventful. But she was glad for her brother, nonetheless. In fact, she had prayed for him the night before that he would have an easy transition into his new school, and that prayer seemed to be working.

Her classmates seemed friendly, but not very personable. No one really inquired at all about her past life or where she came from. She met a pretty brunette named Holly Ivy who sat next to her in three of her five classes. They had a lot in common with each other. Not only did they both enjoy writing, but they also had the same admiration for the latest rock groups. Holly gave her all of the juicy tidbits about the dance club uptown. She mentioned that the local bands performed free shows a few times during the month. The hottest group was Dezire, a quartet of longhaired studs that she was sure Samantha was going to love.

"They really get into their music," Holly replied. "They all run from one side of the stage to the other and climb on top of their speakers. It's really cool."

Samantha was relieved to hear that there was live music in town. She had feared that it would be outlawed here in nowhereville. In Florida, rock-n-roll bands were a dime a dozen: from Hard Rock to Alternative and Pop to Punk, they had it all. Most of them weren't worth a crap, but a couple of them had quite a following. She was one of the devoted fans of these bands. Every weekend she'd gather with friends at the Top Cat, a lounge where bands performed all-ages shows. Often, she would hangout with the groups after the show. All the musicians knew her age and understood that she was just a fan of theirs and not a cheap groupie, so she didn't have to worry about sexual pressure, or alcohol and drugs.

She smiled, reflecting on her club days in Florida, and opened up the bathroom cabinet door and pulled out a tube of toothpaste and a toothbrush. She coated the bristles with aqua blue paste and soaked it under some water, shutting the medicine cabinet door in the process. While brushing, she examined her face for any pimples. As her eyes focused on her skin, a strange sight appeared in the background. Slowly, her eyes shifted from her face to the area in the mirror behind her.

Something was in the library across the hall, but what was it? From her angle, the shape was too indistinguishable to focus on immediately. But with closer inspection, she saw the reflection of a man: his bearded, marble-white face was watching over her. It was the same man who was standing in the backyard by the fence, watching her bedroom window.

She looked on in disbelief, waiting for the vision to vanish like a mirage.

The figure, a good twenty-feet away, suddenly lifted effortlessly off the ground like a balloon and drifted towards her.

She choked with shock and fear, taking in deep breaths as the stone-faced man approached closer.

His arms stretched towards her, and a manic smile came about on his lips. His fingers curled and flexed as his weightless body drifted closer and closer.

Frightened, she spun around in defense but found no haunting specter. The hallway and library were empty.

She turned back to the mirror as her heart throbbed uncontrollably.

The area behind her was empty.

Placing her hands over her face she wept, unable to contain herself.

"What the hell was that! Am I going crazy or did I just see that?"

She looked into the library again, not sure if the man would appear at any moment.

Maybe the lighting was playing tricks with her eyes. *Maybe it was just my imagination,* she thought. *Yeah, and maybe the moon is just the sun at night.*

Walking toward the library, she decided the only way to believe that it was just her imagination tricking her would involve searching the room to prove that it was just a fantasy.

She went to the doorway, unsure if she had made the right decision.

Inside, the room looked normal.

She was scaring herself to death. Her body shook with fear and trepidation.

Edging into the room, she was surprised to find it empty. Placing her hand upon her heart, she exhaled and left the room to finish up in the bathroom.

Lying in bed that night with the covers pulled up to her nose, she felt observed, as though someone was watching her every move. That made her feel vulnerable, and worse, helpless.

She tried to sleep, but it was a restless sleep that came to her. The vision of the bearded specter floating towards her with outstretched arms and zombie-like eyes replayed over and over in her mind like a movie.

What was that I saw? What in God's name is going on in this house, she wondered?

*   *   *

Kelly dreamt during the night about the basement. He was walking aimlessly in search of something, but of what, he was unsure. One moment, the room was pitch black and he had to feel his way forward; the next moment, light would bounce off the wall from some place far ahead and then fade out again.

Suddenly, the rumble of a stampede thundering from behind forced him to run onward. He ran and ran, but the raging force behind still pursued. Stumbling down a slope upon the floor, he rolled into the next room and fell against the well he had seen so many times before in his dreams. The thing chasing from behind got closer and began to scream out like an animal, howling as if it was being ripped apart by the blades of a shredder.

He awoke instantly with sweat glistening on his forehead and remained that way until the morning light.

Chapter 7

Kelly came downstairs, rubbing his eyes from the restless night before.

Going into the kitchen, he grabbed a bowl and spoon, then searched amongst several half-eaten boxes of cereal until he found a box of Count Chocula. Taking these things to the dining room table, he sat down and filled the bowl.

Susan, noticing the darkened circles around his eyes, confronted him.

"Kelly, were you up all night?"

Pouring milk over the cereal, he looked up at her. "I couldn't sleep. I had a bad dream again."

Susan was worried. Now his dreams were affecting his sleep pattern again. There had to be something she could do for him. Talking to him about the dreams just didn't seem to work. Perhaps, she could ask Richard to recommend a sleep therapist to help Kelly with his problem. It was worth a shot, at least.

"Kelly, I'm going to find someone who can help you with your sleeping."

Alarmed, he sat up. "Why? What will they do to me?"

"Nothing. The doctor will try to find out why you're having so many nightmares."

Satisfied he wasn't going to be examined like a test rat, he plunged his spoon into the chocolate milk and soggy marshmallows.

*   *   *

Samantha awoke and crawled out of bed, feeling restless and disorientated. The nasty vision in the bathroom mirror was still etched into her mind and had kept her tossing and turning all night long. She would have major work to do on her appearance this morning, covering over the dark rings around her eyes with makeup to mask her dreary look.

Walking into the bathroom she gazed doubtfully into the mirror.

She felt horrible, and was sure the kids at school would be frightened of her all morning.

*   *   *

The constant rambling of Mr. Conner during the first hour of class went on and on like an early morning television infomercial. Not that what his teacher was saying wasn't important, but Kelly's mind was preoccupied with other thoughts. Such as figuring out why he was being haunted by nightmares in his sleep—that was more important.

As the teacher wrote upon the chalkboard, Kelly tapped Julie on her shoulder.

She turned and whispered back, "What?"

"Do you believe in ghosts?"

She looked at him with apprehension. "What? What are you talking about? Can't this wait until break?"

"Ghosts," he repeated. "Things you can't see. They float above the ground and scare you at night."

Davis Conner turned his head slightly, not certain of where the noise was coming from, and watched the children. Kelly waited for the teacher to resume writing again before he continued his sentence.

"Weird things have been going on in my house lately."

"What kind of things?" she asked interested.

"Things keep moving by themselves. I put something in one place and it disappears and ends up in another place. And I've been having really weird dreams."

"That's normal," she remarked. "I have nightmares all the time. Don't worry about it."

"No. Not like a nightmare. It's like I dream about things that are going to happen in the future. Before we moved out here, I had a dream about a well in a basement. When we moved to our new house, the exact same well was in our basement!"

"Wow! That is kind of creepy. Maybe you're like one of those people on TV who can predict the future. They go out and find killers," she proclaimed excitedly.

"No, these aren't good kinds of dreams. They've all been bad. I'm usually running away from something that's trying to kill me."

"It's too bad," she said somberly. "Psychics get paid really well."

*   *   *

Susan filed a patient's insurance form into a drawer in her desk, then looked up and spotted her tall, lanky brother walking up.

"Hey stranger. How's the learning process?" he asked.

"Not too bad. I think I'm getting the hang of it already. Are you finished with that last patient?"

"Yeah, let's go get something to eat, I'm starving," he replied, sliding his fingers through his thick, curly black hair.

Sitting in the hospital cafeteria, Susan took a sip of diet cola. She gave her brother a look he had seen so many times growing up. It was the look she had when something was bothering her, but she felt uncomfortable bringing it up. So, instinctively, he prodded it out of her.

"All right, Susan B. Adkins, if I didn't know any better, I'd swear there was something on your mind. Now why don't you be a good sister and tell big brother what's troubling you."

She smiled already more at ease. "It's Kelly. He's having trouble sleeping at night. He's been having nightmares since before we moved here, and they are really getting to him. They keep getting worse, and he's been making up absurd stories. He believes he found a doll that's come to life—that it's moving by itself. It's starting to scare me a little, Rich."

Reaching out, he cupped her hands with his. "I don't think it's that big of a deal. But if it's bothering you that much, I think maybe you should talk to someone who's more qualified to deal with these types of situations. I have a good friend that's a psychiatrist. His office is down on Second Street and . . ."

"I'm not taking my son to some sort of shrink! He's not crazy! He'd be scared to death about being sent to talk to some stranger. I thought about taking him to see a general practitioner, to see if there was something physically wrong with him, but a psychiatrist?"

"Sis, I'm not implying that he's crazy. A lot of people see psychiatrists. They help people deal with emotional problems that they're unable to cope with themselves. If he's having problems with something, it might be in his best interests if he had some help. It may even help you deal with the situation better. I'm sure the doctor knows how to ease a child's apprehension with talking about his feelings. And Joe's a really nice guy. He'll be glad to help you in any way he can. Go and see him, all right?"

She felt drained. The words he spoke made sense and had urgency about them. He was right. The doctor would be better suited to help him than her. She would just have to convey to Kelly how important it was for him to give the doctor a fair chance.

"You're right, he needs counseling. I'll make an appointment today."

"Susan, if there's anything you need . . ."

"I promise," she finished, anticipating his next words. "I'll let you know," she smiled.

*   *   *

When Kelly got home from school, his mom was seated at the dining room table. From the look on her face she seemed to be waiting expectantly for him.

"Hi, mom," he said, kissing her on the lips.

"Hi, darlin'. Did you have a nice day at school?"

"Yep. We started reading a book called "Where the Red Fern Grows." That motorcycle guy we met at the diner is my teacher. It's so cool! He's gonna let us read a lot of cool stuff this year."

"That's wonderful," she responded, tickling underneath his chin.

"Kelly, you remember this morning I told you I was going to find you some help with your sleeping?"

He nodded his head in agreement.

"Well, I made an appointment for you with a doctor tomorrow after school."

He swallowed hard, unsure of what she was getting at.

"You don't have to be afraid. He's a good doctor. He's only going to talk to you about your problems so that he can help you with them."

"Is he a shrink?"

She gave him a reassuring smile. "Yes. He's a shrink. But he's a very nice shrink. Where did you hear that word?"

"From Jon Lang back at our old school. He said he had a crazy sister, and that she had to see a shrink all the time," he said, exaggeratedly twirling his finger by his head.

"Well, maybe your friend's sister was crazy, but you're normal, and he's only going to talk to you once or twice to find out what's bothering you so much. He's only going to listen and give you some advice."

"Don't worry, Mom. I'm not afraid," he said, patting her upon the leg.

"That's my brave boy. I'm proud of you."

*   *   *

The next day in the doctor's reception lounge, Kelly sat next to his mom on a hard, outdated 1980s multi-colored love seat.

The office wasn't as scary as he thought it would be. He figured that the room would be all white, with folding chairs to sit upon, and that some huge woman would be sitting behind a desk, painting her nails and smiling.

This office was far from that. It was warm and cozy. The walls had wood paneling; the carpet was ivory white, and several colorful paintings hung upon the walls. One picture was of a voyaging sailboat, and another was of a dense green forest. There was even a painting of a cabin on a snowy mountainside and a frozen pond that had children ice skating upon it.

The door to the doctor's office opened and a young, clean-shaven man appeared. He walked over to Susan.

"Hi, I'm Doctor Ramsey. You must be Susan and Kelly?"

They stood up, with Susan extending her hand. "Pleased to meet you, Doctor Ramsey. My brother, Richard, has told me so much about you."

"Is that right? Oh dear, I was afraid of that. Only good things I hope."

"Yes. Only good things," she laughed.

"Kelly, if you wouldn't mind following me into my office, we'll get started."

"Doctor?" Susan interrupted. "Would you mind if I came in and, sort of, sat in. I won't be any trouble, scout's honor, I promise. I'll be very quiet."

"I'm sorry, Susan, but I find it much easier and rewarding if I have a patient's complete and undivided attention. That way they're not distracted one way or another. He might feel more enticed to speak freely if he is not being monitored."

After escorting Kelly into his office, Joseph Ramsey closed the door behind him. Although he was only forty, he had been pursuing a career in psychology ever since he was eighteen. It was a yearning that persuaded him to apply himself in the field. Ever since childhood, he had loved to solve other people's problems: from family to friends or even complete strangers, if he could help, he would. He loved hearing interesting stories, the crazier the better, and often gave useful advice for the troubled person who sought it.

"Kelly, if you'll have a seat," he said, pointing to a plush white chair in front of a large oak desk.

As Kelly sat down, Dr. Ramsey opened up a small refrigerator positioned on top of a counter against a wall.

"Would you like something to drink," he offered, revealing the inside of the box. "I've got Coke, Diet Coke and root beer."

"Root beer, please," Kelly replied, hoping the cold drink would help coat his dry throat.

"I'll bet you've probably heard wild stories at some point in your life about psychiatrists. Maybe stories about how they treat people with severe mental problems, or so-called crazy people. Well, I'm here to be a friend to you. I'm here to listen to what's bothering you, and to try to offer the best advice I can about your problem. The only way I can help you is for you to be totally honest with me, and let me know exactly what you're feeling and what is bothering you, understand? You have to trust me."

"Yes, sir. I won't lie," he said, taking a sip of soda pop to wet his parched lips.

*   *   *

Susan's mind raced with wild thoughts while waiting in the reception area. The Vanity Fair magazine she held was just a distraction for her concerned mind. Although she read a few paragraphs of an article, her mind was preoccupied with Kelly, and what was going on in the next room.

What if he held this against her for the rest of his life, or if he felt self-conscious around other people from now on? She would never be able to live with herself if he hated her. But what else could she do? She had worn out every possible avenue. This had seemed like the smartest thing to do at the time, but now she wasn't quite so sure. The doctor and Kelly had been hidden together behind a closed door for nearly forty minutes—and it seemed like an eternity to her.

When anticipation finally got to a heightened state and she felt as though she was going to explode, Kelly emerged from behind the closed door, with Dr. Ramsey following behind.

Kelly quickly smiled, which brought her great emotional relief.

"Susan, can I talk to you in my office for a moment, please?" he asked, displaying a relaxed demeanor.

"Sure, Doctor. Kelly, honey, wait right here until I get back."

Still clutching the drink in his hand, he sat down upon the love seat and grabbed the nearest fishing magazine.

Susan walked into the office and sat down, curiously watching the doctor's face to gauge whether he seemed pleased or displeased with their meeting.

"I think Kelly is a wonderful young man. He's bright, witty and respectful. But I believe there is some trouble that seems to stem from the break-up of your marriage and your move out of state away from his friends. He's having a rough transition from breaking ties with his old acquaintances, to learning how to make new friends here."

"But why does he insist on making up these farfetched stories, and why does he keep having nightmares? I don't see any connection," she asked, concerned.

"It's symbolism. You see, when he claims to witness bizarre events or dreams about frightening images, it represents resentment to your separation and the daunting task of making new friends. It's a very intimidating challenge for him, I'm sure you can just imagine. And instead of attempting to make new friends, he substitutes or associates it with fear, and uses these imaginary events as replacements to his real frustrations. The problems and issues manifested at home are his way of not dealing with what's really bothering him. He's deeply frightened of change, understand."

"What can I do to help him adjust?"

"Encourage him to be more socially active with his friends at school. Maybe he could invite a few classmates over to spend the night. Once he develops his own identity with the other children, he'll be more comfortable and his dreams will subside. He mentioned to me that he likes to play practical jokes on his sister. He has quite an imagination. Maybe he's just using the animation of the doll as an output of his creativeness. For the time being, just humor him and then see how it transpires in a month or so."

Susan shook the doctor's hand and smiled, but inside she still felt hollow, as if something more was at hand that neither she nor the doctor could fathom.

"Call me if you notice any change, Susan."

"Thank you, I will," she said hesitantly.

*   *   *

During the drive back home Kelly filled her in about all the questions the doctor posed. He told her that he wasn't really afraid and that he felt fine talking to the man.

"How would you feel about having a party this weekend at the house? You could invite some of your friends from school for a sleep over. We could get pizza, watch some movies and play games. What do you think?"

"What if no one wants to come over?" he asked, looking up with sad blue eyes.

She beamed with pride. "How could they not want to come over to our house? We've got Sassy the wonder dog!" She tickled at his stomach, causing him to burst out laughing.

*   *   *

Samantha slammed the side door shut. She was still in a daze after being asked out on a date by Steven Bentley, an athletic blond boy in her Algebra class. She had agreed to go without consulting her mom first, but why should she? She was sixteen years old and ready to start dating guys, and didn't need approval.

But just to be on the safe side, she figured it couldn't hurt to ask permission first. Her mom would like that. And if her mother said no, she would have to deal with it then.

She had liked Steven the first time they met in class. His chiseled, handsome face and beautiful eyes reminded her of Orlando Bloom. And when she heard he was the star quarterback on the Junior Varsity football team, she almost squealed in delight.

She was caught totally off-guard when he asked her out. But she still had enough wits to play the coy game: "I don't know, let me think about it," she told him. Before the end of the school day, she tracked him down and told him yes emphatically!

That afternoon, after placing her school bag upon the chair, she went into the living room and picked up Feisty, her kitten. The cat purred as Samantha stroked the back of its neck.

"Have you been a good kitty?"

The kitten lifted its head and purred warmly in approval.

She set the kitten back down and went upstairs into the bathroom. Lifting up the drain lever in the bathtub, she began to fill the tub with hot water. After the desired water temperature was set, she clicked on a small portable radio.

Closing the bathroom door, she began unbuttoning her top as an Aerosmith ballad began. The shirt dropped to the floor as she started to unfasten her jeans. She slid her pants down to her ankles and kicked them off into a heap in the corner. Looking into a full-length mirror upon the back of the door, she studied her body, then sighed wearily.

She wasn't gifted with huge breasts, like some of her friends, but at least she was in very good shape. Her stomach muscles and legs were toned. She was confident about her appearance and kept herself active. But as confident as she was about her appearance, she wasn't as confident about how guys perceived her. The only time she'd been in a relationship with a guy was last year, and he was just a close friend who she had gone out with a few times for fun. Kissing was as far as it developed, because she didn't really care to take it to any other level. But as the year moved on, her girlfriends teased her, and repeatedly told her that boys in high school expected girls to go a lot farther than that. Her friends kept pressuring her, and said that if she wasn't at least willing to try and experiment, she was never going to keep a boyfriend. She hated the thought of having to sacrifice her beliefs in order to keep someone's interest. But if she didn't at least attempt to go farther with a guy, there would be a million other girls standing in line who would.

She shut off the water as it rose toward the top of the tub's edge, while Steven Tyler sexually crooned in the background.

Steam rose as she slid her sleek frame down underneath the water's surface. The hot water soothed her body and she closed her eyes in pleasure, tuning out her worries.

Stroking the surface of the water, she relaxed into a state of tranquility. Her hand rested over the lip of the porcelain bathtub, as the radio lulled her into satisfied peace.

But peace was ripped away as the bathroom light shut off, leaving her in darkness.

She sat up in shock and waited, unsure of what to do or how to react. She had a strange feeling of being watched, although she had no sight.

A chill crept over her, as though icy fingers were sliding their way down her body.

She stood up in the bathtub and reached for a towel that was hung against the wall. Feeling in all directions, the cloth was no where to be found.

She stepped out of the tub and walked forward blindly. Dripping with water, she stumbled over her clothing scattered on the floor. Again, frozen fingertips began to probe over her body slowly, and she trembled within. The invisible fingers slid down her legs, up to her shoulders and then traveled slowly across her breasts and nipples.

She frantically flailed her arms into the air, hoping that would cease the touch.

Then she heard the voices. Soft little voices creeping inside of her ears, whispering several words at a time.

She couldn't comprehend everything they were saying, just playful, sexual, threatening sentences. A continuous whisper of words: "KISS ME . . . LICK ME . . . TOUCH YOU . . . WANT YOU . . . NEED YOU . . . GET YOU . . . KILL YOU," a man's voice whispered softly into her ears.

"Stop it! Just stop it!" she screamed, covering her ears with her hands.

Lurching forward, her kneecap slammed hard into a brass handle on the sink drawer. She winced in pain, but kept moving, determined to get out of the darkened room.

Her hand stubbed into the door and she felt frantically up and down for the knob. When she finally grasped it, the bathroom light turned back on by it's own accord.

She looked quickly behind and around her. She was alone.

Shaken with fear, she ran naked out of the bathroom and into her bedroom, slammed the door shut, covered herself in a bathrobe and sat down upon the bed, sobbing uncontrollably.

Chapter 8

The next morning at school, Kelly passed out party invitations with directions to his house to the few friends in class that he had just gotten to know.

There was Philip Nichols, a raven-haired boy who sort of resembled Alfalfa from the Little Rascals, without the stiff horn of hair. Phil, like Kelly, had a passion for Army men and Star Wars action figures. He had every Star Wars' character except for the Emperor and a few non-significant aliens. Phil, excited about having the chance to do battle against Kelly's Storm Troopers, accepted the party invitation, although he said he would call later that night after he verified it with his mom.

Chris Dwyer was a little reluctant to show up at the party. He didn't know Kelly very well, and it took him by surprise to have a new kid in school offer him an invitation. Chris was the timid type, who usually followed along and did what everyone else did. If one person agreed to something and egged Chris on, then he usually followed suit. Whenever it came to making his own decisions in life, he tended to shy away and retreat.

Remembering that information, Kelly came up with a great idea. Since Chris was a close friend of Matt Spellman, he went directly to Matt and proposed the invitation to him, knowing Matt could convince Chris to come along. Matt was up for anything, understanding that his evening would probably be spent alone otherwise.

Matt had never been very social. Since he was overweight, lazy and hated competitive sports, athletic kids ignored him. And lacking a scholar's mentality, he was an outcast with the intellects. He felt like he was stuck going nowhere and left alone on an island.

"If you come over do you think you could bring Chris with you? I don't really know him well enough to ask." Kelly pressed Matt.

"Sure; if I go, I'm sure he will," he said confidently.

Now that he had three confirmations, there was only one more person left to ask. He was positive she would go; nevertheless, he wanted to be careful how he asked her. If he made if appear that it was a boy's party, she might refuse. Yet, if he didn't mention that three other boys were showing up to spend the night, she might be furious.

He popped the question to her at the end of their last class. "Julie, I'm having a party at my house this Saturday. It's kind of like a sleep over. There's going to be pizza, and we'll play some games and . . ."

"I'd love to go," she answered, before he even finished. "I have to ask my mom first, though. Who's all coming over?" she rambled on.

Stunned that she had decided without even considering it, he began naming off the list: "Matt, Phil Nichols, and probably Chris Dwyer."

"What! Only boys are going to be there? What's up with that? I have the feeling I'm walking into some kind of twisted trap," she teased. "Well, okay. I'd be happy to be the lone girl representative. Maybe I'll learn how to become macho. I'll ask tonight and call you later. My mom will probably want to speak to your mom."

He nodded, then handed her a sheet of paper:

**PARTY THIS SATURDAY NIGHT AT 5 P.M.
PIZZA AND POP PROVIDED. BRING A
SLEEPING BAG AND PILLOW.
185 DENTON.**

*   *   *

Samantha bit into an edge of a burnt crusted pepperoni pizza slice she had bought during lunch. The hard, blackened dough snapped sharply as she sank her teeth into it.

"Ewww!" she exclaimed, wrinkling her nose at Holly Ivy, her closest friend. "Why can't they feed us anything that doesn't threaten our health?"

"The school probably overstocked on cardboard for the Art class and decided they could pawn it off on the lunch crowd. We're like guinea pigs," Holly joked.

Samantha laughed, barely keeping from spitting out a mouthful of pizza. As she covered her mouth with her hand, Stephen Bentley casually walked up to them.

"Don't tell me you ate a bad piece of charcoal driftwood, too? That happens all the time around here. That stuff goes down pretty rough," he said, flashing a big smile towards the girls.

"No, not this time. Sammy and I were just comparing our food to paper plates," Holly teased, as she bumped Samantha with her shoulder.

"Are we still on for Saturday night?" he asked shyly, squatting down to eye level with her.

"Sure. I wouldn't miss it for the world." she said confidently, even though she knew she still hadn't asked her mom yet.

"Great. Then I'll pick you up at your house, say at seven o'clock?"

"Sure, that'll be great," she nodded, admiring his pretty face and not hearing a word he spoke.

As Stephen walked away, Samantha dropped her head down onto the table.

"Ohhhh noooo!"

"What? What's the matter!" Penny asked.

"I just agreed to go out on a date, and I don't even know if my mom will let me go yet."

74

"Do you think she'll be mad?"

"No! Um, I don't know, maybe. It's hard to tell. Who knows if she'll flip out."

*   *   *

Susan pulled into the Caseville Elementary School parking lot and circled the area until an open space became visible.

After shutting and locking her car door, Susan went up the stairs to the main entrance and proceeded to the administration office. The receptionist seated behind the counter got up out of her chair. "Can I help you?" she inquired.

"Yes. I was wondering if I could speak with Mr. Conner?"

"Mr. Conner is probably in the teacher's lounge having lunch right now. Would you like me to page him to the office for you?" she asked, tilting her head to the side and offering a pleasant smile.

"Yes, please, if that wouldn't be any trouble."

"No trouble at all," she assured Susan while picking up the phone.

"Cindy, is Davis Conner there? Okay. No, that won't be necessary, thank you."

She placed the receiver down and looked at Susan. "He's still in his classroom. If you want to just go to his office, I can explain how to get there."

"That would be great."

"Just go straight down the main hallway and then make a left. Second door on the right. Room twenty-three."

Susan thanked the woman and headed off down the empty hall. She felt like a kid again, going to class, except now she was an adult checking on her youngest child. She wanted to convey to the teacher just how much trouble Kelly was having adjusting to the new town, and to see how he was coming along with his studies. And if by chance they happened to talk about other subjects, that would be a bonus, too. It wasn't a crime to be friendly.

She had thought about Davis a lot since they met at the diner. If not for all of the moving and adjustment period, he would have heard from her sooner. Even though she felt weird about calling a guy first, she understood that times were different from when she used to be single, and now women often make the first move. After spending over fifteen years attached to one person, she would just have to catch up with the times.

Passing the first door on the right, she came to room 23.

Davis was seated in a chair with his feet propped upon the desk. He was reading over a newspaper, while eating a sandwich.

"Where can I get a job like that," she kidded.

Embarrassed, he scrambled to get his feet off the desk, almost falling over backwards in the attempt.

"Hey, Susan. Oh, wow. I'm sorry, I wasn't expecting any visitors. I guess you caught me goofing off," he said, his face reddening.

"Don't worry, I won't tell the principal on you," she said, happily strolling into the classroom.

He got up from the chair to properly greet her. "To what do I owe this pleasure."

"Well, I'm sure you're well aware that you have a dangerous, unruly new student on your hands now."

"Oh, I do? I thought that I'd seen that villainous face before," he joked.

"I was a bit curious about how Kelly was doing so far in class, and if he was getting along with the other kids."

"He's doing great. He seems to be attentive, interactive and well behaved. He's completing his homework assignments on time and doing well on his tests. He gets along well with his classmates, although on one occasion, he did have some trouble with an older bully during lunch. Nothing big, just a food-fight incident that led to a brief lecture from the principal. I don't think the older kid ever bothered him again, so I don't foresee any more trouble out of it. May I ask why you're so concerned this early into the school year?"

She didn't want to get into a big discussion about her son's problems; the less said about it, the better it would be for Kelly's peace of mind.

"I'm just a little worried about how he's adjusting. But if you say everything's fine, then I'll take your word for it," she replied, trying to produce a satisfied expression.

"Susan, if there's anything you need to talk about . . . if Kelly's having trouble, please let me know. I'll be glad to help."

"Thanks, Davis, but everything's okay."

"If everything's okay, then how come I haven't received as much as one call from you. Not even a 'hello, nice to talk to you, we should go out for lunch sometime' message. Explain that."

"Would you believe my son's dog ate your number? No? I didn't think so," she said, lifting her shoulders sheepishly. "When I heard that you were Kelly's teacher, I thought the best way to communicate again would be face-to-face. Don't you agree?"

"Yes, definitely." he said, satisfied with her response. "I don't know if you have any regulations against dating your child's teacher, but if you don't, I would love to treat you to dinner," he said.

"You know, out of all of my written laws, I don't think any pertain to dating teachers. How about that! Sure, I would love to go to dinner," she teased, giddy with enthusiasm. Her stomach tickled with the excitement of accepting her first date since the separation.

Looking up at the classroom clock, she became concerned that the next class might begin soon. "I'd better get going before Kelly comes back from lunch and thinks his mom's checking up on him. Here's my number. Call me when you want to go out," she said, scribbling the number down on a blank piece of paper and handing it to him. "I'll talk to you later, Davis. Have a wonderful day!"

Waving goodbye, she sneaked through the hallway corridor undetected and slipped out into the parking lot, where she climbed into her Blazer and sped away down the road.

*   *   *

The yellow school bus rocked back and forth as it turned onto Denton. Once again, the driver took her time driving carefully over the deformed terrain, darting and weaving from side to side to avoid large crevices. The bus continued past the old man's small farmhouse and finally arrived at Kelly's stop.

After reminding the three kids about the party on Saturday, Kelly raced down the aisle and jumped off the bus, waving goodbye to Audrey, the bus driver, in the process.

Standing in the driveway, he watched as the vehicle began to pull away and children at the rear of the bus plastered their funny faces against the window glass. Amused by their antics, he turned and walked up the dirt drive, laughing.

As he was walking, a weird sensation crept upon him, as though he was being urged forward. A voice seemed to call out to him, but he was unable to make out who or where it was coming from. Coming to a stop at the front yard, he studied the house. Something about the house was different—something within.

He looked to the front door, to the living room and then the bedroom windows. Everywhere he looked there was nothing unusual. Finally, becoming perturbed, he glanced higher.

Then he noticed the small round attic window by the top of the roof.

He focused intensely at the window, so intensely, his vision blurred.

Then it became clearer: a doll was on the other side, spying on him.

He ran to the side door and burst inside the house like a rocket exploding into orbit.

Susan, standing in the kitchen preparing dinner, looked on as the speeding boy flew past her and went up the stairs. "Hi, honey, how was your . . ."

Bounding around the corner of the stairs he had no idea that the attic ladder would be down. He stopped abruptly, just short of the attic stairs, expecting the doll to roll out again and make another appearance.

But this time the doll did not come out and the attic remained quiet.

He moved a bit closer, knowing that he shouldn't, drawn by curiosity.

He continued anyway, aware that every time he looked for trouble, trouble found him first.

Why was the doll up there, and how did it get up there again? It had to be a joke.

Standing underneath the opening, with his foot secured upon the first step, he checked above to ensure nothing was waiting to surprise attack him. With an unobstructed path, he continued upward.

His head peered up into the opening of the attic, slowly turning in different directions to measure the area. The storage room was dark, aside from a sunbeam that seeped in through a window at the farthest end of the attic. A light bulb attached to a beam of wood on the roof was just above him, within reach.

Instead of waiting for the menacing doll to jump out at him from a darkened hidden spot, he decided to turn on the light and inspect a little closer.

Scampering up the rest of the steps, he landed upon the wooden floor with a heavy thud, and grabbed the dangling string once his feet touched the ground.

The attic was illuminated brightly, revealing nearly all of the room. The window where the doll had once stood was now empty, and in the corner of the room, cardboard boxes were stacked upon one another. The rest of the room was bare.

Walking towards the boxes, he looked back over his shoulder to make sure he wasn't being watched or followed. Thankfully, he was still alone.

The cardboard boxes were covered with dust and dirt and caused him to sneeze violently as he opened up the first box. After rubbing his watery, itchy eyes and wiping his nose with the back of his hand, he reached into a box and pulled out a colored family portrait.

It must be the people who lived here before us, he thought.

There were three in the family: a short, heavy-set man with curly black hair who wore glasses; a woman with long, flowing straight blond hair; and a young boy, who had an eerie uncanny resemblance to Kelly: same hair color, features and build.

Digging deeper into the box he found more photos, several documents, clothing, and several books, including thick novels, short stories, magazines and a bible.

Enticed, he thumbed through the holy testament. While shifting through the first few chapters, he discovered several pages were missing from the book. The pages were ripped from the spine, as if someone or something tore them out angrily.

The imagery Kelly drew forth sent shivers down his spine. *What could be so wicked and evil as to damage the Holy Bible like this?* He shuttered and placed it down in the corner next to the wall and returned to the remaining boxes.

He grabbed a large, tall box that was taped shut, and pulled off the tape.

Inside was a frail, moth-eaten, white wedding gown that had become tarnished and faded yellow from aging in the humid attic. He laid it down by the side of the box and continued to look for more items. Next he found a brown schoolboy outfit, complete with a vest, knicker pants, and small dress shoes. From the shoe size, they must have belonged to a small child similar to his age. The clothing style seemed unfamiliar and very old.

Placing the items on top of the gown, he returned anxiously to the box and pulled out several black and white photographs that, surprisingly, were in decent condition.

He recognized the first photo instantly: their current house on Denton. The film was in black and white, but the house still had the same structure. The next picture he studied was a black and white wedding photo of a woman with short, dark hair, who was staring ominously at the camera. She was dressed in the wedding gown that Kelly had just retrieved from the box. Her groom, a tall, slender man with a scruffy unkempt beard, looked on emotionlessly as he held her hand.

Kelly wondered why the two seemed so unhappy. He always thought that married couples were supposed to be happy, but the couple in this picture seemed so sad.

Laying down the two photos, he picked up a third. He froze in horror. It was another portrait of the family that had lived here long ago, but it wasn't the married couple that caught his attention this time, it was two others: a tiny, blond boy and an elderly woman who stood close to his left. The old woman was the smiling witch who had awakened him in his bedroom, he was sure of it. She had the same haggard face and menacing glare;

even her clothing was exact! The boy next to her in the photo was identical to Kelly. They were strangely alike, and it felt like he was looking into a mirror.

With that revelation hammering against his chest, the attic door lifted and locked into place, trapping him as light evaporated instantly from the room.

Jumping up, he raced a few feet towards the door, but froze when he realized he couldn't see a thing and, worse, felt as if he wasn't alone.

"Hello? Who's there?" he called out blindly.

The attic was quiet.

Kelly was aware that whatever had closed the door was probably up there with him. His body quivered and his pulse quickened as darkness engulfed him. He closed his eyes and wished that whatever was lurking in the corners would just reveal itself. He couldn't stand not knowing what was there, and he hated that he couldn't see a face or a body.

"Please, don't hurt me. Please," he sobbed.

A chill of wind began to circle around him, yet the intruder remained invisible.

Covering his eyes, Kelly fell to the floor and buried his face in his lap. He couldn't bear to think of what was about to happen next. If the thing was going to break his bones or suck out his blood, than he'd rather not be aware of its first strike, he determined.

But instead of feeling the pain of sharp teeth penetrate his skin, he heard a voice just in front of him. "Kelly, I'm not here to hurt you," the voice spoke in a child's hush. "I want to be your friend. I can help you. Can I be your friend?"

The voice scared him even more than an attack. He was now confronted with something that was expecting an answer.

Still trembling, he began to look up.

The doll hovered directly in front of him, four feet above the floor, eyes open and alert.

Kelly's mouth opened slowly, unsure if he was going to speak out, scream or just throw up.

The doll reiterated. "Will you be my friend? I promise I won't hurt you. I won't let anyone hurt you, if you'll be my friend."

Its safe, child-like voice helped to ease Kelly's fear, and he found himself gaining the nerve to respond back. "But why me? Why do you want me as your friend?" he asked skeptically.

"Because we are the same. No one understands us, Kelly. We are different from other people. I know of your fears. I want to be your friend, and no one else's."

"Nobody believes that I saw you move. My mom thinks I'm making it up. She thinks I'm crazy. Why won't you talk or show yourself to other people?"

"No one else can see or talk to me. I will only speak to you because adults lie. They always lie to us. Your mom doesn't believe you because she doesn't trust you. No one does, except for me. Your mother says that she believes you and wants to help you with your problems, but deep down she thinks that you are lying. Why would she take you to see a stranger who has no idea of what you've been through? They are not to be trusted with your secrets. Do not tell them anything. I believe in you, but you must never tell another person about me, Kelly. If you tell anyone else about our secret, I will never visit you again. Understand? You can talk to me about all of your problems, and I will help you. Promise me that our secret will be kept safe."

"I promise," he agreed, confused about his mother.

"Will you be my friend?" the doll asked again, more sternly.

"Yes, I will," he said, still uncertain.

Kelly's emotions were pulled in opposite directions over his love for his mother, and the soothing words from someone who understood what he was going through.

He was uncertain which path to follow. He just hoped that in the end, he would choose the right one.

* * *

Samantha envisioned a conversation between herself and her mother as she walked up the driveway to her house. She was sure her mother was going to demand that Stephen come inside and introduce himself, because parents always interrogated their kid's first few dates, afraid they might be hooking up with the neighborhood serial killer. What if Stephen took offense to the entire hassle, she wondered? What if he called the whole date off? She would just die!

She opened the screen door and entered the house, discarding her shoes in the process on the landing to the basement. Upon entering the kitchen, she noticed her mother was stirring a pot of chili on the stove. Samantha slid her arms around her mother's waist and kissed her on the cheek. "Hey, Mama, how's it cookin'?"

Susan continued to stir, adding a few dashes of chili powder to the pot. "Fine. Are you hungry?"

"I'll say. You wouldn't believe what kind of crap they try and feed us at lunch. It's totally criminal!" she said, leaning back against the counter. *If there was ever a good opportunity to ask, it was now,* she thought.

"Mom, I need to ask you a favor."

"Sure, honey, what is it?"

"There's this really cute guy at school. His name is Stephen Bentley.

"He sounds pretty expensive."

"Very funny. Anywho. Well, he kind of asked me if I wanted to go out this Saturday night . . . and, of course, I told him that I had to ask you first . . . because I know . . . well, that it's the right thing to do, and I want to make sure it's cool with you first . . . so is it cool with you? What do you think?"

Susan's eyes lit up in amazement. "Kind of asked you out on a date? He didn't even give you a full invitation. Just a half hearted one? That sucks."

"You know what I mean," Samantha whined.

"What do I think? You want to know what I think. Okay. I think it's great. I hope you both have a fun time."

Samantha shrieked with delight, wrapped her arms around her startled mother and gave her a kiss. "Oh, thank you, thank you, thank you," she said excitedly.

"What's with the outpour of emotion? Didn't you think I would let you go out him?"

"I didn't know what to think. I just knew that I really, really wanted to go out with him. I'm sorry," she said, still clutching.

Stepping back, Susan looked deep into her eyes. "Sweetheart, I know it's been tough for you to meet people here. I want you to meet people. Believe me, there's nothing I want more than to see you happy. I don't want to see you repress your feelings."

Samantha buried her head into her mother's chest and hugged her.

"I love you so much," she said, forcing herself not to well up and cry. "I really do!"

Susan held her tightly and stroked her long black hair. "I know, baby. I love you, too."

As they held each other, Susan leaned forward and whispered into her ear, "But, I still want to meet him first before you go out."

*   *   *

The door to the attic lowered down slowly, and from it, Kelly and the doll emerged and went into his bedroom.

Annie will help me through good times and bad, Kelly thought. He wouldn't feel embarrassed telling the doll any private thoughts, because it wouldn't judge him.

Placing the fragile figure in his rocking chair, he sat down on his bed where Sassy lay asleep. "Sassy, I don't want you to be afraid of Annie. She won't hurt you. Annie's my friend now."

The dog awoke and released a deep woof in acknowledgment.

Kelly petted her on the head. "Good-girl."

The name Annie came to him because of a commercial for the Broadway play. It was the only girl name he could think of on short notice, but it seemed to suit the doll perfectly.

Kelly walked into the living room with his new friend and stood before his sister. She was oblivious to his presence, and sat in the recliner chair, petting her kitten's stomach.

"Sam, this is Annie."

As he held the doll out for approval, Samantha looked up from the kitten.

"God! That thing's creepy looking. Get it away from me!" she shouted, recoiling.

"She's not creepy!" he yelled back. "You don't know what you're talking about!" he shouted, running off upstairs with the doll.

Susan, witnessing the ruckus, came into the living room. "Sam, don't talk to him like that. If he wants to show you something, just look at it. There's no need to make snide remarks."

"I can't help it," she said angrily. "Did you see it? It makes me really uncomfortable. It's freaky looking."

The image of the ghoulish specter still burned fresh in Samantha's mind, and the pale dead-like face of the doll only brought back the painful memory.

"I know it is," Susan agreed. "It makes me a little edgy, too. But, for the time being, we're just going to have to accept it. It's just a doll, honey. That's all. If Kelly's happy with it, leave him be. I'm sure, after a while, you won't even notice that it's here," she said, offering a warm smile.

But even Susan had to wonder; if there was nothing to worry about, then why did she feel so nauseous.

Chapter 9

Saturday afternoon was a day of patience for Kelly: the morning had gone by quietly, much to his dismay, and the afternoon was going just as slowly, if not slower. He tried to amuse himself by watching television, but it was devoid of entertainment; he attempted a little reading, but his head was too congested with random thoughts. By the time his first party guest called to confirm he would be at the party later on in the evening, Kelly was relieved, but exhausted from worrying. At least something was finally happening.

At 5 p.m., Kelly sat at the window watching for any sign of a car approaching down the street. His heart skipped a beat when he finally eyed a shiny car speeding towards the house from a distance. The car pulled into his driveway, and out popped Philip Nichols, carrying a grocery bag in one arm and a sleeping bag and pillow in his other. Kelly greeted him enthusiastically at the door, then took him into the living room area to meet his mom.

"Mom, this is Phil. Phil's a buddy of mine in my class," he said, presenting the boy to her like an award.

"Hi there, Phil. It's nice to meet you. Let me hang your coat up for you."

"Thanks, Mrs. Adkins," he said, promptly taking it off.

"I brought some Star Wars action figures and some army men, too," Phil said excitedly.

"Cool," Kelly burst. "Let's take them up to my room and then I'll show you the rest of the house." The two scampered upstairs, leaving Susan in charge of monitoring the arrival of the next guest.

Upstairs, Kelly began showing Phil each room. "This is like a small storage room. I don't really know what it's used for," Kelly explained, lifting his shoulders. Walking on, he pointed to a closed door. "That's a bathroom, and that's my older sister's room . . ."

"How much older?" Phil butted in casually, weighing his chances.

"She's in high school," Kelly replied, catching on to his buddy's intentions.

"Oh. That is pretty old," he said, discouraged.

They walked away from the door as the sound of loud, hard-driving music emanated from within.

"Here's the library," Kelly pointed, showing his friend the next stop on the tour.

"Wow! Do you guys read a lot, or something?" Phil asked, amazed by the volumes of books upon the shelf.

"These were all here before us. I read some of them now and then. Let's go into my room," he said, directing him away from the library.

Just as they were about to enter the bedroom, Sassy followed closely behind on their heels, curious about the commotion.

"Sass, you're gonna have to stay downstairs tonight. I've got friends coming over, and I don't want you getting in the way. Okay?"

The dog looked somberly to the ground, then back up at the two boys and continued to walk with them towards the bedroom.

"No!" Kelly demanded firmly, pointing towards the staircase. "Go!"

Taking the unwelcome hint, Sassy turned around and left with her tail between her legs.

"Come on, let's go," Kelly insisted.

Phil dumped the contents from his grocery bag onto the floor, and the two began rummaging through the mass of action figures to find their selected alliance.

*   *   *

Susan, standing in the living room, heard a knock at the door. When she got to the door, Chris and Matt were waiting outside.

"Hi, guys, come on in. I'm Kelly's mother. He's upstairs with Phil."

After taking their coats, she showed them the way to the bedroom. No sooner did she send them rambling up the stairs, then a car door slammed outside.

Last of the Mohicans, she thought. Except this one must be the squaw.

Tending to the door again, she opened it to find a bright and cheerful Julie.

"Hey, Mrs. Adkins, nice to you see you again."

"Hi, Julie. How are you today, sweetie?"

"Just fine, ma'am. Thanks for having me over," she giggled.

"Don't thank me, thank Kelly."

Susan waved out to Corina Baker, who was seated in the driver's seat of an Eagle Talon. The woman flashed a smile and waved back. Satisfied that her daughter was safe, she drove the vehicle around the circular dirt drive and left the house.

"C'mon, Julie. I'll show you where the boys are."

Julie carried her sleeping bag and pillow and followed after Susan.

When they arrived at the bedroom, Kelly and Phil were poised on the floor arranging a Land Speeder, with Luke Skywalker and Han Solo as the pilot and co-pilot for the cruiser. Matt and Chris sat on the bed looking over additional accessories.

"Hey, guys, Julie's here," Susan announced.

All four boys looked up, but three looked on with total surprise at the female visitor. Matt and Chris gave each other an inquisitive and shocked look.

"I'm going to be ordering the pizza soon, so let me know what kind of toppings you guys like or don't like. Is pepperoni, hamburger and ham all right?"

Each kid glanced back and forth among one another, then gave the thumbs up sign to Susan.

"I'll let you know when it's here," she said, closing the door behind her.

Each boy understood what the other was thinking . . . and it wasn't good.

Kelly knew exactly what they thought. He dreaded this awkward moment, and wondered how in the world he could get them to accept her as he did.

Then Julie broke the silence. "Boba Fett! You've got Boba Fett! How cool is that," she said jumping to the floor to get a better look. "That's an old action figure!"

Astonished, Phil looked at her questioningly. "You know who Boba Fett is? I'll bet you just saw a picture of him or something." Positive he had stumped her, Phil looked back over his shoulder at his friends with a Cheshire Cat grin that implied "Am I cool or what."

But instead of hearing her sob and whimper, as he had expected, he heard her lash out. "Uh-uh! Boba Fett's the greatest bounty hunter in the whole galaxy. Darth Vadar gave him Han Solo because Jabba the Hut had a price on Solo's head. Unfortunately, Han got the last laugh by knocking Boba Fett into a giant sand monster's mouth, where he was digested for several thousands of years. What a stupid ending for such a great bounty hunter!" She said, shaking her head in disgust.

"Cool," the boys responded in unison, mesmerized.

$$*\qquad*\qquad*$$

Samantha finished applying the final touches of make-up to her face. She still had half an hour before Stephen would arrive, but the nervousness ate away at her stomach and she decided to keep herself preoccupied before her mind went crazy. The electric alarm clock upon her dresser changed from 7:03 to 7:04; time seemed to move like a calendar. No matter how hard she tried to avoid watching the time, the anticipation of Stephen brought her eyes back to the clock after only a few brief minutes of resistance.

Why were butterflies in her stomach? She had gone out on dates several times before, it was no big deal. Spend a few hours talking about each other's personal thoughts and habits, and then come back home. Simple.

But as much as she tried fooling herself, she couldn't. This was her first love experience in a town where, possibly, everybody knew one another, and the thought of blowing it repulsed her.

7:06

Sighing, she went over to the stereo and put in a CD. Shrill laughter resounded from the next room. She smiled, happy to hear Kelly's party was such a success. Not only was it a big day for her, but for him, also. He was making a first impression as well. Hopefully, her first impression would go just as smoothly.

$$*\qquad*\qquad*$$

At a quarter after seven, the pizza man arrived. Susan brought the boxes inside and tipped the young boy four dollars. She called upstairs to the frolicking kids, announcing the food's arrival. One by one, they scuffled down the steps, and each was handed a paper plate by Susan, who administered them in assembly-line fashion at the archway of the kitchen.

Two large boxes of pepperoni, ham and hamburger pizza awaited them in the kitchen and they greedily stacked their plates with hot greasy pizza slices. Each one took a seat at the dining room table, while Susan brought them plastic glasses and a two-liter bottle of Coke.

"Mrs. Adkins, do you have any diet? My mom won't let me drink any stuff that's gonna' have me getting any fatter," a concerned Matt asked.

"She won't?" Susan asked surprised. "Well, don't worry, Matt, I have some diet in the fridge, just in case of emergencies." She ruffled the top of his hair, as he looked up with tickled amusement.

Susan was just filling a glass when a knock on the door interrupted her.

"Oooh," she announced happily. "Sam's date's here."

She trotted to the back door and pulled back the side window curtain to gain a peek at the young man who had wooed her daughter's heart. After satisfying her curiosity, she went to the back door and opened it.

"Hi, Mrs. Adkins. I'm Stephen. I'm here to pick up Samantha."

"Come on in, Stephen. Sam's still upstairs getting ready. Why don't you come into the living room."

As they walked back into the dining room, the children looked up in curious wonder. Phil, sensing what was taking place, leaned over to Kelly. "Is that your sister's boyfriend?"

"No," Kelly responded, while scarfing down his second slice, "that's just her date."

"Oh," Phil nodded. "He's a pretty big dude."

Stephen and Susan stood in the archway of the dining and living room while awkward silence prevailed, then she finally broke the tension.

"Stephen, would you care for some pizza?"

"No thank you," he replied, placing his hands into his pants' pockets bashfully.

"You sure? We've ordered plenty."

He shook his head in embarrassment. "No, really, I'm not very hungry."

"Okay. Suit yourself. Make yourself comfortable, and I'll go tell Samantha that you're here," she said, heading up the stairs.

Stephen glanced all around the living room, biding time. Turning back towards the dining room, he noticed four young faces watching his every move. He offered a quick smile, which went unreturned. He quickly went back to his routine of observing the living room.

"Hi, I'm Kelly. Sam's my sister and these are my friends from school: Phil, Chris, Matt and Julie," he said, introducing them in their respective order.

"Hey. Nice to meet you all. I'm Stephen," he said, thankful for the hospitality.

*   *   *

Samantha was seated on the bed listening to the radio when the knock on her door sounded. Instantly, she knew what it was. Hopping to her feet, she opened the door and let her mother in. Samantha waited impatiently, as her mother's stone face revealed no details about Stephen.

"Well!" Samantha demanded. "What do you think?"

A smile grew and curled upon Susan's lips. "He's gorgeous," she blurted out.

Susan gave her daughter a long hug. "Honey, I hope you both have such a wonderful time tonight."

"Thanks, Mom. I better get down there before he runs away," she said with sudden urgency.

Stephen looked up as Samantha glided down the stairs. He had considered her pretty in school, but now, she seemed absolutely beautiful. Her hair was pulled back in a bun, showcasing her beautiful high cheekbones, and a pair of emerald heart-shaped earrings. She wore a white lined balloon skirt top and a faded blue jean skirt. The perfume that she had on took his breath away; he had never smelled anything so powerful and wonderful.

"You look really, really great," he said, trying his hardest to sound as sincere as possible.

"Thank you. You don't look too bad yourself," she said, sticking her index finger into his ribs.

"You ready to go?" he asked.

"Ready, Freddy," she replied.

"You two have a safe and fun time, all right? Samantha, I want you home before twelve. Got it?" she said, eyeing her daughter.

"Got it," she answered back.

*   *   *

After finishing eating, the kids went into the living room to play video games. Kelly and Matt started by playing a game of video football, while the others sat patiently, watching and waiting for their chance to dethrone the winner.

Susan, content the kids were preoccupied, decided to throw a load of clothes into the washer.

Rounding up laundry hampers from the upstairs and downstairs bathrooms, Susan went down to the basement and loaded the laundry into the washing machine. She set the cycle to hot, poured in some detergent, and closed the lid.

It is turning into a perfect night, she thought. Kelly and his schoolmates were enjoying themselves without killing each other or fighting, and hopefully, these new friendships will stop his fascination with making up absurd stories. And then there was Samantha, who was taking a first big chance. She had hardly left the house since they moved to

Caseville, and when she did leave, Samantha preferred to go alone on bike rides or long walks. She was finally starting to shed her old skin and baggage to embrace the new community.

Susan trusted her daughter immensely. Samantha had always been a reliable, honest child who rarely got into trouble by running with the wrong crowds, or abusing her privilege of a late curfew; she was always courteous to call whenever there was a change of plans in her night. She was a wonderful daughter with good morals and a strong head on her shoulders, and Susan was extremely proud at how well she had matured, despite growing up in a hostile homestead.

Laying the clothesbasket down beside the dryer, she shut off the light and went back upstairs.

*   *   *

"Not cool! You always kick my butt on this board," Matt protested, getting up from the floor and making way for a new challenger.

"Better luck next time, sucker!" Kelly taunted.

Chris jumped down to the floor and replaced his buddy. He was psyched and ready for a tough battle to the end.

"C'mon, I'm gonna tear your guys to pieces. You're gonna wish your stupid players never stepped on the field. Ha!" Chris laughed with confidence.

"Yeah, yeah. Sit your loser, whiny butt down, and quit yer yappin'," Kelly responded, still eyeing the screen, paying no attention to the newest challenger.

As raucous crowd cheers and crunching hits emanated from the game, Matt Baker decided to go upstairs and fetch a comic book that he had stashed inside his duffel bag. He walked up the flight of stairs, rounded the landing, and paused in the middle of the hallway under the attic door.

Strangely, he felt watched, as if something hidden was conscious and spying on his every move. Looking around the area, he found no trace of another being: there were no footsteps approaching or glowing red eyes peering at him from underneath a bed. It was just a creepy dead silence, the kind of silence that if a pin dropped upon the carpet, it would shatter the calm like glass exploding.

He felt silly. He was a grown boy standing there, frightened of the dark, as if a madman was hiding inside of one of the rooms, waiting to bludgeon him with a knife.

Shaken with a sudden flinch of jitters, he continued into Kelly's bedroom, determined not to be a coward.

Entering the room, he was met with a bitter chill. Nothing seemed unusual in the room, but that sense of being stalked was arising once again—only stronger this time.

He looked to the bed. The area was the same as it had been. *But it was,* he told himself; *something was strange.* It was though something was just waiting to approach, timing a precise moment.

The air felt cold, thick and dense, and he felt confined. The room felt as though it was shrinking rapidly, closing him in a vise.

Still standing at the mouth of the door, he was uncertain whether to grab his book, or just forget about it and return to his friends.

But what would they think if he came back down a nervous wreck?

He shook his head, clearing his mind to wipe out the negative thought, proceeded into the room and picked the duffel bag up off the floor. Setting it upon the bed, he unzipped it and pulled a "Spiderman" comic book out. Placing the bag upon the floor he turned to head back out.

The bedroom door slowly shut.

Undaunted, he went to the door and quickly opened it, expecting one of the other kids to be playing a joke.

The hall was empty.

"Just a breeze, or maybe it was that dumb dog," he reassured himself. "Don't start getting freaked out, idiot."

Looking back into Kelly's bedroom, all remained the same; nothing stood out and nobody jumped out from behind the door to grab him. It was perfectly normal. The only thing he noticed in the room was a funny looking limp doll that was seated upon a rocking chair . . . and what harm could that do? He scoffed.

While leaving the bedroom, a room immediately to his left caught his attention, so he decided to take a peek inside.

"Tons and tons of books," he muttered. "There must be every kind of book in here! I'll bet there's some cool comics, too."

Starting from the front wall, his eyes roamed the huge oak bookcase in search of the best selections. Most of the books were too thick with small printing. Unsatisfied with the choices, he continued down farther along the wall.

The library door slammed shut violently.

The quick jolt threw his heart into a panic. *That was no breeze or dog.*

Slowly walking to the door, he placed both hands upon its wood.

"Kelly? Phil, is that you out there? Come on, guys, knock it off. It's not funny."

Silence.

"Guys, I know it's you. I'm not scared."

He quickly changed his mind as rows of books hurled themselves off the shelf towards his head. Thick books caromed off the back wall of the room and dropped to the floor by his feet. Mortified, he raced over to the handle of the door and furiously tried to turn it.

Unable to free the latch from its locked position, he ducked out of the way of a speeding novel just in time as it smashed against the door just inches from his face. Another hardcover became airborne, skimmed across his forehead and drew blood. Wiping at the gash, he felt the cool sensation of blood ooze out from the open cut and run down his face.

The books began catapulting in pairs, then by dozens. Once they hit the floor, they were soon in the air on another assault run. Soon they were hurling from all directions, engulfing and circling the room like a swarm of locust.

Staggering, he fell against the back wall, away from the door.

Books beat upon his plump body and nicked at his pudgy face. A severe shot hit the side of his head and sent him down upon wobbly knees. Covering his head with his arms, he let out one massive scream, so loud and piercing that his throat ached with rawness.

Lying facedown upon piles of leather and paper, the sound of thumping became continuous in his ears. Looking up, he was horrified to see the frame of the shelf banging back and forth repetitively against the wall.

It was an unbelievable sight as the wood smashed against the drywall with monstrous power: each burst brought more force than the previous.

With a final surge the large shelf fell forward and crushed its massive weight down upon his pinned body.

He was unable to scream. With all his might and strength, he summoned up the courage to cry out for help, but it was impossible to draw enough breath to do more than whisper. His plea would not be heard, and no one would know that he was trapped. The mass upon his chest was much too heavy to move and it was suffocating him, leaving him gasping for breath. He was quickly running out of air, and time.

*   *   *

The haunting scream that erupted from upstairs resonated downstairs. The children, who were gathered around the television, looked upon each other in frightened wonder. Susan, who was resting comfortably in the recliner chair, jumped up immediately and ran after the sound. The kids, understanding the urgency, followed closely behind.

When she arrived at the top of the landing, the door to the library was wide open. Inside, the bookshelf rested on the ground with several books spread out upon the floor.

At first she didn't notice him, but going into the room she saw part of his legs from underneath the wood.

"What in the hell. Oh God, please don't let him be dead," she begged. "Please no."

She pried her fingers underneath the top of the shelf and lifted; thankfully, the weight of the frame wasn't as heavy as she thought it would be, that was because the bulk of the main weight, the books, were upon Matt.

She lifted the bookshelf back against the wall and started digging out the trapped boy. Kelly, Julie, Chris, and Phil raced into the room.

"Mom, is Matt okay?" Kelly spoke, winded.

"He's not going to die, is he! Matt's my best friend, Mrs. Adkins," Chris shrieked, trying to talk between panicked, irregular breathing.

"Help me get these books off him," Susan snapped back, trying to clear her mind as it started to race with horrible thoughts.

The children crouched down next to her and began shoveling books from atop Matt. When his body became unobstructed, Susan bent down next to his face.

"Matt. Matt, can you hear me? Matt?"

He laid still, out cold.

"Matt, if you can hear what I'm saying, nod your head."

No answer.

Oh God. What if he's paralyzed? What if he's in a coma? What if he's hemorrhaging from the brain, she began worrying in her mind. *What if he's dead!*

Suddenly his legs began to move.

Thank you, Lord. Thank you, she thought.

"Oww," he moaned. He gradually began to move his arms and legs.

Finally, with full consciousness, he spoke, "I was looking at the books . . . and things, books . . . started flying around the room. They started hitting me on the head!" He was fully alert now.

"I'm just glad you're all right now, Matt," Susan said, rubbing his shoulders. "Oh, honey, you're cut. I'll get you a wash cloth to clean it up," she responded, going to the bathroom.

"Matt, what happened?" Chris asked, curious to know the truth.

"This place is haunted! It has ghosts!"

"That's ridiculous!" piped in Phil. "Did you see any of them?"

"You don't see ghosts, they're invisible, dummy. But they were here. I know it! They kept throwing the books at me. Then when I fell on the ground, that shelf fell over on top of me! You explain how a big thing like that could just fall over!" he argued, red in the face, turning towards each kid.

Susan returned with the washcloth and wiped away the blood from Matt's face. "I'm afraid your gonna have a little bruise here," she said, touching his cheek lightly.

"Mrs. Adkins, I really wanna' go home. I don't want to stay here."

Susan was surprised to hear the boy's request. It was a terrible accident, but with time, she was sure he would have been fine. Nonetheless, if he wanted to leave she would have to oblige.

"Matt, I know what happened scared you, but the bookshelf fell over accidentally. I'm sure you realize that, don't you," she suggested, trying to make him comprehend.

"No! It's not true. This place is haunted, and the ghosts tried to kill me. I really want go home!"

"Ghosts?" Susan blurted out, almost laughing, looking upon the child with bewilderment.

"There's no such thing as ghosts. All right, if you don't feel safe, we'll go downstairs and call your mom." She knew it was futile trying to reason with him just after the accident.

Susan took Matt by the hand and the two went off to use the phone. Chris waited until they were out of sight, and then began. "Kelly, I don't know what's up here, but I don't like it. If that thing almost got Matt, then what about us? It could get us in our sleep or something!"

"I'm telling you guys, I don't have any ghosts here!" Kelly insisted. "Matt knocked the shelf down upon himself and he got freaked out. That's all!"

Kelly knew his guests were on the verge of leaving, and he was afraid that if they didn't feel safe in his house, they might never come over again or be his friend. So the only thing he could do was lie, deny the existence of whatever did lurked in the house, and hope to God that it would not repeat itself.

*   *   *

"So, do you wanna go to the club? They've got a really good band up there tonight." The club was a slang term the kids used for the Coffeehouse.

Samantha heard the question as she fidgeted with the powered window. Did she mind going to the club? Hell, she didn't mind going to the moon, as long as she was going out and getting away from that freaky house.

"The club sounds great. I've heard a lot of cool things about it," she said, still occupied with the button.

"Yeah, we hang out there a lot. It's got pool tables, dart boards, a dance floor. It's probably not as fun as the clubs in Florida, but it's all we've got. I mean, hell, if we didn't have that I'm sure the kids would go nuts with boredom!" He said, cracking a smile.

"No, it sounds fun. The bars in Florida aren't so great. I mean, there are a lot of them, but they're all the same. It's too monotonous. A friend of mine told me that I'd like the bands out here. She mentioned there's a band called Dezire."

"Yeah. They're playing tonight. I'd say they're the best band in the area. They do a lot of new stuff, plus some cool older songs."

Stephen's red Probe turned down Main Street and then stopped in front of the historic white Town Hall office building. The parking lot next to the coffeehouse was jammed with cars, so they parked in the street. Even as they pulled in, people were exiting their cars and heading towards the main doors with a rush of adrenaline.

Samantha was struck with a sense of excitement. She was attending the main event for all the kids in the area. Laughter could be heard in the air, while music and flashing lights filtered from out of the building. A large neon sign above the roof flashed "Coffeehouse" on and off in bright pink letters.

Samantha ran hand in hand with Stephen across the street, in a rush to get to an open table, and quickly avoided oncoming cars.

Stephen paid the two-dollar cover charge at the door for both of them, then escorted her onto the open floor.

The room they entered was the pizza parlor. At the main bar, stools were placed for those who wanted a malt or a soda. Giant television screens showed videos of songs that were being played by the DJ in the adjoining room. A dance floor was situated in the middle of several surrounding square white tables in the parlor.

The room was full of kids talking and laughing as they consumed large pizza pies and poured pitchers of pop into chilled mugs.

"You hungry?" Stephen yelled over the pounding bass from the state-of-the-art P.A. system.

"Kinda. How about you?" she screamed back, not wanting to let on how hungry she really was.

"I'm starving!" he said, looking around the room. "I see an open table against the back wall. Come on," he said, escorting her by the hand.

They crossed over the baby-blue and white tiled dance floor and headed toward the open table. It was close enough to the opening of the next room that Samantha could make out some moderate details of the stage.

"This is great," she said, bobbing her head up and down to a Velvet Revolver song. "It's so bright and colorful in here, and full of life."

"I'm glad you like it. It's really a cool place," he said, his blue eyes gazing deeply into hers.

They sat motionless for a few priceless seconds, reading each other's thoughts.

Samantha knew she was falling hard for him. And by the way he looked at her, she was sure he felt the same way.

The silence was broken when a teenage waitress popped in between them. "Hi, I'm Penny. What can I get you guys?" she squealed in her perkiest tone.

Stephen looked to Samantha. "Pepperoni pizza sound all right to you?"

"Divine," she nodded.

"Awesome. That will be about fifteen minutes. Would you like something to drink?" Penny asked.

Again, he looked over. "What do you like?"

"Coke," she responded, more like a question than an answer.

"Bring us a pitcher of Coke, please," he told the diminutive, bubbly blond.

"Awesome. Back in a flash," she said, skipping away.

"Bring me what she's having," Samantha laughed, wide-eyed. "I don't know if they pay her to act that way, or if that's just God's gift."

They both chuckled.

"Thanks for asking me out," she said, looking down bashfully.

Her timidness excited him. A tingling sensation churned inside of his stomach, and the palms of his hands began to sweat.

Am I the luckiest guy in the whole world, he wondered? *I'm sitting here with the prettiest girl in the whole place, and I think she likes me,* he relished, lost in thought, with a dreamy smile.

*   *   *

After Matt Baker's mother picked up her ailing son, the other children went back upstairs to Kelly's room to play. Susan shut off the television wearily and went into the dining room. The evening had drained her of all her emotions and she still had to await Samantha's return.

Picking up the empty cardboard pizza boxes from the dining room table, she took them in the kitchen and discarded them into the trash basket. Realizing it had been over an hour and a half since she last placed a load of clothes in the dryer, she went down into the basement, clicked on the light and walked across the freezing cold concrete floor.

She pulled the basket up to the dryer, opened the door and reached in. While squeezing the clothes together, she felt another object lodged between the sheets. It was thick and heavy, yet soft and flexible, and immediately she knew what it was. Drawing back the clothing, she found Feisty, Samantha's kitten. Its spine was snapped, which left its body mangled into a twisted shape.

She recoiled, stunned as she looked into the open eyes of the kitten. How in the hell did it get in there, she wondered? Surely, she would have noticed the animal inside of the dryer before she loaded clothes in. Could it have jumped in when she wasn't aware? It was possible, but highly improbable; she wasn't that clueless.

Looking down, she contemplated how in the world she would tell Samantha. The obvious response would be the truth: tell her where she found it and how it died. But how it died, she still couldn't comprehend. The compassionate response would be to tell her the animal escaped out of the house and ran away. She could save herself the embarrassment of guilt, and protect her daughter from the heartache of the gory details of its death. But she didn't want Samantha to spend all of her time worried and searching for a pet that she wouldn't find. She would tell her daughter that a car hit and killed the cat. She could bury the animal in the backyard behind the shed, and tell her about it the next day. There was no reason to spoil Samantha's night and make her restless; it could wait until the morning.

She picked up the limp kitten with an old towel and carried it up the stairs and outdoors. Its head dangled out of the cloth and bounced from side to side uncontrollably, while its fractured vertebra lied twisted in her hands underneath the cover.

Susan brought the carcass out to the barn and placed it down on the dewy grass. Entering the shed, she found a shovel immediately to the left upon the wall, grabbed it and headed to the back of the small shed. She found a patch of ground that had softened from the previous day's rain and began to dig. When the hole was sufficient enough to keep another animal from resurrecting the kitten, she stuck the blade of the shovel deep into the ground, and retrieved the towel. Tossing the whole kit-and-caboodle down into the hole, she filled it with dirt until it was fully covered and packed tightly.

As she began making her way back towards the house, she stopped momentarily and looked back. Out in the field, past the old frail wooden fence, a fog began to gather in the distance.

Strange. Only moments ago, the area was clear.

A thick, misty, gray smoke crept closer and swallowed up the fence in its path like the moon eclipsing the sun. The silent invader slithered along the moist grass, inching over the backyard on a distinctive collision course with the house.

Susan stood in awe of the spectacle, spellbound by its flowing hypnotic effect. The patch of fog rolled closer and covered the shed.

She felt a twinge of nervousness. Something dangerous and significant lurked deep inside that blanket of mist—she felt it.

94

As it crept closer on the ground towards her feet, the child inside of her screamed to run—and she did. Never looking back, she darted back towards the house to seek refuge from the invisible force.

Entering the house, she slammed the door closed and peered out of the window. Realizing windows were open around the house, she moved in a mad panic to the sunroom.

She ran up the landing stairs into the kitchen, went into the sunroom, and began slamming down windows and bolting them locked as quickly as she could, while gazing outside fearfully.

The sky was clear. She blinked in disbelief. The fog had passed.

How? That quickly? Was it possible?

She went to the other end of the sunroom and looked out the side window.

Clear.

Sitting down upon the love seat, she stared blankly through the window out to the wooden fence.

I saw it. I know I did. It was there. It had to have been.

The sky remained clear.

*　　*　　*

The opening guitar riff of the first song sliced through a smoke screen of fog as the music erupted. Thunderous drums pounded from out of massive stacks of speakers—which were aligned against the five-foot high stage—as the floor underneath the feet of the standing crowd rumbled.

Teenage boys slam-danced in the middle of the dance floor as the mighty driving beat roared on with anger. Slam-dancing would seem like a violent sport of bumper cars used with human bodies, but to the young, or whoever simply liked physical pain, it meant nothing more than enjoying the music and letting aggression out.

Samantha and Stephen strayed away from the rough crowd and stood by the side of the stage. The decibel level was ear shattering. Every beat of the bass drum seemed to crush against her chest cavity, yet it made her feel so alive! The atmosphere was buzzing. If she had to sacrifice her hearing in the future for the sake of youthful pleasure and colorful memories, so be it! It was all worth it.

Stephen, noticing the sweeping motion of the crowd, took her by the hand and led her to safety against the side of the wall, away from harm's reach.

His large hand in hers felt warm and endearing, and she was relaxed with him like she was with no other person.

They stood together during the rest of the show, holding hands and smiling at the sight of the exuberant crowd.

It was a perfect night, she told herself over and over—a perfect night.

*　　*　　*

After several minutes of disputing, Kelly finally succumbed to Julie's stubbornness. He had pleaded with her to take the bed instead of the hard floor, but she simply shook her head and said, "I'm no wuss. I can take it."

Her rebellious antics were starting to weigh heavily on him. She was insistent that the only reason he was offering the bed to her was because she was a small, feeble girl, and, since that was the case, he could go sit on a rusty nail as far as she was concerned. Okay, maybe he was treating her differently from the rest of the group, but it was nothing to be ashamed of. *Girls were supposed to get the easy breaks, weren't they? Why was she complaining?* As long as he lived, he would never understand a wishy-washy girl's mind.

Feeling a bit sheepish, he looked down from the bed to Julie. She was lying on her back with her arms folded in silent protest. Her eyes focused upon the ceiling, and she refused to acknowledge his stare.

Checking to see if Chris and Phil were eavesdropping—which they weren't, as both were enraptured by their comic books—he spoke out softly to her.

"Julie, you mad at me?"

No response.

He frowned dismally. As he lay upon the bed and sulked, she quickly sat up and snapped back with a suppressed tone, "how could you treat me so differently! You know I'm not like the other girls. I'm just as tough and smart as you boys."

Her quick temperament sent him reeling for answers. "I know, I know," he said, finding himself on the defense. "Julie, there's no one that's tougher than you in class! I seen you take care of those goons at lunch, remember? I'm sorry I tried to give you the better bed. I guess it was stupid of me," he said, still stymied over being declared the bad guy, even though he was trying to be nice.

Chris and Phil briefly looked up from their books as the shouting escalated, then returned to reading as the argument was quelled.

"It was a nice gesture you made, but you shouldn't have bothered," she said, chewing on her bottom lip for a minute while in thought. She smiled. "Oh Kelly, I could never be mad at you, silly" she responded, swinging her pillowcase to the side of his head and toppling him over.

He bounced back up with a pillow in his hand and returned the favor.

"Take that!" he yelled, kneeling in a musketeer position.

"Oh yeah," she said, responding to the challenge.

Drawing the pillow back behind her head, she stared Kelly in the eye, smiled, and gave him a wink. He got the message instantly, and they both silently counted to three then delivered swipes at the two boys on the floor. As they were struck, the boys bounded backwards, while their comics flew upward into the air and landed in separate corners of the room. Mayhem followed, as all four began beating one another with their pillows. After ten minutes of rough housing, they called a truce and lay back down, exhausted.

*   *   *

At three o'clock in the morning, the Adkins house rested in unbroken silence. An early October wind howled outside against the windows of the house, as the occupants slept comfortably inside. Outside, the leaves tumbled effortlessly upon the cold grass as the wicked wind lashed its tongue upon the fragile plants. A light rain began to bead on the windowpane. Inside, the calm house breathed with deep slumber. The furnace kicked on and released a warm passage of air from within the heating ducts; Sassy, resting beside it, basked in its warm glow.

Upstairs in the bedroom the children slept peacefully, as sounds of their heavy breathing resonated through the room. A moonbeam shone through the window and shed light upon the motionless rocking chair that hosted the devilish doll upon its wooden frame.

Instantly batteries upon the dresser top flew off and struck Chris upon the back of his head. Still sound asleep, he muttered and brushed at his body. A book dropped off the nightstand and slammed into Julie's back.

"Cut it out, you dweeb," she commanded, restless.

The ceiling light clicked on for a few brief seconds, just enough to wake the bewildered, groggy kids, then shut off.

"Whoever's messing with the light, stop it and go to sleep!" Kelly yelled, with his face buried deep into the pillow.

The light flicked back on; then went off again for ten seconds. It turned on again and quickly off.

Raising their heads, still groggy from deep sleep, they watched in amazement as not a soul touched the switch upon the wall, which was lifting up and down on its own in quick repetitive bursts.

Julie sat up. "Kelly, what's going on? Why are the lights all freaking out?" she said, turning her head back and forth from Kelly to the light switch.

"I don't know," he responded in disbelief.

The closet door opened slowly then slammed shut.

The rocking chair began to rock quickly while the rag doll sat upright and complacent on it.

Kelly, Julie, Phil, and Chris watched in horror as everything in the room that wasn't bolted down began to move. The three kids scrambled and climbed up on the bed next to Kelly, while picture frames turned around in circles, army men shot rapidly through the air, and doors, chairs, and light switches moved without assistance.

"Matt was right," screamed Phil, "your house is haunted. It's going to kill us!"

"No one's going to die!" Kelly insisted. "Just wait till it calms down," he said, holding on to Julie.

"Calm down?" Phil continued. "Calm down! What, are you nuts, Adkins? We're in the middle of some sort of Poltergeist movie and you expect us to remain calm. Screw you!"

Phil was just about jump off the bed and run, when the stereo blasted on at high volume and stopped him cold.

"Holy shit!" Chris blurted out, not worried about minding his tongue.

Phil jumped back into position on the bed with the other terrified children, who were now scrunched tightly together against the corner of the wall as far back as they could get.

The ceiling light was flickering on and off so fast that the room appeared to be masked in a strobe effect. Anytime something moved it seemed as though it was traveling at half the speed. Objects began to smash into them, as they were too slow to react from being disorientated.

Kelly watched as the onslaught of flying waste continued to soar. Looking to the right, he gazed suspiciously at the doll that was rocking back and forth, seemingly oblivious to his presence.

But the doll knew he was there and returned his stare, and its icy eyes bore deeply into him and forced Kelly to look away.

*　　*　　*

Susan awoke on the couch after hearing the blast of music from upstairs. She had fallen asleep sometime during the night while waiting up for Samantha, but what time she had drifted off, evaded her. The last thing she remembered was watching the news around eleven o'clock; Samantha must have come home shortly after that and shut off the television without waking her.

Getting off the couch, she stumbled hazily while trying to wake up and find her way in the dark. Then hearing the music again clearly, she turned and headed up the stairs. As she rounded the top landing of the second floor, the music coming from Kelly's room suddenly ceased.

*　　*　　*

The rocking chair continued to rock rapidly, moving with great speed. Army men lifted into the air and hovered in a swirling cyclone motion, while dresser doors opened and shut repetitively in systematic order from left to right.

Julie buried her head into Kelly's shoulder and sheltered her eyes from the demonic display. Phil and Chris cowered back against the wall next to one another.

The madness died just as instantaneously as it began, and every thing ceased at once.

The kids looked around the room in horror, unsure if the invisible force would manifest once more.

The room remained quiet, with toys and clothing littered on the floor, and dresser drawers pulled partially out. Not a thing moved, including the frightened children who still clung to one another.

As they sat shaking with fear, the bedroom door swung open and all four let out a frightened scream. But to their surprise, Kelly's mother, not a specter, appeared in the room.

"What in the world is going on in here?" she demanded.

"Mom, we didn't do it," Kelly began.

Samantha entered the room on the heels of her mother. "Mom, what happened? What was that scream?" she asked, rubbing the sleep from her eyes.

"Nothing, honey, go back to bed."

"Holy shit!" Samantha blurted, noticing the damaged room.

"Sam! Go back to bed now!" Susan yelled.

Samantha went back to her room after a bit of prodding. When the door shut, Susan began again. "All right. I want to know why this room is trashed, and what you're all doing up at three o'clock in the morning," she said, sternly looking around the room.

They all spoke out at once, talking as fast as they could.

"Whoa, whoa, whoa, whoa," she calmed them. "One at a time, please."

Chris began first. "Mrs. Adkins, this place is very weird. Can I go home? I don't like the idea of sleeping here, or the thought of being killed," he said sarcastically.

"Yeah," Phil added. "Chris is right. Ghosts were throwing things against the wall and moving doors. It's spooky here. I want to go home, too!"

"It's way too late to call your parents and have them pick you up. If you don't feel safe then you can sleep downstairs in the living room. Nothing will happen to you there."

Susan didn't really believe this crazy tale about supernatural forces in her home, so instead of arguing about its existence, she simply humored them and made the best of the situation at hand. Kelly was surely up to no good again, as usual. He thrived on a good scaring, no doubt about that. He probably underestimated himself this time and was surprised to find them all begging to go home. Unfortunately, he was still making things up. The doctor said it would be a slow transition, but she had hoped this sleepover would have cured him of his infatuation. For the time being, she would have to listen and understand his problem.

"Come on kids, grab your sleeping bags and pillows."

The children gathered their belongings and followed Susan. As the children approached the bedroom door, they moved cautiously past the porcelain doll, and its devilish smile seemed to wish them well.

*   *   *

Darkness surrounded the children like the inside of a buried coffin. The tight grip of fear had them at its mercy, and the silence of the house crept inside of each one's ear. Four little hearts thumped nervously, for their only means of security from the invisible force was a thin, flimsy peace of cotton sleeping bag. They scurried deeper inside it, drawing the fabric up to their noses.

"Kelly, are we safe down here?" Phil asked.

"Sure," Kelly responded, trembling inside of the bag.

"It's so quiet," Chris responded, looking around the darkened room. "All I can hear is my heartbeat."

RRRRRR. RRRRRR. A sound rumbled from somewhere below, in the basement.

Chris' eyes grew large. A lump formed in his throat and his body tightened with dread.

"What wwwas ttthat?" he stuttered.

"I don't know. Probably nothing. It could be the house settling," Julie suggested.

"That was settling? It doesn't sound vvvery sssetttling to me. It sounds like a mmmonster," Chris responded.

"You're just being a baby!" Julie cut in.

"Baby nothin'. Remember Matt? The monster got him!"

"Kelly, I swear, if I ever make it through this night, I'm never going to speak to you again. Ever!" Phil insisted.

Kelly slumped deeper into his sleeping bag. His heart ached with sorrow. It wasn't his fault. He didn't want the ghost here, either; he didn't even want to be here himself.

"I'm really sorry, guys. I didn't know this would happen. Please, don't be mad," he apologized, as his voice broke up.

"You're weird, Adkins. And your house is weird!" Phil said angrily.

"Its okay, Kelly. I know it's not your fault," Julie whispered, lying beside him.

It was of small consolation, and he sighed wearily.

RRRRRR. RRRRRR. The noise bellowed again.

Outside, the wind picked up and pressed against the window, howling like a wolf at the moon.

The frightened children moved closer against one another and alertly monitored the dining room and kitchen area.

Footsteps creaked slowly upon the staircase.

Sassy, lying beside Kelly, lifted her ears with sudden alertness, aware of the strange noises that were going on in the house.

Each child's heartbeat intensified dramatically.

The floorboards snapped with life as the sound moved from the upstairs level toward the kitchen.

"Something's ccccoming," Chris whimpered.

The steps continued to squeak in the darkness.

"Kelly do something! Do something!" Julie begged.

Closer and closer it approached. It was now only a few, small steps away from the dining room.

Phil's head became dizzy and he shook uncontrollably.

Go away! Just leave us alone! Kelly screamed within.

The room was quiet.

Each child focused on the dining room, waiting for the Devil's shiny, blood red eyes to appear.

They waited. They watched; even Sassy, tight with anticipation, kept still, listening.

Silence.

For the remainder of the night, the children lay awake motionless in their sleeping bags. Their gaze never wavered from the dining area as they prayed for daylight and sanctuary from the creeping invisible force.

For three children, the night was one that they would never forget.

For Kelly, it was one he would relive again and again.

*　　*　　*

At eleven o'clock in the morning, Susan sat at the dining room table sipping on a hot cup of coffee while she waited for the juicy details of her daughter's big night. Samantha, as usual, was still sound asleep.

Kelly's friends, with the exception of Julie, had been picked up well over an hour ago. The two kids sat in the living room playing video games.

They seem to be growing closer as the days went by, Susan thought.

*　　*　　*

Kelly was glad that Julie was still hanging out at the house. He wanted to talk to her alone, without the other guys listening.

"Julie, how come you didn't leave like the rest of them? Aren't you afraid of being in this house?" Kelly asked, tapping the fire button on the controller.

"I'm not afraid, like they are," she responded, staring at the screen.

Kelly turned his head towards her, then paused the game.

"Not scared?" he asked sarcastically.

She returned the look, instantly catching on to his disbelief.

"Okay. Maybe I was a little scared last night. Who wouldn't be? As long as you can put up with it and deal with it, then I guess I can, too. I mean, if you thought you were in danger you wouldn't be here right now. Would you?" she asked, trying to rationalize the situation.

"No. If I thought we were in trouble, we'd be gone."

Deep down in his heart he knew he was lying. How could he tell her that he didn't have a clue as to what was going on? Anything could happen at any given moment—and it usually did—there was nothing he could do about it.

*　　*　　*

Samantha shuffled merrily down the stairs with a content smile upon her lips. Normally, her movement in the morning would be wavering, as she groggily bumped into walls and searched blindly for the kitchen. But today, she felt like a new person.

The whole world seemed to be singing to her. The sky was a brilliant blue, a sunbeam happily lit the house with warmth, and the day seemed destined for greatness.

So, when her mother calmly explained the misfortune of her kitten, she was heartbroken. She was shocked and saddened to hear the news, but she didn't lay any blame upon anyone. If it was an accident, it was an accident. Hating the world would not bring Feisty back.

Samantha took a drink of orange juice and finished off a raisin bagel. *It was just a baby; it barely had enough time to live and enjoy life. Was she being heartless for not mourning Feisty?* She wondered. *Was she so cold and callous that her own happiness drowned out her ability to feel compassion? It was just an animal,* she reminded herself.

"What did you do with Feisty, mom?" she asked, ashamed of her behavior.

"I buried her behind the shed. I didn't want him to lie on the side of the road."

Samantha nodded her head in agreement.

"Are you all right, honey?" Susan asked, concerned.

"Yeah," she responded, pausing to understand her mixed feelings. "Mom, should I be a little more emotional right now? I don't really feel torn up about it. If something you love dies, then you grieve, right? But I kinda feel empty inside. Is that bad?" She looked to her, distressed.

"No, sweetie. You're not bad. People grieve in different ways. Some get all broken up and teary eyed, while others bottle it up. You loved your kitten very much. Don't be so hard on yourself." She reached over and kissed her on the forehead.

"Okay," Samantha smiled. "Thanks, Mom."

They sat at the table watching Kelly and Julie play Sega, then changed the discussion to the big date. Samantha admitted she was half an hour late because the band played several encores. Susan shrugged it off with a brief warning of "Just this time" and prodded her daughter for more details.

They talked that whole afternoon about boys, school, and everything in general. It was the first time the two had such a heart to heart talk. It was something they both needed, and relished.

Later that evening, Susan received a call from Davis. They talked for an hour as he made good on his promise and asked her to dinner and a movie. She accepted graciously. It was kind of ironic that he had called her. Samantha had hit off with her date, Kelly and Julie were becoming quite the cute little couple, and now it was her turn to be struck with Cupid's flying arrow. She welcomed the change: a little love spread throughout was just what they all needed.

Chapter 10

After marking the last chapter that he read, Kelly closed the book and set it upon the night stand. It was a drab Saturday morning on November the 23rd. Sam was in her room asleep, and his mom was still at work. She had been spending a lot of time at the hospital recently, but she said that would change because her boss was going to offer her a full time position on the day shift with fewer hours. That pleased Kelly to no end. He hated that he never saw her, and he also hated staying alone in the house. There were always weird and bizarre sounds that often woke him up. He could be sound asleep one moment, then hear movement and laughter in the hallway the next and be wide awake the rest of the night. As strange as the noises sounded, he had distinctly heard the shrill of children playing and running around. The noises usually lasted for a couple of minutes then slowly died out. He was way too frightened to even attempt to go out and investigate them. The only thing he really could do was sit, listen and hope it didn't shift into his room.

The sounds weren't always happy, though; sometimes they were quite sad. A few nights back he had heard the soft sob of a woman. That was really scary. He was tucked away under the sheets when the soft moans began. It seemed as though she was in the attic right over the top of his bed. He wondered: *could it have been the wind that made those faint noises?* It seemed impossible because he was sure the voice filtering through the floor was weeping.

Kelly looked around the bedroom. He felt the raging power of the room pulsing with energy.

He kept a watchful eye on his dresser drawers, but they remained motionless, although coiled tightly, prepared to spring forward.

The windows refused to lift upward, yet his legs still trembled with fear.

Pulling Sassy against his body, he waited for the unexpected.

The task of waiting was killing him. He was going crazy, his mind repeated over and over, and he wished that his mom would come home soon.

A million tiny invisible eyes seemed to watch over him.

The doll sat silently in the rocking chair, directly facing him.

Kelly looked over to it, and his trembling increased.

He had thought about putting it back into the storage chamber, or any other place besides his bedroom, but a terrible premonition of the small figure finding its way back crept into his consciousness, and he didn't want to upset the doll in any way.

Above, in the attic, a creaking emitted.

Kelly put his cheek against Sassy's fur and embraced the dog even tighter.

Footsteps began to pace from one side of the attic to the other.

Kelly's heart could stand no more. Racing out of the bedroom, he went downstairs to the phone and started dialing; the line rang four times, then Julie's voice answered, "hello?"

"Julie? Hi, this is Kelly."

"Hi, what's up?"

"I was wondering if you were doing anything?"

"No, not really. Why?"

"I was kind of feeling a little, well, you know . . . bored, I guess. Do you think you could come over as soon as possible?"

"Sure, I'll have my dad bring me over right now."

"Thanks, Julie. I owe you big time," he said, hanging up the receiver.

When Julie arrived, Kelly thought it would be safer if they stayed away from the house and just went for a walk. It was just after six o'clock and the warmth of the November sun was slowly fading away. Kelly zipped up his Detroit Lions jacket, and the two stepped out into the brisk eve.

Walking along Denton, Julie turned to face Kelly.

"Is it getting worse?"

"Yeah. I can't stop it. I hear noises in my room all the time now."

"I wish there was something I could do. Anything," she replied sadly.

"There's nothing you can do. I'm trapped and no one believes me. I thought mom would, but she doesn't! And I told you before about that doll I found. I know she's alive, because she talks to me. Her name is Annie, and she told me my mom doesn't believe anything I say, and I'm starting to wonder if she's right. I'm not even sure if Annie's on my side or not, though. At times she's really cool, but other times she scares me."

"Don't listen to her, Kelly! It's just a trick! It's a lie! She's only trying to keep you from telling anyone the truth. You've got to keep trying to tell your mom!" she pleaded.

"It's no use! I'm scared. I know that if I make the ghosts any madder they're gonna' kill me, or someone in my family! I can't let that happen, Julie."

"I really think you should try explaining it to somebody. You're just a kid and you can't handle this all on your own."

The two stood in front of the old man's small house.

Kelly stopped abruptly and watched the yard carefully.

"What's wrong? Why are you stopping?" Julie asked, concerned.

"The old man. This is where he lives. My sister's seen him, and she thinks he's really evil. I think he's done something really bad, but we don't know what it is yet. Sam says he probably has some kind of secret hidden inside of his house."

Both studied the house.

The front door opened and the old man stepped out onto his porch. Moving forward, he peered at the stationary kids and continued closer.

Kelly's eyes met the old man's eyes, and the rest of the world seemed miles away as their stare continued.

"Kelly, let's go," Julie shouted. Her words sounded like a distant wind.

The only sound that he could hear was the old man's voice, chanting in his mind. *You must leave here . . . You will bring the evil back upon us all. The spirits are always watching you and will not give up, and I cannot fight them again.*

"I won't bring them here . . . wait, you know what's going on in my house! You've got to help me. Please!" he said aloud.

I can't help you. It is not my battle anymore. You are in grave danger at that house, boy . . . Leave now, before it's too late.

"Run, but where? I have no where to go. Who are you? What battle? I don't understand what you're saying," Kelly replied.

"What? Who are you talking to?" Julie asked.

They're going to kill you and your family, just like they killed the other families. Run, boy . . . do not tempt fate.

"Kelly!" Julie's voice echoed loudly as she grabbed him by the shoulders and shook him hard.

He turned to her, still dazed. "Huh?"

"Are you all right? You were in some kind of trance, talking to nobody," she said.

"Yeah. I think so."

Suddenly he became aware of row after row of tall corn stalks behind Julie.

The imagery began painting in his mind once again: the vivid dream of the two of them playing together in the field, running through a maze of corn.

Grabbing her by the wrist, he turned quickly and ran back towards his house.

"Kelly? Where are you going? What's wrong!"

"We've gotta' get out of here. It's not safe here. Julie, I could hear that man's voice in my head! We're all in danger."

The two crossed over the grassy field back toward Kelly's house.

*   *   *

Susan pulled out some coins from within her purse and slid them into the change slot of the soft drink machine. After pressing the glass button, a can of Diet Coke tumbled from inside and appeared at the bottom of the machine. Reaching into the holder, she withdrew the soda and took it to a small round table away from other occupied seats. She plopped down into the chair, exhausted, and lifted open the tab of the can. It hissed, releasing tiny snapping and crackling noises from within.

Placing an elbow upon the table, she propped her head on the side of her hand and nonchalantly watched as other nurses spent their lunches gossiping or reading smutty novels. She was too wiped-out to do either of those things. Although the new job was coming along rather nicely, the long odd hours and night shift were tougher than she expected.

The only real job that she ever held was as a cashier at a grocery mart, and that was when she was seventeen. She had almost forgotten how hard work really was! After having the luxury of vegging at home watching game shows and soaps, she grown increasingly lazy and content with the homebody routine, not that motherhood was anything to scoff at. Naturally, when she joined the workforce once again, it wasn't as easy a transition as she had hoped.

Susan's eyes just began to drift shut when her station buddy, Ida Allison, pulled out a chair and sat down next to her.

"Wake up, girl. You better not close your eyes in front of me."

Susan looked up and smiled groggily at the tall blond.

"And don't even think for a second that you're gonna pull that 'I'm so tired, would you do my work' routine on me," Ida kidded, while giving her a serious look. "I invented that routine."

"I wouldn't dream of it, your highness." Susan took a drink and then looked around the cafeteria. "Don't any of these old hens have anything better to do than talk about the daily trash?"

"Honey, that's what holds them together like glue. If they didn't get their fix, they'd become ornery bitches," she said, leaning in. "Why are you so worn out? Did you do some crazy partying last night?"

"No. I went out with that guy I was telling you about, Davis."

"Oh yeah. I forgot all about it. Where did you guys go?" she asked, applying a fork to a plastic container of salad.

"We went out to the Tavern Steakhouse and then to a movie."

"What did you see?"

"That new Mel Gibson flick. It was pretty good. You should check it out."

"So what's the report card on your first date?"

Susan turned red and bashfully looked around the room.

"Come on, Sue, you can tell me. I have an unconditional right as a work associate, and as your only true friend in this small gossiping town. Don't make me hear it on the street. I'll haunt you forever if I do."

"It was great. I have to admit it. As nervous as I was to go, we really clicked and had a fabulous time. We seem to have so much in common, too."

"Ooh! I'm so happy for you," her girlfriend squealed with delight. "What's he like?"

"He's a perfect gentleman. He opened the car and restaurant doors for me, and I was in heaven, I swear! He's a schoolteacher. In fact, he's Kelly's teacher."

"Oh, I see how it is now. That's why you're dating him, you're trying to help your kid's grade point average," she teased.

"Shut up! You're just jealous, that's all."

"Hell yes, I'm jealous! My boyfriend's fastidious attitude makes me sick. He's too compulsive. Everything has to be perfect. Where we go out, the way we go out, what time we go out . . . its way too much calculation!"

"Oh, you love him," Susan chimed in.

"Yeah. So what if I do? After spending three years with the bum, how could I not?"

Ida was such a card. There wasn't a day that she failed to entertain and keep the nursing staff in stitches. She was the funniest person Susan ever met. One time, when the two first met, they went to a pub that had live music. After a few hours and a few brews, Ida let loose and danced on their table to the song "Land of a Thousand Dances" in front of a full house. After hamming it up on the table, she took to the stage and provided back up vocals on the chorus. The crowd roared with delight. On the ride home, Susan asked Ida what the hell had gotten into her to do that. She simply smiled and replied, "I thought it was amateur night."

The tall blond shuffled her fork between tomatoes and croutons. "So when's the next time you two are going out?"

"This weekend. We'll probably get a bite to eat, then hang out at the pub."

"The pub? You want me to come along and entertain you guys? Maybe provide some candlelight table dancing?"

"No thanks! I finally find a man, and you want to scare him off."

"What? I hope you know I made good tips that night. I could have gone on the road with them," she said coyly. "How's Sammy doing?"

"Good. She has a boyfriend named Stephen. He's a sweet, well mannered, cute, athletic kid. You should come over and visit more often. Then you can catch up on all the current events."

"Why? What tirades are taking place now?" Ida asked.

"You know that Kelly believes the house is haunted and that I took him to see a doctor?"

"Yeah."

"Well, he still believes it. I think he's getting worse, though. Last week, a few of his friends from school stayed the night. Kelly reverted back to his old pranks and scared the hell out of them. Kids were crying, and the room was trashed. It was a big fiasco and I don't even know what time they went to bed. Then I was downstairs when I heard an awful scream from above. I ran upstairs and found the library bookshelf on top of one of Kelly's friends, who was so scared and shook up that he tried blaming it on a ghost and wanted to leave. So I called his mom and she picked him up. It was totally embarrassing. After that, at three in the morning, Kelly's stereo blasted on. So I ran back upstairs and found his whole bedroom destroyed. I mean ripped apart like a tornado ran through it. Once again . . ."

"The ghost?"

"Yep. They were positive that's what it was. I could have strangled Kelly for that. Each kid wanted to leave. I had to keep them downstairs in the living room so they wouldn't freak out anymore. You know what kind of flack I'm gonna get from their parents! I'm surprised that I haven't heard any word from them yet. Shit, Ida! I don't know what I'm gonna do about that boy."

"Sue, what if they're telling the truth? What if something strange is going on inside your house? I've seen stories about that kind of stuff."

"Oh, right. Like the X-Files, or some Saturday night sci-fi show. I really don't believe in that nonsense. I never have, and I never will. It's just his silly little imagination, that's all. Nothing more."

Ida Allison shook her head in bewilderment. "I don't know. If I had kids screaming in the dead of night, you bet your sweet bottom I'd investigate it," she said, still concerned.

"Then how come I haven't had any trouble with it? Or why hasn't Samantha? How come it only presented itself to them?"

"Who knows. Maybe it thinks you're gonna get pissed off and punish it. How should I know, do I look like some kind of Ghostbuster?" she laughed.

*   *   *

"Do you feel scared staying here?" Kelly asked, setting a bag of chips on the living room coffee table while sitting cross-legged on the floor.

Julie reached into the bag and pulled out a greasy handful, and replied nonchalantly, "Not really. As long as we're together."

He nodded his head in agreement.

"Tell me what it was like in Florida. I've never been there," she asked.

"It's really hot and sticky. Everybody has a pool at their house. You know how it's hot here during the day, but cool at night?"

"Yeah."

"Well there when you go outside at night you start sweating. Can you believe that, you sweat at night!"

"Ewww! That stinks! Did you ever see any alligators?"

"Sure. One time I was at a friend's house and this big ol' gator was getting a tan in his backyard. It was really neat."

"Did you have a lot of friends?" she asked curiously.

"I had a few, especially Andy. He was my best buddy. We used to catch snakes and play ball together," Kelly recounted fondly.

"Oh," she replied, a bit distraught.

Kelly noticed her sudden change in demeanor.

Great, now what did I do or say wrong? he wondered.

"Andy was my best friend. It's funny though. When I moved out here, I swore I'd never meet anyone as cool as him again, and I was right. Because when I met you, I found someone even cooler."

She blushed with embarrassment. "Kelly, that's the sweetest thing anyone's ever said to me. You're such a goofball. But yeah, I feel the same way about you."

He smiled, happy that she wasn't upset anymore and pleased she felt the same way inside as he did.

Julie reached into the bag and withdrew more chips. Noticing that the power indicator light for the stereo boom box was on, she asked, "Were you listening to something earlier?"

"Huh? Listening to something? What do you mean?"

She pointed toward the radio. "It's on."

Confused, he got up and went over to it. The record button was depressed and the reels of the tape inside the deck were turning.

"What is this?" he said unsure. I never touched it. Hey, it's recording us. I'll bet Sam put it here to trick me."

Julie pointed alertly. "Look! It's not even plugged in!"

Holding up the dangling chord, he unfastened the battery compartment door on the back of the player. "If you think that's weird . . . There's no batteries in it."

*   *   *

The knock upon Samantha's door frightened her slightly. Although she didn't actually believe a ghost would be gracious enough to knock before entering, the hard thumps became a cold reminder of days past.

"Sam, you're not going to believe it. This place is haunted, I know it!"

"You woke me up from a nap to start with this again?"

"I've got proof! Julie and I both witnessed it."

"Witnessed what?" Samantha asked.

"This!" he replied, extending the tape.

As the cassette played, only static emitted from out of the speakers.

"Are you sure you put it on the right side?" Kelly asked.

She flipped over the tape. The dead hiss persisted.

"Kelly, if you ever pull this stunt again!" Samantha warned.

"I'm serious. We saw it! I've seen a lot of things like that. In the attic, I found some old pictures of the people who used to live here before us. That's when I found the doll again."

"Stop it! I don't want to listen to any more. And don't go running off telling Mom about it, either. It's bad enough she has you seeing a shrink, she'll surely think your nuts."

Kelly looked over at Julie with despair. "Come on, Julie, let's go downstairs," he said miserably.

Samantha sat down on the bed and looked at the closed door. *Why was she so angry and why did she snap at him?* She didn't mean or want to, it just sort of built up inside. She couldn't control it. Those creepy stories were too much for her to handle. It was bad enough she couldn't sleep lately, but to know there were more incidents going on in the attic. That thought disturbed her. The less she knew the better off she would be.

*　　*　　*

Kelly and Julie returned to the living room and sat back down at the table. "I'm sorry. I thought Sam would've believed us. The only reason I'm seeing a doctor is because my mom says he will help me sleep better. I'm not crazy or anything."

"Kelly, I know you're not crazy! There's nothing wrong with seeing a doctor. I hope he can help you. And don't worry about what your sister said, I was there and I seen it too. I believe you."

Chapter 11

The time since the sleepover incident was relatively quiet. Only a few occurrences of moving or misplaced objects took place.

Samantha continued to date Stephen. The two were now in the elite crowd of couples dating at the high school. She also began working for the school newspaper, writing columns about events or other newsworthy stories going around in school, or in town. She fancied her newfound talent. It gave her a chance to excel at something she enjoyed and was good at. It also gave her an opportunity to invest time into other areas.

Kelly still remained close with Julie, although the holiday season had separated them for a brief period while she visited relatives out of state. Chris, Phil, and Matt still hung out with him, but it wasn't the same. They had made it a point to let everyone in the community know what went on at the Adkins' house, although no one believed them.

Susan was hired full time at the hospital. She worked long hours and learned the ropes quickly, and the board decided she was an asset to the facility and gladly welcomed her. Acknowledgment of achievement was something that she had strove for since leaving her husband in Florida. She sought self-respect, and now having it, life was finally fulfilling. Her relationship with Davis was blossoming. They had dated continuously during the last two months, and were falling head-over-heals for one another. Davis looked after Kelly's well-being as promised. He was not only a teacher but also a good friend that the boy could talk to and confide in. Susan believed Kelly desperately needed a father figure in his life, and Davis helped fill part of that void by taking him places, like the time they went to a football game in Pontiac to watch the Detroit Lions play. The two hit it off, and after the game spent the remainder of the evening having dinner and taking in a movie.

Christmas was one of the best celebrations in quite some time. Richard took the kids out to get a tree and helped them decorate it, while Susan went shopping with Davis for outside lights and a mechanical Santa Claus and elves. The house was festive: lights were draped across the rooftop and blinked on and off in splendid colors of red, blue, green, and yellow. She had a lighted plastic snowman that sat on the front porch and merrily waved to passing cars. Inside the house, a large, fresh Christmas tree full of bulbs and lights filled up space in the living room; its mass barely squeezed into the corner of the room, or fit under the ceiling, with the point of the star inches away. They even had an electric train that rumbled over plastic tracks, which then prompted an alarm of bells and whistles the moment it passed by its destination stop.

On Christmas Eve they sat and listened to holiday songs, and watched classic animated specials of "Rudolph the Red Nosed Reindeer" and "Frosty the Snowman," while they drank eggnog and ate popcorn.

On Christmas morning, Kelly and Samantha raced downstairs to their awaiting presents and fumbled through them, determined to predict what was in the box before it was opened. Kelly eagerly wakened Susan and dragged her out of bed, while Samantha fixed her a pot of coffee. Susan videotaped the kids opening their gifts that morning for John, who had called the night before, asking for a copy. He called again on Christmas day to find out if had they liked the presents he sent. Kelly still harbored bitterness towards his father. In his mind, his dad had betrayed and abandoned him, and the presents were only a mere consolation prize that made him feel bought off. Samantha, on the other hand, was old enough to understand separations. She realized the two of them were unhappy together and welcomed his call and gifts without any hang-ups.

That afternoon, Susan fixed a ham, complete with a buffet of side dishes. Richard, Stephen, and Davis were all invited over for dinner. Afterwards, the group played board games through the night. It was a memorable evening uninterrupted by the spirits of the house. Either the unknown forces felt compassion for the holidays, or they had sneaky intentions planned for later on.

*   *   *

Thursday night Kelly sat on the bed with the doll. He tried once again to entice it to speak—as he had done several other times—but it was still mute.

"Come on, Annie, why won't you speak to me? You said you'd be my friend."

The doll remained lifeless.

"You only come out when there's trouble. Don't you!" he yelled emphatically.

Placing the rag doll on its back upon the bed, he got up from the mattress and began to walk away when he heard his stereo click on from behind.

"Annie?" he asked, turning back to it.

Incredibly, the limp doll lifted to a sitting position and turned its head slowly towards Kelly.

Apprehensive, he gradually walked back to it. "Can you talk?" he asked.

"Yes," a whisper like the wind answered back, "I'm here Kelly."

"Annie, why are you scaring me and my friends, like you did when you threw the army men and the books around the room? And you dropped the bookshelf on Matt. Why, I thought you wanted to be friends?"

"Kelly, those actions did not come from me. I am your friend. You must realize that there are other presences in this house and that I am not the only dwelling spirit. Just as I am good, there is also evil. And unfortunately, Kelly, evil exists here. The spirits are resisting any outside interference, for I have tried to reason with them. It is not in their manner to be told what to do. Whoever steps upon this unholy soil is in extreme danger from the darkness that occupies it."

"Am I in danger? Is my family in danger?" he asked, frightened.

"No, I will protect you. Only outsiders who do not live in this house are in danger. You and your family will not be harmed unless you try to leave," the child-like voice spoke.

"Why will we be hurt if we leave?"

"Because, they want you to stay here with them; they need you."

"I don't understand," he questioned.

"All I can tell you is that you are safe here with us. You won't be harmed unless you deceive them and try to leave. Everything will become clearer in the near future."

The doll fell limp.

"But why does it need me? What did I do? Annie. Why me?"

The doll lay motionless upon the bed.

*   *   *

As the last hour of class began winding down on Friday, Davis Conner handed out a pop quiz on mathematics. He distributed the papers as he walked between rows. The childrens' faces turned white with shock, for they had expected an easy final class before the weekend. Davis smiled with delight. He loved doing the unexpected and was intrigued to see how well the children concentrated in moments of pressure.

After he finished handing out the quizzes, he returned to sit upon the front edge of his desk.

"All right, boys and girls, enough moaning and crying. Just a little quiz to see how alert and awake you are this week. Nothing hard, just the basics we covered during the past two weeks. If you've been paying attention, you should have no trouble at all. Okay, begin."

Simultaneously, the pencils began scratching upon the papers. Davis returned to his seat and briefly watched the class, then started thumbing through a basketball section of a Sports Illustrated.

Kelly stared blankly at the numbers on the page. His mind was discombobulated. All last night and all during the morning, he had thought about the doll's warning. *Why would they hurt people who intended on coming over to his house?* he pondered. If he tried to explain to his mom about the threat, she would just laugh it off, or worse yet, take him back to the shrink. He had already tried telling Sam, but she was adamant about her feelings. There was no one he could turn to, no one.

He looked up from his paper to Davis at the desk. Back in December, Davis had taken him to a Lion's game. They had had such a great time together, just like they were buddies. He remembered that Davis had promised that any time he wanted to talk about something—anything—he should feel free to simply ask.

It was clear now. He had to tell Davis. If anyone could help his situation it was he.

Realizing he was losing time, he began writing down answers to the quiz questions, unsure of whether they were right or wrong, just as long as they were answers.

The bell sounded at three o'clock and the children filed out happily as the weekend was officially started. Kelly waited in his seat as the class emptied. Julie was halfway to the door when she noticed him behind. Turning around, she went back.

"Kelly, what are you doing? It's the weekend. Nobody sticks around. You should be running out of here," she joked.

"I need to speak with Mr. Conner for a minute. It's important."

"You want me to wait for you."

"No, Julie, you go on. I'll be all right," he said somberly.

"Okay. Why don't you call me later tonight?"

He nodded his head in agreement.

After she left, he got up from the chair and addressed the teacher.

"Mr. Conner."

"Please, Kelly, we're not in class anymore, you can call me Davis."

Kelly smiled bashfully. "Sorry. I forgot. I was wondering, can I talk to you about something personal?"

"Sure, I told you anytime you needed to talk, I'd listen."

Kelly looked around the room for a second, then shifted his feet into a different position. "Well, it's kind of different. It's really weird. Like different weird—"

"Kelly, I'm not sure what you're trying to get at. You're not making much sense. Why don't you start at the beginning and tell me what's on your mind," he said, cutting the boy off in mid-sentence.

"Davis, do you believe in ghosts and stuff like that? Do think bad ghosts live in people's houses?"

He was shocked at how candidly the words came from the boy's mouth. Davis looked at him for a minute then remembered how Susan had mentioned the stint with the psychiatrist, and about his inability to distinguish fantasy from fact.

"Yes, I believe there is some form of spiritual world. I think anything's possible. To rule otherwise would be ignorant. There are many things that go on in life; we're just not wise enough or receptive enough to understand them. Kelly, some people are afraid to believe in something they can't touch, or can't see. For instance, many people have faith in God. Can we see him? No. But that doesn't prove he isn't present among us. If people can put their faith into God, then why can't they open their minds to the possibility of another spiritual world of ghosts or alien life forms in outer space? Anything is possible as long as you have an open mind. Why are you so curious about this?"

Kelly looked down at the floor. If he told Davis what he saw he probably would get laughed at, or it would just confirm that he really was insane.

Looking up with despair, he spoke hesitantly. "I . . . saw them."

Lifting his eyebrows in anticipation, Davis replied, "You saw what?"

"Ghosts," Kelly responded softly. "At my house. There are several of them. I didn't actually see all of them, but I know they're there."

"Are you positive they were ghosts, Kelly? Could you have mistaken what you saw?"

Kelly felt resurgence in his confidence to tell the story. "No, I'm sure. When we first moved into the house, I found a doll in a storage closet. After that, I found it moving from room to room by itself. Then things in my room started to disappear or move, like books and doors. I was asleep in my room one night and I heard this noise; it woke me up. I looked across the room, and there in my rocking chair was this ugly old lady, grinning at me. Laughing! She sat in the chair rocking back and forth, tapping her really long, icky fingernails on the arm of the chair. I also found some old pictures in the attic of different families that lived here before us. The old lady I was telling you about was in one of the pictures! Then I had some friends over and one of them got locked in the library. He said books were flying off the shelf at him. The bookshelf fell on him, too! That same night, three of my friends slept over and the ghost started throwing things around the room, slamming doors, and switching on my stereo. Everything in my room was going bonkers." he finished, winded, trying to fit every last detail into one quick burst.

Davis sat silent. *What in the world had happened? Kelly couldn't be that traumatized to concoct such a vivid and luridly detailed story such as that. Could he have witnessed an apparition or a demonic presence? The only way to confirm it would be to find out whether anyone else in the house had any confrontations.*

"Kelly, I believe you. It is possible that the house is haunted."

The boy lit up in surprise. "You believe me? Really? Everyone thinks I'm crazy. I'm not crazy am I, Davis," he asked.

"No, definitely not. But, Kelly, before we go telling everyone about your experiences, you've got to give me time to figure things out, all right?"

Kelly looked up at Davis with confusion. "But you told me you believed me," he responded sadly, shrinking back depressed.

"I do. But I need to talk to some people and find out a thing or two about your house. I need to know everything that's happened there."

Kelly nodded, satisfied with the explanation.

"Now do you feel any better?"

"Yes. A whole lot better. Thanks for helping me. I'm glad that you're on my side."

Davis smiled. Kelly was such a great kid. Davis never had a child of his own, one who would rely and look upon him for guidance and support. He'd give anything to be that little boy's father, and he wouldn't let him down. Not like Davis' own father. That man was a joke as a father. As long as he lived, he would not repeat his dad's mistakes; he would be the strong, loving, caring father figure that he'd never had.

He looked at Kelly and smiled warmly.

Kelly, sensing the strong bond, smiled back, then hugged him.

"Oh, and one more thing I forgot to mention about the doll. It speaks to me. It told me that if I try to leave, or if someone gets in their way, the spirits would kill them."

Davis turned pale. He couldn't believe what he had heard. The words echoed in his mind: *kill them.* A chill ran wild down his spine.

"Come on Kelly, I'll give you a ride home," he said, staring off into the distance.

*   *   *

That night, Davis decided to treat Susan and the kids to dinner, figuring it would give them all a chance to grow closer and get Kelly's mind away from the house. He arrived at the house to pick them up at six-thirty. Earlier, he had made reservations at the Tavern Steakhouse, an extravagant restaurant that catered to wealthier clientele.

The car idled in the driveway as Susan, Samantha, and Kelly—who escorted Sassy by the leash—emerged from the house.

"Kelly, I don't want you bringing her along, she doesn't need to go."

"Aw, but Mom, Sassy's part of the family, too! I always take her with me now. She's my protector."

Ever since the sleepover, the need for safety haunted him daily. There wasn't a moment he was caught alone without the dog—especially upstairs. Sassy's guiding presence and fearless courage helped ease him through the torment of living in the confines of a spooked house.

"Davis doesn't need dog hair all over his nice, clean car," she responded firmly.

"She doesn't shed! I won't let her," he begged.

Davis lowered the window. "Susan, it's no problem. It'll be fine."

"Are you sure? I'd hate to have your car get smelly."

"Naw. I smell it up all the time. I don't think she can do much worse," he smiled.

Samantha climbed into the back seat, followed by Kelly and the dog. Susan locked up the side door of the house and got into the passenger seat.

Reaching over she gave Davis a quick kiss upon the lips, which enticed smooching sounds from behind.

"You're-just-jeal-ous," Davis teased back like a schoolboy who was taunting another kid.

As the car began to pull around the circular driveway to leave, Kelly looked back to the front of the house. The light inside the attic window was on.

Kelly's eyes widened. He studied the attic closer.

A dark, looming shadow seemed to dart past the window.

He was about to open his mouth to let the others know about the incident when the light shut off.

Kelly felt cold and shaky. *The ghosts were never going away—never! They were going to eventually kill somebody; it was only a matter of time now.*

He decided to keep the bad thoughts to himself.

*   *   *

Richard Tanner switched the radio station as he steered his 2006 Mustang along State Street. He skipped from one frequency to the next, dissatisfied with the lack of variety on the Caseville airwaves.

All that he stumbled upon was country or light rock; even jazz found its way on a station somehow. What he really wanted to hear was rock: not soft rock, alternative rock, or 50's rock, but unadulterated guitar orientated Rock-n-Roll music. The kind of music that smashed you in the face, kicked major ass and didn't hold back.

For a man in his forties and a respected doctor, he sure lived life on the wild side. He had never married, was unable to keep a steady relationship for more than three months at a time, dated younger women, partied in bars and was a thrill-seeker. He was the perfect picture of rebellion. His office even had pictures of James Dean and Marlon Brando on the wall. Back in school he was a partier who stayed out late, drank with the guys, and lived a promiscuous lifestyle. He was the total opposite of his younger sister. Susan was always pristine and well mannered. She had rarely dated and barely left the house, only to go over to her cheerleading friends' homes to practice routines. He was proud of her for that. Even though he was a bad role model, she had the presence of mind to avoid following in his footsteps. That was something he always envied.

Once, he passed out in their parents' front yard after a drunken night of bar-hopping. There he was in all of his glory, comatose for the neighbors to bear witness to. But his sister saved him from public humiliation by pulling him off the ground and carefully walking him past their parents' bedroom and up to his room. The next morning, she covered for him by claiming to have seen him walk in before his curfew. Even now, as he reminisced, the amazing thing about that night wasn't the fact that she saved him, but why she did it! That afternoon he had been a bastard, telling her off in front of her friends and condemning her virgin qualities. It was a stupid and disgusting display from a young man who was too out of control and frightened of his own destiny to give a shit about hers. Yet, she managed to forgive and help him in his time of need. He had changed after that experience. He was frightened of what he was becoming—a selfish, alcoholic loser, plain and simple. She had rectified his life. It was her love and understanding that prompted him to clean up his act and pursue college. For that, he would always be grateful to her.

That's why he pushed for her to move away from that son of a bitch in Florida. She continuously made excuses to him on the phone, saying that she just couldn't bring herself to go through with it, or she wouldn't for the sake of the kids. But he had kept after her and pleaded with her to be strong, if not for herself, then for the kids. Eventually, she had listened. He felt moderate satisfaction, but it was trivial compared to what she had done for him. It was the least he could do.

The red Mustang turned right on Denton and began down the rocky road. Richard envisioned what a nice surprise it would be to drop in on them unexpectedly, since he rarely had the luxury of time to do so. And the kids would probably enjoy the little visit as much as he would. After all, he wasn't doing anything that night; he didn't have any dates lined up. Why not get to know his sister and the kids a little better.

The headlights of his car pulled into the driveway and shone upon Susan's Blazer.

Great, they're home tonight, he thought.

Shutting off the engine, he pulled the keys out and stepped away from the vehicle. The kitchen and upstairs hallway lights were on. Walking up to the side door, he raised his hand to knock, then decided against it. *It would be more of a surprise if I snuck in and scared them,* he laughed, turning the doorknob.

The house was quiet.

Strange. Two kids in the house and not one noise. "What's up with that?" he mused.

Walking through the kitchen, he noticed that dishes sat stacked in the sink and a skillet rested on the stovetop. He continued through the dining room and then into the living room.

Nothing. The house remained still.

Susan's bedroom door was open, but the light was off.

He scratched his head, befuddled. "Where in the heck are you guys?"

Overhead, a stereo cranked on. The sound vibrated from the upstairs ceiling and resonated into the living room.

"Ah-ha!" he shouted. "I knew I wasn't all alone."

*   *   *

Kelly looked over the menu. It was filled with items he had never heard of, let alone tried before, like prime rib, lobster and filet mignon. It all seemed Greek to him. So instead of being brave and carefree, he turned chicken and conservative and ordered a cheeseburger with fries.

"All this great diverse food on the menu and you pick a burger. Well, you might not be considered refined, but you sure are American," Davis said, grinning.

Susan chuckled and slapped him on the shoulder.

Kelly looked at both of them as if they were crazy. He had no idea what Davis was talking about once again, but it couldn't be too bad since they were laughing about it.

"Samantha, how's the journalism department doing? Make any big waves?" Davis inquired, taking a sip of water.

"Great. It's pretty hectic, but nothing I can't handle," she bragged.

"Good to hear," he beamed.

"The last article I wrote was about the county roads. They're all mangled. Look at Denton, for example. It's like driving through Vietnam. You need a jeep or a tank to make it across. Hopefully the piece I wrote will turn some heads. Who knows, maybe we'll get a petition going or something," she said with a broad smile.

"You never know. Once you put your mind to it, you can do anything," he said, pointing a finger to his head.

"Mom, do they really serve lobster here?"

"Yes, Kelly. Why?"

"It's gross! What about the claws and tentacles? How can people eat such yucky stuff?" He grimaced, sticking out his tongue.

"Don't worry Kelly, it all tastes like chicken," Samantha replied wryly.

*   *   *

Richard walked up the stairs as music echoed from above. Reaching the top level, he paused and listened to determine which room it was coming from.

The hallway was illuminated and he noticed that Samantha's door was wide open, but the room was dark inside.

Taking a couple of steps forward, he stood underneath the attic door when the music ceased behind Kelly's door.

That's it. That's where they're hiding. Smiling, he took a small step forward, keeping his movement silent. Edging closer to the door, he listened intently for an advantage in surprise.

Nothing. The room was dead silent.

What are they doing in there, he wondered? *Maybe they heard me?*

Moving one step further, he came nose to nose with the door. As his foot rested down upon the carpet, the floorboard creaked softly. He cringed, realizing the sneak attack was thwarted.

Time to catch them off guard before they caught him.

Placing his hand slowly to the door, his palms glistened with sweat as it wrapped around the brass knob.

Taking a deep breath, he counted slowly as he prepared to charge in.

Quietly turning the knob, he pulled the door open with great velocity and shouted as he burst in. "Gotcha!" he screamed.

An old woman's apparition hovered a foot and a half above the ground. Rolling back her head, exposing a bare outstretched neck, she extended her arms outward in a crucified position, laying the palms of her hands upward, while stretching her fingers apart from one another. A loose flowing black gown covered her frail bones and rippled in the air.

A deep, constant moan began to emit from the throat of the floating specter, then rose to an ear-shattering intense pitch.

The wicked siren forced Richard to cower. His face drained of blood and his wobbly knees buckled, leaving him in shock, frozen in place for the wrath of the hovering witch.

The shrill faded, but underneath it came a low, vicious animal growl; a deep cry from within the bowels of Hell.

The old woman's decomposed grayish face lowered slowly until it was level with his.

Richard felt paralyzed. The once young and nimble man was now helpless and immobile. Even a scream for help failed to emerge from his quivering lips. He was now at the mercy of the unimaginable demon manifested before his very eyes.

The hag's head rolled from one side to the other then lowered until she was eye to eye with the trembling man. A slow curving grimace formed upon her face. The old woman's eyes suddenly widened with anticipation as she carefully studied, and then relished, the sight of his frozen body. She reveled in the supreme power and revered herself for having such immense strength and control over the frail man, who sat cowering inside the doorjamb, terrified and too afraid to move.

Sweat beaded quickly upon Richard's white face and then slithered down his forehead and cheeks, covering his parched dry lips.

The hovering figure drew in her arms and crossed them over one another upon her chest. The specter's ashen gray flesh-tone contrasted with her bulging white oval eyes, as the light of the room displayed the hideous woman in all of her splendor.

Richard was scared senseless. For the first time in his life he was truly afraid. If this demon didn't kill him right now, a heart attack surely would.

If only he wasn't here alone. God, why couldn't someone else be here with him now? He had branded himself a proud loner, a cool guy without any baggage of a partner to deal with. And now, standing immobile and beaten against a force he was no match for, he was going to die alone.

*　　*　　*

Davis started up the blue Taurus and the vehicle instantly reacted and idled unerringly.

"Guys, isn't there something you'd like to tell Davis?" Susan asked, looking over her shoulder to the kids sitting passively in the back seat.

Kelly looked over to Samantha and the two exchanged glances for a moment. Suddenly they both lit up, aware. "Thank you for dinner, Davis," both responded sheepishly, embarrassed by their rude behavior.

"You're both welcome. It was my pleasure," he said, touched.

The car continued down State Street and headed for Denton Road. It was eight-thirty and the sun had gone down a few hours ago.

An idea popped into Susan's head, while watching oncoming cars pass by.

"Davis, do you have to go home right away?"

"No. Why?"

"Well, since we're all together, I thought maybe we could rent a movie or two tonight. What do you think?" She smiled.

"I think you're one smart cookie."

He turned onto Denton and did a U-turn off the shoulder. When a few cars passed across State, he punched the gas—throwing rocks behind through the air—and reentered the main road back into town.

Susan looked back at the kids. "All right, let's decide what kind of movie you want to watch, okay?"

"Scary ones! Let's get Saw!" Kelly shouted, hyped up.

Samantha wrinkled her brow. "Get real, you're way too young to watch that kind of stuff. I'm not watching a blood and guts flick."

"Fine," he replied, crossing his arms.

"How about that new war movie," Samantha proposed, knowing his weakness for action and adventure.

Kelly smiled. "Yeah! That's cool."

She laughed at his delight and tickled his side. He thrashed and wailed, gasping for air as she poured on the torture.

Davis watched from the rear view mirror and smiled with pleasure. Turning toward Susan, who sported her own glowing smile, he responded, "I think everything is going great."

"It can't get any better than this," she concurred.

*   *   *

The hovering body of the dead woman began to move closer towards Richard. Aware of the danger he was in, he instinctively slid backwards on the carpet and got up off the floor.

The pale, transparent face of the figure inched closer and closer. With every step he made backward, she gained two.

"What do you want from me? You're not real," he shouted, attempting to dispel the truth before his eyes. "Leave me the hell alone!" he demanded, shielding his face.

The floating spirit passed through the bedroom door's archway with hands outstretched and her dress flowing in mid-air.

The withered, snake-like skin of the hag's face stretched from ear to ear as she erupted into laughter, gurgling amidst congested snot drainage, revealing dark yellow decayed teeth. Hissing vehemently, she snarled, wrinkling the bridge of her nose as saliva ran wildly down into the corners of her mouth.

Richard shrank back as the ungodly beast continued forward. His breathing became labored as he forced himself not to succumb to sheer panic, and his pulse quickened out of control, pounding excessively against the wall of his chest. The more he tried to remain calm, the more his lungs craved oxygen. Soon he became winded and light headed, on the verge of unconsciousness.

The fright was inches from his face, intent on scaring the living shit out of him before it even touched him. For the figure to be only an apparition, he could swear it had repulsive, pungent breath, and as it wheezed and snarled, he turned to face a different direction away from its ghastly scowl.

He stepped back once more with his left foot, then with his right. As his last step swung back, the heel of his shoe caught against a dresser in the hallway and abruptly stopped him. Suspended in awkward balance, he looked down, confused by the sudden stop and noticed the object.

He cursed under his breath for being so clumsy and careless in his quickened path.

Looking back up, he was startled to find the woman's discolored face inches away from his as she reached for his jugular with her long, splintered fingernails.

Richard let out a blood-curdling scream as he fell backward against the dresser and bounded helplessly over the railing of the stairs. Spiraling down head first, he slammed into the third step and snapped his neck as the weight of his body followed. He tumbled down the remaining steps and sprawled out onto the kitchen floor upon his stomach. His head, twisted completely around, focused upon the ceiling with terror frozen in the eyes.

*   *   *

Samantha and Kelly took the key from Susan and immediately ran to the side door in a competitive foot race. After unlocking it, they squeezed together into the house and went out of sight.

Picking up the two movies, Susan began to open her door. Stopping, she glanced back at Davis and planted a passionate kiss upon his lips.

"What in the world brought that on?" he asked surprised.

"It's just something I've been wanting to do for a long time," she said, with a sexy grin upon her face.

She was just about to give him an encore kiss, when Samantha screamed from inside the house. Startled, they both jumped out of the car and ran to the house. When they entered, Samantha was leaning against the wall with her hands covering her mouth and tears streaming down her cheeks. Kelly stood like a statue by the kitchen sink staring off towards the dining room. His face was white as he remained in a trance.

Now what? Susan thought as she went to Samantha.

"Honey, what is it? What's wrong?"

The girl shook her head back and forth violently as she continued to sob and shake.

Suddenly Susan felt that awful knot form in her stomach that warned her when trouble loomed. She walked closer towards Kelly, but instead of talking to him, passed, understanding that whatever was around the corner would explain everything.

Susan gasped and covered her mouth as the bile in her stomach rose. She turned her head quickly from the grotesque sight and fell back against the counter. Her legs wobbled and gave out as she tried desperately to move away; unable to, she fell back against the counter's edge, overcome with grief.

Davis rushed over to her quickly and caught her before she fell. Taking a brief glance to the floor, he wrapped his arms around her tightly and shielded her from the sight.

"Come on, Sue. Come over here," he said soothingly, walking her towards the side door.

Davis looked back, remembering that Kelly was still consumed by the horror.

"Susan, stay right here," he said, going after the boy.

Kelly's eyes were as big as saucers and fixated upon the twisted frame of his uncle. As soon as he saw the body, he knew what had happened: *the bad thing*. The evil spirits had taken his uncle's life, just as they had promised to do. They said it would kill if someone interfered, and they did. Just like that.

Kelly felt as if the weight of the world was on his shoulders, crushing him into the ground like a spike. A huge black cloud resided over him and all he could do was watch. He wanted to cry, sob and break down like his sister, but he couldn't; he was numb. It was his fault his uncle was dead. He had made the mistake of telling Davis about the secret, and now he was paying the price.

"Kelly, it's all right. Don't look at him."

The boy refused to acknowledge.

"Kelly, please come over here," Davis pleaded.

Kelly heard the voice off in the distance, but he didn't respond; there was no need to bother or even care; he had failed his uncle. He simply stood and stared at the fallen figure.

"Kelly," Davis tried again.

Nothing. The boy remained lifeless.

Susan, hearing Davis' attempts, snapped loudly, "Kelly!"

The boy shook from the spell and faced her.

She looked lost and in shock, as if someone had reached into her chest with their bare hands and pulled her heart out. Kelly saw glistening tears begin to well inside of her eyes and he ran to her, placing his head upon her stomach and wrapping his arms around her waist. "I'm so sorry, mama! I'm so sorry! It's my fault. It's all my fault," he sobbed uncontrollably.

Susan cradled him tightly. "Shhh. Shhh. Don't cry. It's all right. It's all right. I'm here. Shhh. I'm here, baby."

He held onto her tightly and released all of the pent up frustration and anger built up inside.

Samantha walked over to them and put her head upon her mom's arm and embraced Kelly. Susan hugged her close and all three rocked back and forth.

Davis looked at them somberly, then asked, "Susan, why don't you and the kids spend the night over at my place tonight?"

She sighed wearily, then nodded yes.

"You guys go wait in the car and I'll phone the police and let them know what happened."

The three went to car as Davis watched and waited. After they were safely in the vehicle, he dialed the number to the police station and told the officer every necessary detail.

He glanced down at the body again. A grim chill overcame him as he studied the dead man's haunted expression. Davis looked away towards the kitchen and then into the living room to distract his mind. He felt monitored. *Was something watching him at that very moment? Some kind of invisible force with eyes in the night?*

Seated in the passenger seat, Susan gazed out into the blackness of the night. The car was still; not a soul breathed a word. Reality seemed such a long ways away.

*   *   *

Kelly could still see the frozen look of horror upon his uncle's face, crying out for help before the beast killed him. Once again the icy feeling of being watched came upon him and he directed his view back to the house. He knew where the eyes were coming from and he knew what they wanted—recognition. They wanted to be feared and respected for their act.

It was a stern warning to Kelly of things yet to come: *listen to the bad thing, or else.*

The boy looked up the side of the brick house until he came upon the small library window. There in the light of the hallway appeared the face of the rag doll, waiting to be admired.

Chapter 12

It was a somber, chilly, overcasted afternoon as light drizzle began to sop the earth's soil. A small crowd of family and friends gathered to pay their last respects to Richard Daniel Tanner, while thunder clapped and echoed from beyond the hilltop.

After Susan and the children said their tearful farewells, they trotted out of the building rainstorm to Davis' car. Susan looked back at the grave sight and shook her head with disbelief. She had just started to get to know him again, and now he was gone. Her closest family relation was now gone, and it left a lasting bitter taste in her mouth.

She rested her head upon Davis' suit coat. "I don't know if I can stay in that house alone anymore, after what's happened. I think I'll see his face every time I'm in that damn kitchen. I can't deal with that yet."

Davis watched her affectionately, then stroked her long hair.

"Would you stay with us at the house, please, for just a little while?" she asked softly.

"You know I will," he said, looking deep into her eyes, bearing the pain she was feeling.

When they returned inside the house that afternoon it was dark and gloomy. Samantha went around to every window and drew back the curtains, filling the house with additional lighting.

Susan stopped short in the kitchen and looked upon the floor by the stairway. Her heart ached and her stomach churned.

Davis put his arm around her. "Come on, let's go sit in the living room."

As they started, footsteps from the top of the stairs ensued. The two stopped short of the opening, watched and waited.

Sassy trotted past them through the doorway, wagging her tail with delight. She approached Susan, sniffed her leg, then trotted off into the living room to greet the children.

Susan and Davis followed behind. As they went past the opening of the stairs, a cold gust of wind blew upon Susan's exposed arm, giving her goosebumps. She continued forward without glancing upward, unwilling to give in to her suspicions.

*   *   *

After spending an hour on the couch watching television, Susan nodded off to sleep. Kelly had taken the dog upstairs to bed, and Samantha went to her room a half-hour later.

Davis slipped out from Susan's sleeping grasp, got up from the couch, and went upstairs.

Something very strange was going on in this house, and he was interested in hearing Samantha's recollections or opinions.

He approached her bedroom door, and as usual, music came from within.

He rapped twice upon the wood.

After turning down the radio, she opened the door.

"Sam, do you think we could talk? That is, if you're not doing anything important," he inquired.

"Sure, come on in."

He closed the door behind him and pulled up a chair that was next to her writing desk.

She sat down on the edge of the bed and listened with interest.

"Sam, I hear some strange and bizarre things have been going on around this house. Have you noticed anything unusual? Anything out of the ordinary that you might consider odd."

She looked around the room in silent thought. *If you consider seeing a floating ghost, a stranger in our backyard watching my bedroom window, or being felt up in the bathtub by the invisible man odd, well then, yes, I guess I'd have to say this house is pretty strange.*

Why was he asking her this? Kelly is the one who is seeing a shrink, not her. Maybe Davis was simply trying to trick her to find out whether or not she was making stories up as well. She was not about to be laughed at for telling an outlandish tale.

She envisioned the tall, bearded man in the trench coat who had watched her in the bathroom—and probably the same man, no doubt, who stood outside her window. *What man,* she thought? *He wasn't real; he wasn't there.* She recounted how terrified she had been after that creepy bath experience, the way it had made her feel violated, and how every night from then on she had slept with sweatpants and a sweatshirt on, regardless of the temperature that night.

She wanted to tell Davis the truth, or what she thought was the truth. But deep down inside, she didn't trust her feelings to him. Would he take her seriously? She didn't know him well enough to know that for sure. If she was honest with him and admitted everything, he might dismiss it with a laugh. She wasn't about to be embarrassed and belittled.

"Nope, nothing that I can think of," she heard herself respond.

"You sure? If anything happened, you'd tell me, wouldn't ya?" he asked her, still unsure.

"Of course. I promise," she smiled, nodding her head up and down.

"Okay," he said, getting up from the chair, satisfied with her answer. "Thanks, Sam. Sorry to bother you," he said, shutting the door behind as he left.

She watched him walk away and a frown emerged from her face as she realized his good-hearted intention.

I'm sorry, Davis, she thought. *I'm really sorry.*

* * *

Susan and Davis lay side by side in bed. Neither had any impulsive sexual desires, only shared needs to be close to one another.

Davis relished the companionship he had been seeking for so many years. He yearned to be involved with a woman of her stature: intelligent, sensitive, beautiful, and charismatic. She was everything that he dreamed about.

Her golden, blond hair fell across the pillowcase and rested upon his shoulder. He lay there in complete fulfillment, oblivious to the madness around them. He reflected back to when they first met in the diner: how she had thought of him as her knight in shining armor. He laughed out loud.

She turned her head at his sudden movement. "What?" she asked, looking up smiling, curious to know his pleasure.

"I was just thinking about the first time we met. You know, how you thought I was this big hero to you. Your prince."

"Yeah, and I still do. Why?"

"The truth is . . . I think I was just as scared as that guy was. I was scared shitless!" he said, throwing his hands to his forehead.

"What? My big, brave man, afraid. That's preposterous. I don't believe it. You mean you were putting up a front to intimidate that guy?" she responded, sitting up in bed with a smile a mile long.

"Yeah, that's about the gist of it. If I wouldn't have acted so quickly, I probably would have froze standing there. I'm lucky I didn't piss my pants."

"I don't care. You're still my hero, no matter what you say, regardless of how you felt. You saved us and I'm forever in debt," she reached over and kissed him warmly on the lips.

She felt over his smooth cheeks with the palms of her hand, stroking passionately. The masculinity of his face excited her.

"You know, I never thought that I would be able to say this again, what with everything John put me through, but . . . I think I'm falling in love with you," she said, looking at him in awe, her green eyes shining like diamonds in sunlight.

"Susan, you know that I would never do anything to hurt you, and I promise, I'll always be there for you. Before I met you I was really a lost soul. I didn't have a clue to what I wanted out of life, nor did I know who I was. It was the hardest thing, you know, living life alone, without having someone to care about, laugh with, or share every wonderful detail of life with. When you and your family entered my world, I knew right away what a lucky guy I was. I thank God for bringing us together. No matter what happens, I will always cherish our time together. I never want to lose you, Sue."

He kissed her softly.

She arched back, enjoying the sweet taste of his mouth upon hers.

Prior to that day, she was lost and confused also, crushed by the sudden death of her brother. Davis was able to ease her mind and help her realize she could be loved and that she could give love, also. It wasn't impossible, as she once had thought.

That night, the horrible visions of her brother and the uncertainty of the future gave way to her heart, and she felt love truly for the first time.

*　　*　　*

Noticing it was ten-thirty at night, Samantha told Stephen that she was going to say goodnight so that she could get ready for bed.

He reluctantly agreed to let her go, since they had already been talking on the phone for two entertaining, engaging hours.

"I love you so much, sweetie. I'll be dreaming of you all night until we see each other again tomorrow at school," he told her.

She seconded the sentiment, and added another "I love you," and then hung up the receiver.

Lying upon the bed, she heard his warm, sensitive voice echo through her mind. Though they had only been dating a mere few months, she yearned and thirsted to be with him like a flame needed oxygen; his name and voice was etched into her mind eternally.

She sighed with satisfaction and drifted off the bed with wild emotions. Drawing her journal out of the desk drawer, she brought it back to the bed and added another poem.

What is love?

> Not a courtship, nor a system, nor a struggle for truth.
> What is love?
> But a wisp, and a dream, everlasting from youth.
> What is love?
> Come the dusk, just as sure as the day.
> What is love?
> Just a touch, from my angel, just a heartbeat away.

Closing the book, she set it back and left her room.

After brushing her teeth, she closed the medicine cabinet door and left the bathroom. Stopping short of her bedroom door, she looked up to the attic and remembered how cruel and insensitive she had been to Kelly in front of Julie. That childish, stupid display had been eating at her conscience like crazy since.

She should have apologized to him; he deserved it. Supernatural events were going on here constantly and she had witnessed several of them. If only her big bad ego didn't prevent her from telling the truth. The way her mom looked at Kelly every time he brought up the subject of ghosts, she'd think Samantha was crazy as well, and she wasn't about to lose her mother's trust and respect now.

She looked over to the attic door. Kelly said pictures were up there. If there were some proof I could show her, then she'd have to believe us.

She edged closer to the rope.

What was in the attic? She had never been up there before, and as far as she knew, he could be making everything up. But it was worth a try. If she could find anything that would help their situation, she would have to go up there.

She looked over to Kelly's bedroom where he lay asleep. "I hope you're having pleasant dreams, while I'm on some sort of crazy detective case."

Grasping the knotted rope, she pulled the ladder down.

The darkness was even greater than she had imagined. Not a single object was detectable above.

"Great, I don't even have a clue to where the lights are at."

Going to the hallway closet she withdrew a plastic flashlight, clicked on the beam of light and began to ascend the stairs. The white spotlight illuminated and trailed across the ceiling as she made her way upwards. Nearing the top step, she redirected the flashlight beam at multiple angles inside of the attic, but revealed nothing significant. She crept up through the door opening and stood upon the attic's wooden floor, peering around in the dim room.

She felt foolish. Why was she doing this? She should be fast asleep in bed, not roaming around in a dusty dark attic during the middle of the night. "No one would be crazy enough to do this," she lamented, "not even Nancy Drew."

The beam of light passed over a stack of boxes in the corner of the attic. Finding them, she turned the light back upon it.

"Yes, there they are! Cool." Walking forward, the floorboard squeaked underfoot.

Her stomach felt queasy.

There are only boxes up here. Only boxes and nothing else, she repeated calmly to herself as she approached them.

Then she heard a sound that froze her heart in mid-beat: the sobbing of a woman.

Samantha stopped abruptly; the noise was right behind her.

Coldness touched upon her shoulders, almost hand-like.

Her lips trembled. Afraid to move, she kept the light directed upon the boxes.

The crying of the woman's voice ceased, but was immediately replaced by a rubbing noise above in the rafters

I have to get out of here. I can't breathe! I can't breathe! She panicked as claustrophobia began to overcome her.

As Samantha turned around, the flashlight beam struck directly upon the bluish face of a short, brunette woman who was hanging from the ceiling by a noose. The dead woman's eyes were opened in tortured shock, and her purple, split lips were apart in silent scream.

Sickened by the repugnant cadaverous face, Samantha dropped the flashlight to the floor and ran past the ghoulish sight. She trampled recklessly and noisily down the short flight of stairs, lifted and locked the ladder back into place and ran into her room. Shutting and locking her bedroom door, she turned the light on, then curled up into a fetal position on the bed. As if on cue, a loud, deep guttural moan arose somewhere in the attic just above her, which was then followed by heavy footsteps that seemed to wander aimlessly back and forth, pacing restlessly.

Oh God, this can't be happening. But it is, Samantha repeated to herself, shaking with chill. *My God, it's real!*

*   *   *

The light over the well swung back and forth and then smashed against the side of the basement wall. Drops of water dripped slowly down the side of the inner well wall into a darkened abyss, and as they landed in a small pool collected below, a reverberation echoed back up.

The beast slowly placed its hands upon the outer edge of the well's rim and pulled itself upward out of the base. Its misshapen head appeared, deformed and mutilated as though a sledgehammer had beaten the skull. Bulging white eyes darted and scanned the small furnace room, searching for anything in its path to pull down into the darkened hole. Inch by inch, it clawed and pulled out of the well to the surface, straining with every muscle to be free. Hunched in the shadows, the creature lifted its head, sniffed the air for its victim's location, and then began to walk through the darkened corridor. Its three-inch long sharpened claws dragged across the concrete wall, screeching like a knife upon a chalkboard.

Its milky-white moist flesh smeared fresh blood and pus upon the walls as it slithered up the basement stairs.

Moving through the dimly lit kitchen, the beast dragged its infected, deformed leg as it continued and headed upstairs, leaving a trail of blood soaking into the kitchen carpet. The beast licked at the corners of its mouth with a dark green eroded tongue as it ascended the stairs. Creeping onward, it stalked slowly, cautious of not waking a single soul, and its eyes were alert and focused intensely. Sniffing the air with its pig like snout, it recognized the smell of human blood and quivered with delight.

The reptilian face studied the first door. There was life inside of the room, but not the life it was interested in taking.

It reached a second closed door and grinned with delight, dripping saliva from its fangs.

The door opened slowly, and there in deep slumber slept the boy, unaware of the silent force within his room.

The beast's huge eyes transposed into slanted snake eyes as it moved in on the child.

Directly over him now, its chest heaved with uncontrollable excitement, and strands of hot mucus dropped from its cracked nostrils onto the blanket covering the sleeping child.

Kelly's eyelids fluttered and then lifted once he felt the hot, vile breath of the beast upon his face.

Still grinning, the creature placed its sharp fingernail upon Kelly's throat and began to stroke his soft, white skin gently.

Its eyes were staring and piercing through his skull like a laser as it stood over the bed, watching patiently.

What was it waiting for, he wondered? Why wouldn't it finish him off?

Kelly's skin was sheer ice as his body shook underneath the covers.

The tight muscles in the creature's jaw twitched spastically.

Its sharp claw continued to stroke over Kelly's skin and the roughness of its edge caught and sliced, drawing blood down the side of his neck.

He whimpered and grimaced from the pain, but remained still, trying not to make much noise.

Tears began to well up in his eyes. He desperately wanted to scream or run, but he knew it wouldn't do any good.

Blood began to trickle out of his wound faster and in larger spurts.

The bed sheet was sopped in crimson red fluid.

The massive creature stood over the top of him, pleased at the sight. Its eyes darted back and forth from the sliced wound to Kelly's eyes.

Kelly looked down at the bloody sheets; terrified, he finally gave in to panic and thrashed and kicked his feet upon the mattress of the bed and screamed for help.

Blood gushed from his cut like an active volcano and covered his face and body in a warm pool. The pain was excruciating and unbearable. The more that he tried to scream out, the faster blood would spray out of his neck onto the bedroom wall.

Still the beast stood calm, unaffected by the sight and sounds of the child.

Kelly's pale, sweaty face stared back into the creature's solemn eyes. He was sure that it was waiting patiently for him to die.

Blood spilled upon the floor and stretched out toward each corner of the room. The white carpet was masked in red.

Kelly tried to scream once more, but only blood gurgled out of his mouth.

With his last attempt futile, the end was only a heartbeat away.

The last thing Kelly remembered before succumbing to darkness was the wicked grin of the satisfied beast as it licked and tasted its dampened red finger.

*   *   *

Davis rolled over on the mattress fighting restlessness. For the last half-hour a tense feeling of confinement consumed him, and since first waking during the night a presence of some kind seemed alive in the room. He was unaware of what it was, but he was sure that it was there.

Lying upon his back, he listened to Susan's peaceful breathing and her lull confused him. *How she was able to sleep so well with the recent traumas that had changed her life?*

He reached for a glass of water on the nightstand and placed it to his lips. The cool liquid went down in large gulps and quenched his dehydration.

Moonlight reflecting through the window highlighted features in the small bedroom and brightened the corner walls by the door.

He loved moonbeams. They reminded him of an old werewolf story that his grandfather used to tell. He recalled the story about a mansion in the deep woods of West Virginia during the late 1800s, where some distant relatives lived in a small town with a "so-called" werewolf. Every full moon the beast would run rampant throughout the woods and terrorize whoever crossed its path. Town folks were aware of the legend and always bolted their doors and latched their windows, even if they publicly disbelieved it.

One foggy, full moon night, his distant teenage cousin, Karie Higginson, retired to bed. After undressing and brushing her long, black mane, she climbed into bed and blew out the candle upon her stand. While she lay there, the wind picked up mightily, howling and wailing with a fury. A shutter started banging against her bedroom window. For a brief moment the wind would subside, but it would soon return and roar back with intense power.

The frail, young woman squirmed under the sheets as she watched the window with keen interest.

A gray mist of fog curled upon the outside pane of glass and obstructed her sight beyond the house.

She felt cornered.

Suddenly, an awful trebly screeching noise started from outside her window.

It sounded like a piece of metal sliding against the glass. She jerked, alarmed by its harsh pitch, and climbed out of bed to shut the loose shutter before it snapped off its hinges or cracked the window. Crossing the wooden floor bare-footed, she came to the window to investigate.

Staring back at her from the other side of the windowpane was the most hideous-looking beast, scratching its splintered fingernails against the glass like a cat would a wooden post. Its fire-red pupils studied her like a piece of meat on a platter.

The werewolf's face was covered in matted dark brown hair and showcased several layers of razor sharp teeth.

She could hear its venomous howl slicing through the raging wind.

Terrified, she screamed for help, but it was to no avail; she was alone and defenseless in the room.

By the time her father had raced up the stairs to save her, the beast had broken through the window and carried her off into the night.

The only thing left in the aftermath were tattered threads of clothing, shards of glass upon the floor and the constant thump of the wooden shutter against the house, nothing else. Fortunately, a neighboring farmer, who was hunting in the woods, scared off the beast by firing a warning shot into the air, and saved the young girl's life. The werewolf was never seen or heard from again.

The unbelievable thing about the tale, Davis was told, was how the werewolf got up to the second floor window. There was no means of support for the beast to climb or keep itself steadied upon—no ladder, ledge or nearby tree. There was only the side of the house, which it had grappled and scaled.

Davis stared out of Susan's bedroom window, half expecting the werewolf's shiny red eyes to appear. They didn't, and he knew they wouldn't. The story his grandfather had told him was just an old spooky tale, handed down through generations to scare kids.

A light wind picked up and began to gently sway a tree branch outside the window. He watched and smiled; amused by the visual the old man had placed into his mind.

A strong chill rushed upon his bare chest and made him flinch in surprise.

Odd, one moment the room was cozy warm, the next it was freezing.

Rubbing his arms to warm up, he looked down at Susan who was still resting in the same position against the wall, unconscious to his fidgeting. He started to lay back down on the bed when he looked over to the door and raised quickly off the pillow with trepidation. Looming in the corner stood a massive black winged demon with flaring red eyes. It was so enormous that its back was arched forward to avoid hitting the ceiling, and its massive body stretched to both sides of the room.

The demon's head was long and dragon-like and attached to a sleek extending flexible neck that bobbed and darted as its breath became visible in the chilled room. Its chest expanded and contracted rapidly, while the wings upon its back unfurled and stretched outward into each corner of the room, confined and unable to fully expand. It curled its long, thin muscular arms upon its chest. The demon's overwhelming size seemed like an illusion inside of the tiny room.

Davis shifted his weight slowly until he was sitting in an upright position. Unsure of what he was seeing, whether it was dream or truth, he kept his movement to a minimum.

The monstrous beast remained unmoving, breathing heavily into the icy room while staring at the startled man. Its leathery-skinned jaw opened slowly with a hiss, revealing rows of fangs.

Sweat began to pour down Davis' forehead. The salty juice streaked down his cheek and filtered into the corner of his mouth, leaving a bitter taste that made him queasy. His mind raced back again to the discussion with Kelly about the evil spirits of the house. The last words the boy had mentioned were, "Whoever interfered with the house would be killed." He was looking for proof of its existence, and now he seemed to have found it in the most inopportune way, if in fact it was reality.

Saliva that drooled in pools from the demon's mouth became structured into hot foam, as the beast gnashed its teeth together in rage.

Davis' heartbeat was thrashing out of control. His shirt and shorts were drenched with perspiration. Closing his eyes, he desperately tried to wish the illusion of the figure away, but even with his eyes closed, the beast's rumbling breath became deafening.

In a brief moment of darkness and wonder, Davis felt a pain like none he had ever felt before. A force like a wrecking ball slammed into his side and knocked him backward onto Susan against the wall. He cried out in agony as a wave of pain coursed through his body. Instantly, he reached for his ribs, feeling for blood or a wound. His skin wasn't wet, but the moment his finger touched his rib area he recoiled from the pain.

Susan, hearing the commotion and feeling sudden weight upon her body, stiffened upright off the bed.

"What is it? Davis what's going on?" she cried out, nervously looking around in the darkness.

"Oh, God! Shit. Damn it hurts," he screamed out.

Susan attempted to calm him, but he was unaffected by her words and continued to thrash upon the sheets in agony.

"Oh, God," he screamed, "we've got to get out of here now."

*   *   *

CLICK CLICK CLICK CLICK.

The shifting noise continued to sustain through the darkness in Samantha's room.

What was that funny sound, she wondered, fidgeting in sleep.

The noise had been occurring for more than three minutes. Was she dreaming or awake?

CLICK CLICK CLICK CLICK.

The sound was becoming increasingly irritating. She crinkled her eyebrows and burrowed her head into the pillow, intent on ignoring it.

CLICK CLICK CLICK CLICK.

Perturbed and disoriented, she sat up in the bed and studied the dark room. It was coming from her closet. *But what was it,* she wondered?

The room was suddenly disturbingly quiet: too quiet, in fact. Now that her attention was upon it, the noise had playfully stopped. It was teasing her.

The thing she saw in the bathroom, the same thing that Davis was asking her about, was that the culprit? Was it there in the room with her?

It couldn't be, she willed herself to believe, because there were no such things as ghosts. If her mother didn't believe in the possibility, then why should she?

CLICK CLICK CLICK CLICK. The doorknob to the closet turned quickly back and forth.

Something in the closet was attempting to get out. But what, though? Could Kelly be in there? Why would he be? It was almost three o'clock in the morning; he should be asleep. But she also knew Kelly's ingenious and devious mind. If he wanted to wait for hours, or even days, to pull a good prank, he would.

She wanted desperately to believe that it was Kelly, but she didn't. The constant frights that she had witnessed before were proof enough. If this was Kelly, then she could try to rationalize all of the other crazy things that went on, and maybe, just maybe, this wasn't the scare it appeared to be.

She wasn't fooling herself; she had seen the dead women in the attic and she had witnessed everything just as Kelly had. He wasn't in the closet.

CLICK CLICK CLICK CLICK.

Placing her feet on the floor, she threw back the covers and walked towards the door.

Why wouldn't it come out? As levelheaded and skeptical as she proclaimed to be, she was afraid and reluctant to know the answer.

She reached for the light switch by the door, but before she could touch it, it turned upward on its own volition. Startled, she took a step back and looked at the fixture in amazement. "That was crazy."

Looking back at the closet, she studied the knob.

CLICK CLICK CLICK.

The handle turned furiously as if something had dire need to get out immediately. Hard pounding raps began to strike against the wood from inside, and she cried out, alarmed.

The overhead light flashed off and on repeatedly, illuminating the room in short intervals.

Samantha backed away from the closet and reached out for the bedroom doorknob.

It was locked. With all of her strength, she turned the brass handle, but something held it firmly. Exasperated, she pulled on the knob, then turned it back and forth again. Panicking, she banged upon the doorframe with her palms to get anyone's attention.

Her concentration shifted as she heard the closet door click and open. She looked back in horror. The door began to move.

She was going to die like her uncle. The thing in the closet was coming for her and the only exit from the room was bolted shut. "Go away, please, just go away."

As the light switch continued to change, Samantha kept her eye upon the closet, waiting for something to come forth. Nothing appeared.

All of her dresser drawers slid out at the same time, then slammed back into place.

She jumped at the sudden movement.

The closet door widened opened further, revealing darkness within.

Sobbing, she tried to turn the doorknob with her damp, sweaty palms, but was once again let down.

"Mom . . . Somebody, please help me," she cried, with her forehead resting against the door. "Get me out of here." she yelled louder, pounding her fists hard upon the door.

The madness of the room became deafening in her head. Drawers were slamming, knobs were turning, and the room was in a surrealistic strobe effect.

She dropped helplessly to her knees and curled up against the door. As she lay trembling with despair, the light above her stopped its constant strobe and remained on, the dresser drawers ceased instantaneously, and the closet door closed and latched shut.

She sat on the floor, shivering with fear. Her once shiny, glossy hair was damp and matted. Her heart rate continued above normal as she waited for the next wave of violence to arise. But to her bewilderment, the room remained still and empty.

Lifting out of the crouched position, she staggered to her feet, her eyes wide with dismay.

"Why are you playing with our heads? What do you want from us?" she demanded.

She looked around for a drawer to move, but nothing did.

As the breathing in her lungs slowly returned to normal, she gathered her wits and attempted to leave the room once more. As her hand approached the door, the knob turned, released the lock, and opened for her to pass through. Mesmerized by the demonic display, she walked forward through the door and out into the hallway. She stopped, curious of a noise from behind, and turned around.

An opened crystal music box was on her bed playing the melody to "Mr. Sandman."

*   *   *

Davis sat on the edge of the bed shaking his head with dismay. The room was fully lit and no demon was hunched over in the corner. The pain he had felt earlier had subsided greatly, but his ribs were still tender.

"I don't know," he began again for the third time, "I'm not sure what the hell it was. Honest, Susan, I'm telling you the truth. I was having trouble falling asleep, so I had a sip of water and laid back down. The room got tremendously cold, and I had this odd sensation that something else was in here with us. When I looked over by the corner of the room I saw this incredible huge demon. It was massive! God, I know it sounds ridiculous, baby. You probably think I'm crazy. But God as my witness, I saw that thing!" he emphasized, shaking with consternation.

Placing a hand to his forehead, he swiped away at building sweat.

"Honey, you were asleep, that's all. You were just having a nightmare. I heard you screaming out, and when I turned on the light nothing was there. There wasn't anything in the room. It was just a dream," she repeated softly, rubbing her palms against his back.

"No it wasn't!" he snapped back, startling her. "Listen, Sue, we were ignorant and naive about this house. Maybe you should have taken Kelly a little more seriously, and not that damn doctor," he said restlessly.

"What? Oh, come on, Davis. What on earth are you saying?"

"I'm saying that I believe supernatural things are going on inside of this house. I don't know much about demonic forces; in fact, I don't know shit about them, but what I do know is that there is enough evidence not to rule it out."

"Davis, you know how I feel about all that paranormal and demonology crap. I think it's all bullshit! There's an explanation for everything. I think you've gotten all caught up with Kelly's horror stories and the tragedy with my brother, and you blended them into a nightmare last night. That's why it seems so real," she said sympathetically.

Davis' face grew stern and increasingly impatient. He sat up off the bed, turned with the right side of his ribs facing her and pointed.

Her expression turned blank. A dark black and blue bruise, the size of softball, engulfed his right mid-section. Staring at the mark in disbelief, she grew perplexed as she noticed puncture wounds like teeth prints deep into the skin.

"Davis . . . what . . . what . . ." her words sputtered as she tried to speak out.

She felt like a fool for doubting him and was overcome with shame.

136

Bowing her head in frustration, she responded sadly. "I don't know what to say, really. I'm so sorry for doubting you."

He lifted her chin up to look her eye to eye. "It's not your fault, and I'm not mad. It's very hard to swallow. I didn't want to believe it myself. But I do now. I had to, for the safety of you and the kids. I'm sorry I snapped at you like that. But I didn't know of any other way to tell you."

They embraced one another. She held him close and relished the warmth of his body against hers. "Oh, Davis, what are we going to do?" she asked, looking up at him from his hold.

"We'll think of something. Don't worry, we'll think of something," he said, protecting her.

A knock at the door broke them of the embrace. Susan looked up at Davis, displaying the same hesitant look that he had. They held their breath and listened intently. When the second knock came, a voice behind the door spoke out. "Mom? Are you up?"

"Sammy. It's Sam!" Susan replied happily, going toward the door.

The girl was a mess. Her eyes were bloodshot from crying as she stood at the door trembling.

"Honey, what's the matter? What are you doing up at this hour?" Susan asked.

Samantha ran directly to Davis. "I wasn't telling you the truth. Earlier, when you asked me if I noticed anything going on in the house, well I did! I was just too scared to tell you because I was afraid of what you'd think of me. But it did happen, and it just happened again! I can't take it anymore, Davis. I had to tell someone."

Davis hugged her tightly. "It's okay, sweetie, tell us everything, okay," he asked.

"Things in my bedroom started moving by themselves. I couldn't believe it. It was happening right in front of me and scared me half-to-death. A few months ago, I was touched by something when I was in the bathtub, but I couldn't see it."

"Oh, baby." Susan went to console her. "Why didn't you say something?"

The girl shook her off, determined to finish the story.

"I could feel icy fingers touching over my entire body. I felt so sick to my stomach. After that happened I felt dirty inside," she said looking at both of them. "I was too embarrassed to tell anyone, and who would have believed me?"

"Samantha, this in no way is your fault, do you hear me," Davis urged.

"I know that now," she nodded.

"Did anything else happen?" he asked.

"I saw a ghost levitating in the hallway. He wasn't totally solid, but I could still see him."

"It was a man? Are you sure?" Davis asked.

"Yeah, I'm positive. I'll never forget the sight of him. He's tall, thin and has a scraggly salt and pepper beard. He had a dirty scowl about him," she remarked. "I remember seeing him in the backyard during the fall, also. It was really foggy out. I didn't know that was him at the time, but I'm sure of it now. He was standing next to the fence out back. I thought I was seeing things at first, 'cause it was so far away and with the bad weather . . .

but as the fog rolled in I lost sight. By the time it cleared a bit, he was gone—vanished into thin air." Samantha looked at them concerned. "Do you think we're in danger? Did they kill Uncle Rich?"

Susan stopped short of answering and looked to Davis.

"I'm not sure. But, I don't think we should take any kind of chances here. Something evil is inside of this house. I think we all can attest to that. I can't tell you whether or not Rich's death is related to this, but I wouldn't be surprised if it was," Davis responded.

Susan didn't respond about the death of her brother out loud, but deep down she knew the incident was related. "I think we should sleep in the living room tonight. If we stay together we should be safe," Susan suggested.

Davis agreed.

"I'll go bring Kelly down," she continued.

As the three turned around to leave the bedroom, they were surprised to find the young boy standing silently in the doorway.

Stricken with grief, Susan placed a trembling hand to her mouth.

Kelly stood in a catatonic state. His eyes were unfocused and distant. The skin on his face was marble white and he was perspiring badly.

Susan went to him quickly and held him by his shoulders. "Kelly? Baby, are you all right?" His pajamas were soaking wet. He continued to stare away.

Samantha, sensing the urgency, knelt down beside him. "Kelly, it's me, Sammy. Can you hear me?"

He spoke out apathetically, "It's coming for me."

"What sweetie? What's coming?" Susan asked desperately.

"The bad thing; the monster that lives in the well. It wants me. It wants to kill me," he responded in monotone.

Susan's eyes welled. "No one's going to hurt you. Why would you say that? Don't be silly," she said, offering him a smile and a hug.

"Susan, let's take the kids into the living room," Davis suggested.

"Okay. Why don't you turn on some lights, Sam," she said, picking up Kelly, taking him into the next room and setting him on the couch.

Samantha flicked on the overhead light above the dining room table, and went back into the living room; Susan went to the closet and pulled down some sleeping bags and blankets. After that, she went into the bedroom and grabbed a couple of pillows. A spot on the floor was cleared out for the two children to sleep.

Kelly immediately fell back into heavy sleep, while Samantha reluctantly fought it and stayed awake longer.

Susan understood the girl's apprehension: she was tossing and turning, alert to every noise inside of the house. Who could blame her? The poor girl had been bottling up her emotions all of this time, trying to deal with the insanity by herself.

Susan detested herself. What type of mother would refuse to believe anything her children say? How could she be so blind as to not see or sense any kind of poltergeist? she asked herself.

138

Was it only manifesting for the children to witness or encounter its presence? A million questions burned in her mind. There were a few occasions when she thought things had disappeared or moved, or the incident when she watched the sudden fog roll in, but she believed it was her own stupidity and stress that caused it.

"Sam, you're safe with us. Try and get some rest for school," Susan replied.

"I have to go to school? Why?" she asked in protest.

"It's not going to do you any good to miss class. We'll figure out something tomorrow."

Susan clicked on the television and lowered the volume. After a while, Samantha's stubbornness turned into drowsiness, and finally to sleep. Soon both children were asleep with only three hours left until they would rise again.

Davis looked up at the clock on the wall and sighed.

"Oh man, I've got to be in class in a couple of hours."

He rested his head against the back of the couch and let out a deep sigh. He felt physically and mentally beat. Every muscle in his body ached, especially his side. His eyes were red and puffy with dark bags underneath them from lack of sleep.

"Are you going to be okay tomorrow?" Susan asked, noticing his appearance.

"I'll be all right. It's amazing what a couple of cups of strong coffee can do for a person in the morning," he said, forcing a smile.

"I think I'm going to call in sick tomorrow. I'd like to find out the history of this house, who owned it and if any kind of bizarre incidents ever took place here," she responded.

"Why don't you and the kids stay over at my apartment until this is all straightened out? I know it's kind of cramped there, but at least you'll be safe."

"You sure you wouldn't mind us? We won't bring our spirit friends with us—unless you wanted us to?" she teased.

"Oh no you don't! I draw the line at uninvited ghosts. They can stay here and haunt an empty house for all I care."

"Can you give Kelly a ride home after school? I'll pick Samantha up when she's out. I'll remind her before she goes out for the bus tomorrow morning."

"Sure, no problem."

"It's weird, you know. I went from one monster in Florida to another here. Out of all the houses I had to find, it figures mine would be haunted," she said despondently. "I don't want to live here any more. I have to sell it. How would the kids ever feel safe here again, and there are way too many bad memories already. It's been a total nightmare for them. I'm selling it and that's all there is to it," she said, unconcerned about his point of view.

"I think you should. You're right. The last thing you should do is stay here. Susan, I know we haven't been going steady very long, but we feel the same way about each other. I love you and you love me, right?"

"Yes, with all my heart."

"Then let's move in together. You and the kids could stay at my apartment until we find a house."

He couldn't believe what he was saying. Words were spewing from out of his mouth, but he wasn't worried, it just felt natural. Rationality was his highest attribute, yet here he was throwing caution to the wind—and for the sake of love. It felt good to feel for once, instead of just think.

Susan's eyes widened with delight. Her heart skipped a beat.

Before meeting Davis she was looking for individuality, a chance to become her own person. But when he asked her to live with him, she was relieved of the burden of starting over. She could still be the same person and still have the same aspirations, yet with someone she loved.

"I love you so much, and I would love to live with you. The sooner we start looking for a house, the better," she responded, full of joy.

He bent over and kissed her on the lips, enjoying the moment until she drew back from the exchange with a bemused look.

"I can't believe that I'm running away from my own house," she said in disbelief.

Placing his arm around her shoulder, he gave her a squeeze. "Everything's gonna work out. Don't you worry about a thing, we'll get through it and live happily ever after."

Chapter 13

At seven-forty in the morning, Susan was the last remaining person in the house. Davis had left an hour earlier, with coffee mug in hand, then Samantha, and finally Kelly, who still looked exhausted as he went out for the bus.

The county library was closed for at least another hour, so Susan decided to have another cup of coffee to add life to her depleted energy cells. The library would be the best place to find any kind of useful information about the house. There had to be some old newspaper clippings or records of the previous owners. *How many people had occupied this place before,* she wondered? *Did they have the same problems?*

She went to the refrigerator, pulled out a carton of milk, then poured some into her coffee. Before, she'd had no quarrels about spending time alone in the house, but now she felt watched and studied under a microscope. As a little girl, she never believed in the boogie man, or monsters and witches. Her friends used to tell horror stories during slumber parties to make one another cry, but she wasn't as superstitious and naive as they were; she was too mature and level-headed to be scared by nonsense. Now, some twenty years later, that same girl was having a change of heart. She was totally unnerved about spending any time alone in the house, recounting how shaken Kelly seemed the night before. It had to be those damn nightmares. He had the same disoriented look last night as he did the first time he mentioned being bothered by dreams: pale complexion, glazed eyes, hypnotized stare. He was adamant that something what was after him, but what, something in the house? *Was it a ghost or a demon?*

Taking a sip of hot coffee, she placed it upon the kitchen sink. As she did, she heard a tumbling noise erupt from the stairs above. Startled, she listened closely.

One step after another, the object bounced down the flight of stairs.

She stood next to the stairway entrance, anticipating the emergence of the noise. She swallowed nervously as the sound grew louder and closer.

The porcelain doll somersaulted off the third to last step and replicated the exact position of her brother, Richard, as he had fallen. The fragile head was turned 180 degrees around and its powder white face gazed at the ceiling mockingly.

Susan stumbled awkwardly to the doll. Her eyes filled with tears from the sick reenactment, yet she couldn't turn away from it.

"You bastard! You cold son of a bitch!" she screamed hatefully.

Her breathing became rapid and furious. Looking at the doll, all she could see was the face of her brother, twisted and aghast. If she could have vomited, she would have, but the shock of the devilish joke left her cold and numb inside.

When she thought it could get no worse and that her fragile mind was ready to explode with anger, the doll lifted up and faced her. Its baby blue eyes stared keenly upon hers. "He belongs here with us, Susan. Bring him back."

Susan rocked back on her heels and moved backwards into the kitchen. Grabbing her purse off the counter, she ran out of the house and climbed into her blazer. She fired up the engine and sped recklessly out of the drive and down Denton road.

*   *   *

Kelly watched the overly fat child stuff a third hot dog down his throat. The last part of the bun crushed up against his short plump fingertips as he worked it in amongst the full mass of chewed up wreckage already compiled in his mouth. The grotesque kid began to chew with great difficulty and stamina, while the sides of his cheeks were expanded out like a scavenging squirrel transporting acorns.

To Kelly's distress, the boy opened up a pint of chocolate milk and added it to the collection of food, while trying not to gag on his own stupidity.

"Man, that's the sickest pig in the whole school," Kelly said, sticking his tongue out as he watched the other boy.

"Sick? You wanna' know what sick is? Those sad things they call hot dogs," Julie responded, matter of factly. "Those things are gross. Do you know what they put in them things? Garbage! Nothing but garbage!"

"No!" Kelly shot back. "You're making it up. You don't know that for sure."

"Oh yes I do," she insisted. "My uncle used to work for a wiener company. He told us what they put in 'em. Pig snouts!" she blurted out, nodding her head up and down with satisfaction. "Oink! Oink! Oink! They even put in the feet, eyes, and intestines. All kinds of nasty stuff. It's all in there."

"You're crazy," he scoffed.

"Nope, I heard it straight from the horse's mouth. Come to think of it, that's probably in there too! You won't catch me eating a pigs butt," she laughed, making a disgusted face at him.

Kelly looked over at the gluttonous boy against the wall. The thought of intestines, and Lord knows what else that was swimming around in his stomach, made him want to wretch.

"I heard they even mix dog food in there, just for the fun of it because nobody knows they're doing it. They probably drop guts on the floor and scrape them back up with a shovel and put 'em right back in the pot. It happens all the time I hear."

"Stop it. Stop it. Enough already," Kelly said, standing up and away from the table. "God, Julie, you're really sick!"

"Fine," she said, smiling, delighted by his repulsion.

Holding on to his stomach, Kelly said, "I don't think I'll eat another hot dog ever again."

Julie took a sip of chocolate milk and studied Kelly. He didn't look as alert and upbeat as he normally did at lunch. Instead, he looked drawn and fatigued. His eyes were heavy and dark.

"Kelly, are you feeling all right today?" she inquired, trying not to seem infatuated.

He shrugged his shoulders and stared off into the distance.

"You look like crap. Didn't you get any sleep last night?"

His mind raced back to the hideous beast in his dream that sliced open his throat. He shivered.

"I'm okay, Julie, really."

"Come on, I know you pretty well. I know when something's bothering you. You might as well tell me, or I'll start talking about hotdogs again."

Her words were soothing to him. The thought of telling another person about his dark secrets seemed unappealing, yet, as he looked over to her worried face, he understood that she was concerned and he trusted her advice. That's why he decided to reveal the vision that had invaded his sleep for so long.

She didn't seem quite as stunned as he thought she would be when he told her the gory details. But then again, it was Julie; nothing ever seemed to shock her.

He sat waiting for her response.

"You really believe there's a connection between your dreams and what's going on in your house?" she asked.

"Yeah. I've had a lot of nightmares and they're all about the house. Even before we moved in there, I had a dream about the well in the basement. I think the ghosts in the house have something to do with that well. Maybe that's where they're coming from, who knows? All I know is that I can feel something deep inside that tells me it's not a dream, and that something there wants to kill me."

"We have to get you out of that house. I'm not going to let them hurt you," she said, angered by the stories.

"Yeah, right. What can you do to stop it?" he said sarcastically.

"I don't know, but there has to be a way. Why don't you stay at my house for a while," she suggested with newfound hope.

"I don't think your parents or my mom would let me hang out with you. It would be cool though, huh?"

"Awesome," she replied somberly.

"Thanks, Julie, but I think this is something I have to handle by myself."

They sat silently until the end of lunch; nothing could be said to ease the tension.

In the corner of the cafeteria, the plump boy got up from his table and quickly raced over to purchase another hot dog.

*   *   *

Susan approached the small information desk situated at the center of the large library. A tall, thin woman sat upright typing on a Compaq computer, while reading from an office memo.

Susan stood silently in front of the woman, waiting patiently to be helped, but the middle-aged librarian continued to type upon the keys. Finally, with an exaggerated tone, she coughed roughly to let the busy woman understand her need of attention.

The woman looked up from her screen with mild interest. "Yes ma'am, can I help you?"

Susan, not wanting to seem too pushy and demanding, smiled back awkwardly. "I hate to be a bother to you."

"Don't be silly. That's what I'm here for. Bother away, bother away," the librarian responded wryly.

Susan chuckled hesitantly, then continued on more assertively.

"I'm trying to find some records of the house I own, or past history of the previous owners," she said, abandoning the helpless routine for a more practical approach.

"How far back do you wish to trace?" the woman asked.

"As far as I can, I guess. I'd like to find out if anything unusual has happened there."

"Well, I hate to be the bearer of bad news, but we only go back as far as the late 1960's. You see, back in 1963, the town library was destroyed by fire, and records weren't kept on file again 'til 1968. So, I'm afraid anything you're looking for before then is missing. If you'd like, we can trace the local newspaper wire during the years you're seeking. Or I can dig up the names of the previous owners by contacting the Realtor who sold it to you," the lanky woman spoke, taking a sip of Diet Coke.

"Let's try and find out any events that took place from the seventies 'til now. Maybe I can find something that will shed a little light on what I'm after."

The librarian got up from her roller chair and escorted Susan to a long oak desk against the side of the room. The table offered several different computers to work from.

"This is going to take you quite a while, so what I'll do is show you how to print up the dates from the paper, how to scan the section or page that you want, and how to go on to the next day. If you need any help increasing the size of print or anything else, just let me know, I'll be back at my station," she responded happily. "Like I said, it's going to take you a while. Hope you brought your lunch with you. It must be pretty important if you're willing to spend your day here like this."

Susan looked down at the computer for a moment, then gazed back up at the older woman. "Yes, it's extremely important and can't be put off," she responded, focused.

*　　*　　*

When Kelly returned from lunch, Davis immediately motioned for him to come over. As the other classmates filtered into the room, the boy made his way to the desk.

"Kelly, I'll give you a ride home after school, so just wait here after the last bell, okay?"

Kelly looked at him with trepidation.

"Why? What's going on?" he questioned.

"Your mom and I feel that, for the time being, it would be best if you guys stay at my apartment."

"Will we ever go back to that house again?" Kelly inquired.

"I'm not sure. All I know is that for now you'll be staying at my house."

"What if it follows me there? What if it comes to your house and starts trouble? It can, you know! I know it can follow me. If it wants to get me, it'll follow us!" Kelly exclaimed, with conviction.

"Kell, relax. It's not going to follow us. What ever is in that house, will stay in that house. It's not like it can attach itself to clothing or an automobile and follow us wherever we go," Davis said, noticing the full classroom.

"But Davis, I don't think . . ."

"Kelly. We'll talk about this later. It's time for class to begin."

The boy turned around and found the entire class seated and attentive to the front of the room.

"Yes sir," he agreed, solemnly walking back to his desk.

Davis arose from his chair and picked up a history textbook from which he was reading before lunch.

"All right. Can anyone tell me where we left off before break?"

A bright, smiling blond-haired girl lifted her arm up eagerly.

"Yes Marcia, where were we?" he asked, watching Kelly, who was miles away in thought, instead of the rosy-cheeked girl.

"We were discussing Christopher Columbus and his journey to America, in the year 1492," she said, displaying a vibrant smile.

"Thank you, Marcia. I believe you're right."

The girl quickly raised her hand again in sudden desperation, looking over her shoulders to ensure no one else was challenging.

"Yes, Marcia, something else."

"Mr. Conner, I believe we left off on page four hundred and twenty-three. Chapter twenty, sir," she said, blushing from her own perfection.

"Once again, thank you, Marcia," he replied graciously.

*   *   *

Susan continued to scan over a 1981 article from the Caseville Daily News. Growing frustrated with reading every daily issue, and sick of the monotonous process involved in finding nothing, she slammed her fist to the table and dropped her head in defeat.

She understood going into the project that it would be a lengthy and miserable experience, not to mention potentially unrewarding, yet she still had hope. Surely, if spirits possessed a house, someone would know about it, especially in a town with a population of less than four thousand. Neighbors would talk. It couldn't go by undetected, it just couldn't.

145

"Not having much luck are you?" the librarian asked from behind.

Susan lifted her head up and glanced back. "I'm afraid not much at all," she said, shaking her head with a weary smile. "Have you lived in Caseville long?" Susan asked.

"Oh yes. Born and raised here since 1964. Never had a thought in the world of leaving," she said earnestly.

"Have you ever heard of any wild stories about a haunted house on Denton road. Anything out of the ordinary?"

The tall woman's face turned peaked. She tried to keep a pleasant smile, but the corners of her mouth twitched nervously. "Ah, the house on Denton. Let's see, well, yes, I do recall hearing some strange tales about it. Say, is that the house where you're staying? Is that what you've been trying to find out about?" she asked vigorously.

"Yes, that's right. What do you know about it?"

"Well, mind you, this is all hearsay and gossip, now. But, I've heard some people mention that it's haunted. That certain bad things have happened to whoever has owned it."

"Like what?"

"Talk's been going on about that place since even before I was born. You know, all kinds of crazy stories. They say that people were murdered there. But, honey, in no way am I saying that's true or not, so don't you let that scare you any! You know how stories get stretched out of proportion."

"When? When did people die there? Was it recently, or are we talking about several years ago," Susan's voice rose excitedly.

"No, no, no," the woman reassured. "From what I gather, sometime back in the twenties is when it happened. All I know is that a few people were killed there. It was probably something minor. Stories range from a psychopathic killer, to a quiet couple that committed suicide together. Like I said, they're nothing but rumors, honey. When I was a little girl, I remember my grandpa telling me about a little boy who fell into some sort of deep well. I guess the little guy was left unattended and died from the fall. He must have been playing alone by it. You know how kids can be so curious. My grandpa used to say that it had something to do with your house being haunted, but my mom and dad told me that granddad was just senile and confused. I never took him seriously on that story. Grandpa said it caused a hell of a stink with all the people in town, too."

The librarian bent forward wide-eyed and whispered, "You haven't found any bodies, have you?"

Shocked by the straightforward silly question, Susan stammered, amused, "Uh no, nothing like that."

"Well then, what have you seen, if you don't mind me asking. Is it spooked or not?"

Susan didn't feel like starting more gossip, or enticing the old woman into prodding for more details. "Well, some strange things happen on occasions, but they're minor incidents like misplaced items or weird noises; nothing big. I was just curious about the history of the place," she said.

"You know another strange thing about that place, ever since the time those so-called murders took place, no one has stayed there more than a year or two at a time. Isn't that just amazing? People put it up for sale almost immediately. Oh my, how could I forget! There were a couple of other deaths that were associated to the previous owners of your house. A little boy died in his sleep there, or so that's what they said. Nobody knows what happened—they just found him dead. I think that was in 1986. And I also vaguely remember hearing about a little boy who disappeared, or was abducted, back about thirty or thirty-five years ago.

Susan became light headed. She felt dizzy, nauseated and faint as the woman's babbling continued. *Little kids . . . killed. Boys just like her own.*

Her sweaty hands began to shake.

What killed those children? Was it a something in that house? Could ghosts actually murder a child? Oh God, yes they could, she convinced herself. They killed her brother, and they surely could kill an unsuspecting kid!

Bracing herself against the table, she felt her knees buckle. While her mind jumped with wild scenarios, the voice of the nagging lady played on like background music.

"You know, I'd venture to say at least ten different couples lived in that place. Not one wanted to stick around very long. They couldn't sell it fast enough! Some I don't think even sold it themselves, they just put it in the hands of the Realtor and moved out of town."

The librarian, noticing Susan's distraction, called out, "Honey, are you all right? I don't think you've heard a word I said."

"Huh? Oh yes, I'm listening," Susan responded emphatically.

The woman gave her a candid look, then smiled forcefully. "You know who you should really be talking to, Harold Snippet."

"Harold Snippet?" Susan inquired.

"Of course. I should have thought of that first thing. Harold's your neighbor. The only other person beside you on Denton, I believe. Ol' Harold's lived there all of his life. That man must be in his nineties by now. People try to get him to talk about what went on years ago, but he won't, he refuses to. It must have been something pretty traumatic. He kept that secret all to himself all of those years, can you believe it? Town folks say he was involved in the murder, that he shut up just to save his own skin," she responded, clucking like a hen in a chicken coop. "He is a pretty weird bird."

Susan stared at the overzealous woman, waiting for an opportunity to excuse herself from the conversation.

"Yeah, I'd say the best thing for you to do, honey, would be to ask Harold about your place. I'm sure if anyone could give you the information that you're looking for, it would be him."

With the last of her gossiping let loose, the woman took a deep breath, relaxed and waited for Susan's opinion.

"I can't tell you how much of a big help you've been for me today," Susan replied appreciatively. "I'm sure I'll have better luck over at Mr. Snippet's farm."

"Don't thank me. It's my job. That's what I'm here for," she responded pretentiously, adding a sly grin.

Susan soaked up the woman's smugness and exited the large library.

"Silly old tart," she muttered, going to her car.

Pulling into traffic, she went up Harbor Street and then turned left onto State. She glanced down at the clock on the radio. 3:35 p.m. Davis and Kelly would be home soon. It would be wiser to go home first, pick up Samantha in an hour, then head over to the old man's farm.

Susan slowed down at a railroad-crossing gate, then proceeded over with caution. As she passed over the railroad tracks, she turned right onto a paved road called Elkwood, which immediately led into the Mayfair apartment complex where Davis lived.

She shut off the engine and sat there a moment in thought.

Could she get that eccentric old man to talk? And at what price will she pay for the inquiry? If he's a murderer, what kind of state is his mind in now?

She entered the modest two-bedroom apartment and found Davis and Kelly in the kitchen preparing a snack. Although the living room dimensions were small (twenty by fifteen), Davis made use of bright hues to add depth and rich flavor to the structure. His love of plants added warmth and life to the décor, with ferns and ivy hung sporadically throughout the house. He also had a fascination for Japanese collectibles: fans, carpets, fixtures, pottery, and even a painting of a Samurai warrior. Any time he could get his hands on one, he did. The Orient had always intrigued him since he was a kid. He watched all kinds of television shows and movies that dealt with eastern cultures. As an adult, he continually read extensive novels and articles about the Japanese way of life. The contradictions between Western and Eastern Hemisphere philosophies were extraordinary. In Japan, extreme emphasis is placed upon education, and students are required to take several examinations and achievement tests.

He had visited the country briefly in 1994, touring Tokyo, Nara, Kyoto and Yamagata—a place where he learned the essential way of using a hashi, an eating utensil.

Davis was standing in the kitchen showing Kelly how to maneuver his hashi to a plate of pork and rice. Kelly, intrigued by the notion of not having to use a fork or a spoon, welcomed the challenge of the wooden sticks, but failed miserably and dropped white rice upon the floor. After several unsuccessful attempts, he gave up and retreated back to the counter for a fork.

"How's the oriental orientation going," Susan asked.

"I don't think he's ready for the advanced class just yet," Davis chimed.

Walking into the kitchen, she set her purse upon the table and kissed Davis on the lips.

"I thought you would have been back long ago," he said.

"I did too. I didn't realize how long it was going to take," she said, pulling a Diet Pepsi out of the refrigerator.

"Any luck finding anything?"

"Sort of. The librarian told me all kinds of creepy stories about the place, with a warning that she wasn't sure if it was fact or fiction, though. But we know better, don't we?" she replied.

"So what do you think?"

"I think it's true, well at least most of it. It scared me."

She remembered that Kelly was in ear's reach. "Kelly, why don't you take your plate into the living room and watch some television," she said, smiling at him.

He obliged happily and went into the next room.

Susan waited for the television to turn on, then began again.

"I found out that no one has stayed there for very long."

"How long?"

"Less than a year. It gets worse, though. Rumor has it a murder took place there back in the twenties. A little boy died in a well. You remember I told you about Kelly's dream about the well. Do you think there's a connection?" she asked, concerned.

"Sounds like it to me. I don't think it's a coincidence."

Susan peeked into the living room where the boy sat eating rice, mesmerized by the television set, and then continued on with a quieter tone.

"The librarian didn't know how the murders took place, but she did know that a little boy fell into a well some years later. Oh!" she said, startling herself, as a lost thought surfaced. "And another little boy died in his sleep at the house. Something is connected with children, or little boys. It's eerie, Davis," she said, putting her arms around his waist. "I have to go get Sam in about a half-hour."

"Sam called while you were gone. She's going out with Stephen to do a little bit of shopping, then and they're going to get a bite to eat," he replied, quickly remembering. "She said that she'll be home later tonight."

"Good. That's one less thing I have to worry about. There's something I have to do later. You know that old man who lives on Denton?"

He nodded.

"Well, his name is Harold Snippet. I found out that he's lived at the same address all of his life. I'm going over there to see if he knows of anything significant."

"I'm going with you," Davis said.

"No. It would be best if you stayed here with Kelly."

"I don't think I like the idea of you tracking all of this on your own, especially back by that house again. Do you even know anything about this man?"

"Not really," she lied. "But he's very old. I think he's in his nineties. I'll be all right, honey," she insisted.

She refrained from telling Davis the whole story about the man and his possible connections to the murder out of fear that it would only infuriate him and fuel his desire to protect her.

"Okay. But promise me you'll be careful. And if you get in over your head, come back or call me."

"I promise, sweetie. Don't worry, I'll be fine. What kind of harm could come from doing a little detective work?" she reassured him.

Chapter 14

Susan turned the Blazer onto Denton, and as usual, proceeded with caution.

A strange sense of irony struck her. She was avoiding her house to keep her family safe, yet the allure of the two-storey brick house still loomed large. She was driving right to it and deep down inside knew that she would cross paths again with the evil spirits.

As the car motored slowly over the crevice-ridden road, Susan kept an eye on the old man's shack. The front yard was empty except for an old, beat-up black pickup truck.

She turned the Blazer into his driveway and drove up to the front of the house. Sitting with the car idling, she waited for Mr. Snippet to reveal himself.

When there was no movement at the front door or the curtains on the front bay window, she shut off the engine and stepped out of the car.

Her stomach churned with anxiety and nervousness. Every step towards the house only heightened her apprehension.

A cool breeze played delicately upon her cheek as she approached the front door, and her jaw tightened with anticipation.

Standing upon the front door landing, she waited for some nerve to kick in.

The side window curtain drew back slightly, then closed quickly.

With a small prayer and a deep breath, she knocked assuredly.

She stood there in the perpetual calm of dusk as a frigid air crept over her weary body and sent a tingle down her spine.

The door to his house was in dire need of repair. Constant seasonal weather changes and years of neglect had taken its toll upon the rotted and splintered wood grain, for when it finally began to open, it creaked with resistance.

The old man seemed stunned and in disbelief. It was the first time in over ten years he had received a visitor, the last of which was a young landscaper who offered his services to the dismal lawn.

She took the initiative and spoke first. "Mr. Snippet? Hi, my name is Susan Adkins. I live down the road from you."

The old man looked behind her and then from side to side, inspecting the car and grounds for any other unwelcome visitors.

"Sir, I was wondering if I could talk to you for a minute, if it wouldn't be any trouble," she said pleasantly.

Harold Snippet continued to stare off in every direction but hers, seemingly oblivious to the young woman's request.

A lump formed in her throat, as she watched the discombobulated man twitch with anxiety.

Was he deaf? A mute? Maybe he had suffered a stroke and was incapable of speech. Whatever the case was, he certainly wasn't receptive.

"Mr. Snippet?"

His eyes widened, realizing she knew his name.

"I was hoping you could give me some insight about my house?" she attempted again.

Still, the man was mute.

Susan was now beginning to feel inept, as though she was talking to an invalid.

Just when she was about to offer an apology for disturbing him and say farewell, he spoke. Not a riveting sentence, or a mesmerizing line, just a quick and modest, "Come on in."

He backed away from the door and motioned for her to follow, which she did with a friendly smile upon her face.

He escorted her into a cramped kitchen that was cluttered with dishes, pots, pans, and magazines lying upon the counter and kitchen tabletop. The wallpaper was pale lime and faded from tobacco smoke. Yellow and green flowered curtains were drawn over a window on a side door.

Harold Snippet gestured to a seat by the table. Susan, following behind, graciously accepted, pulled out the chair and sat down.

A small poodle with matted, chocolate-mousse colored hair slept upon a small circular throw rug by the back door. The old dog lifted its head tremulously, with mild interest for her, then rested back down, exhausted.

"That's Pierre. He won't hurt ya'. Hell, the last time he tried to get up, he nearly pissed on himself," the man laughed. "I call him Pierre 'cause he's one of them French poodles. So I figured he ought to have a French name. Pierre's the only one I could think of," he said candidly.

"I think it fits him perfectly," she said, looking down at the dog.

The poor thing looked as old as Harold. Every time it shifted its weight, it whimpered, then trembled and wheezed.

Susan felt sorry for the helpless animal. Age, disease, and lack of medical attention hampered the dog's ability to live happily.

"The darn thing can't hear anymore, and he can barely see a foot ahead. All he does is lie on the carpet and piss. Don't 'ya," he said, shaking his head at the dog.

A whimper came forth from Pierre.

Susan forced a smile for the old man.

"Now, missy, you said you had some questions about your house," his high-pitched voice, slowly, but meticulously asked.

"Yes, if you don't mind?"

"Mind? Are you kidding!'" He jumped. "I haven't had company since, I don't know when. I kind of get bored talking to ol' Pierre."

They both chuckled.

"If you don't mind me asking, Mr. Snippet, do you have any family?"

The old man sighed. "No. Just me and him. I lost my dear wife of sixty-five years about fifteen years ago. Everyone else is long gone. Don't have any children, either."

"I'm sorry. It must be difficult living all alone."

"Naw. I've lived a good, full life. Seen lots of things, met a few interesting people. I ain't got no regrets," he said proudly. "What can I help you out with?"

"I understand that you've lived here all of your life. I was hoping to find out if anything unusual has ever happened at my place."

The old man gazed down at the table. "Can I get you a cup of coffee . . . I'm sorry, I forgot your name," he said cordially.

"That's quite all right. Susan Adkins, and yes, a cup would be fine, thank you," she said, extending her hand.

Harold Snippet shook her hand. "Very nice to finally meet you, Susan."

She looked at him, surprised. "Excuse me?" she responded, uncertain about the comment.

"Oh, just that I met your daughter, and I'm afraid I made a rather bad first impression. You see, I've lived here so long, and because of certain bad experiences in my past, I've become a little cold towards people. A few families have moved into your house. They stay for a while, then leave. It becomes routine. I guess I just got too used to it," he said, pulling a coffee cup from the cupboard above the stove. "How would you like that?"

"Black's fine."

He poured some of the contents of the half-filled coffeepot into a cup and placed it down in front of her.

"Thank you very much," she replied.

He returned to his chair and took a sip from a cup that said "World's Greatest Nobody" on it.

"Mr. Snippet,"

"Harold, please," he interrupted.

"Harold, I was told my house has a bit of history to it. Is that true?"

"Yes. It's very true," he said, leaning back in his chair, reflecting on another place and time that he had tried desperately to forget. He stared up at the ceiling, deep in thought.

"I understand this may be difficult and painful for you to remember, but I implore you to consider how urgent this is to my family."

"I'll tell you everything I can," he responded sincerely.

"Did someone die in that house?"

"Yes," he nodded with dread, "yes, it's true."

"How long ago, Harold?"

"A long, long, long time ago, that's when it first began. I'd venture to say it happened in 1928. In fact, I'm positive that's when it happened. I'll never forget that day as long as I live," he said, lowering his head, pained by the memory.

Suddenly his demeanor brightened, as if he was explaining a concealed piece of history that had been vaulted away from the ears of society. His eyes lit up like fireflies dancing upon a shimmering, placid lake. His crouched, slouched body stiffened upright alertly.

"I was just a boy of twelve, a little ball of energy, pent-up in a small town of unassuming farmers. I was an only child, and it was hard to feed my wild enthusiasm being alone all the time. I had a few friends from school. They were boys three years my senior and we started our own gang. Nothing dangerous like today's kids, just simple country fun. Everything at that time was exciting. Crops were selling, spring was in the air, and I had found friendship that I always wanted. But in the spring of '28, a family from down south moved into the house across from ours. Just a small family of three: the mother, father and a small blond-haired boy, no older than ten or eleven. I didn't see the boy's face too well the day they pulled in, I just saw him step out of that old Ford Model-T car. Well, needless to say, I was tickled pink," he crowed loudly.

Susan chuckled at his enthusiasm.

"Yes, sir. Things seemed to be picking up in the neighborhood. Now I had a kid my own age living across the street. My other friends were at least two miles, maybe more, from my house, so I only seen them on occasion. I wanted to race over to the new boy's house as soon as they arrived, but my mother thought it would be best if I gave them a few days to arrange their belongings and settle in. Reluctantly I agreed. But the next day, whoa, I was down there about the crack of dawn," he said, slapping his withered hands upon his knees. "I remember knocking on the door and seeing this beautiful young woman with hazel eyes, short black hair, and a warm friendly smile. She noticed my excitement, and graciously accepted me into their household. I walked through the house until we got into the living room, and there stood this tall, thick, bushy-bearded man with wild, crazy-looking eyes—almost like the Devil's! He was very straightforward, scared me to death, that is. 'I take it you're here to see our boy. Hmmm? Kinda' here early, wouldn't 'ya say? Does your parents know that you run around town this early in the morning?'" Harold Snippet mocked the father's voice. "I just stood there, silently taking it all in, yet terrified as a bug under a fat man's shoe," he said, grinning at Susan.

Susan took another sip of coffee and smiled back, fascinated by the story.

"The wife told that big, intimidating oaf off. Said, 'Would you mind your manners, and show this young man the proper respect he deserves.' I wanted to crack up laughing, but fear and common sense, thankfully, prevailed. She called upstairs, and that's when I met Luke for the first time," he said, with a far away look in his eyes. "Luke came down the stairs slowly, and when he rounded the corner I could see fear in his eyes. Back then I wasn't aware why, but I know now. He wasn't nervous about meeting a new friend. Naw. It was because Luke had Down syndrome, and he was really sick. We didn't know what that was back then, but I believe that's what it was. I just thought he was mentally

153

slow, or that something bad had happened to him. I was raised properly, where you don't question or discriminate a person for how they look, or how they speak. You get to know what's on the inside of them. And I'm glad I did that with Luke, 'cause although that boy was slow and a bit disfigured, he was a true friend. He had a real heart of gold."

Tears began to fill in his eyes; he quickly brushed them aside and composed himself.

"Yes, sir. Sorry about that," he said with embarrassment. "I normally don't carry on like that, but it's been such a long time since I've talked about the past," he apologized, lip trembling.

"Harold, there's no need to feel ashamed. I'm sure it's quite difficult for you to dredge up the past. Please continue," she urged, placing a reassuring hand upon his arm.

"Thank you, Susan, that's very kind of you. Luke and I got along well for quite a few months. I visited him, and he came over to my house. Unfortunately, school started back up and Mr. and Mrs. Smith enrolled Luke. Now, I'm not qualified to judge whether a physically impaired kid should interact with other children, but in Luke's case, it was a bad mistake. When those other kids got a whiff of poor Luke's handicap, they tore him apart, mentally and physically. At first I tried to stick up for him. But in a class of thirty kids, all different ages, it's hard to maintain order. Whenever we went outside for recess or activities, I stood by his side. I couldn't always be there for him, and the other children knew it, especially my own gang, who were putting pressure on me left and right to explain my sudden interest with a crippled child. Oh, they were so vicious and cruel. They spit, pushed and punched on him, and called him names like "monster" or "creature." The poor boy took it all. He didn't know what friendship was about," the old man's voice tremored. "All he knew was that his mama and papa told him to go to school and behave, and he did. That's when I began changing. I started breaking off my friendship to Luke to prove myself to the gang. They got me involved in teasing and tormenting him. Oh, why was I so stupid!" his voice rose angrily and he slammed his fist down on the table. "I could have stopped it, I could have did so much for that little frightened boy, but I didn't! I was a coward! I left him to fend on his own. A poor invalid, and I led him to the wolves, to die."

Harold Snippet reached forward with trembling fingers and picked up the coffee cup; placing it to his lips, he slurped eagerly and quenched his parched throat. The ceramic cup clanked harshly upon the table as he brought it back down.

"The gang wasn't through by no means, though," he said, looking Susan square in the eyes. "They wanted revenge. Certain older members of the group thought that Luke was getting special favoritism, that he was becoming the teacher's pet. That's when they devised a plan to scare him into leaving school. It was mid-fall, a pleasant, warm morning. Back then, everyone walked to school no matter where they lived. Reluctantly, I agreed to walk Luke to school and persuaded him to use another route, where I knew four of my other friends were waiting. It was in town by the old church, near a twelve-foot deep water well.

"When we reached the church, the other kids came out from behind the building. Luke was frightened; I could see it in his eyes. The look of terror, realizing he was involved in something deceitful, and that I, his friend, was setting him up. John Davidson—I think that was his name—the leader of our pack, stepped forward and made up some hair-brained story that we wanted Luke in our very private group. He made up a test that would initiate Luke; a simple task that would have to be completed in order to become an elite member. John informed him that his days of being picked on would be far behind, that the gang would watch and protect him. The bastard!" Harold hissed. "The test involved climbing into a bucket that was attached to a rope and pulley. Two kids would lower him down into the depths to retrieve a golden egg, and then pull him back up to the surface to be commended for his bravery."

Harold Snippet sat still for a moment, reflecting on the tragic event. His face was drawn and tired, as though the story aged him another ninety years.

Looking up at Susan, he sighed, "There was no egg. It was all a lie. We were going to lower him down and leave him for a few hours until lunch, to scare him, and then bring him back up," he said with regret. "We began lowering Luke into the well. When we got half way down, Johnny yelled, 'Now,' and the other two boys who held the rope let go. I wasn't involved with the lowering, but that's only a feeble excuse. I was there, so I share the blame. When the other kids ran off, I stood by the side of the well for a moment and listened. I heard him hit the water, after a delay of at least three, maybe five seconds. I ran. I ran as hard and fast as I could, and caught up with the other boys at school. I sat in my chair all through class with remorse, guilt, and pity for that poor kid. At one point, I begged Johnny to tell the teacher because I feared Luke had been injured in the fall. He refused, and I sat quietly in despair. The teacher questioned about Luke's absence, but everyone went along with John that the boy had taken ill and went home. During lunch, the five of us went back to the well and called down to him. Not a word came back up. When we called to him again and received no word, we pulled the rope up. To our dismay, the bucket had broken during the fall. I remember everyone panicking, including John, who now sought my advice in the matter. Scared, shocked and bewildered, I sent one of the boys back to the school to fetch the teacher. We waited next to the well for ten minutes of pure hell. I tried calling down to him again and again, hoping he was just playing possum to get even with us, but he never answered back. The teacher arrived with a few of the local townsmen, and Luke's parents were summoned. Mr. Smith was lowered into the well. As darkness enclosed around him, he found Luke in six-foot deep water and was pulled back up. When he emerged from the cold, dark well to the warm, sunlit sky, a hush fell over the watching crowd. Mr. Smith stepped out of the well with the body of his little boy clutched in his arms. I'll never forget that moment as long as I live—the glossy, vacant eyes of Mrs. Smith when she saw her lifeless child . . . it was heartbreaking to say the least. I wanted to beg their forgiveness right there. I wanted to plead for their mercy. Instead, I stood paralyzed by the sour taste of death."

"We never knew what killed him: the fall, the water—it didn't matter. To all of us kids, we felt it was ourselves that took his life. The next morning, the day that Luke was to be buried, Mr. Smith found his beloved wife's body hanging from a rafter in the upstairs attic. The pain of losing her only child was too much to bear. Townspeople rallied around him. Everyone attended the funeral for the mother and son, but deep down inside that man burned with such wrath and vengeance. His eyes during the funeral were cold and bitter—his fury unconcealed. He continued to live in the house and two months later his mother, a gray haired, old woman moved in to help him get by. Or so we thought. In actuality, the most diabolical and sinister plot in our town's history was being prepared. The elderly woman pushed the crazed man into a vengeance that fixated on the children of Caseville. Oh she was such an evil, evil woman. She worshiped a darker faith, and practiced black magic. It was known around town that she had the power to conjure up spirits, demons and bring to life these horrible, horrible creatures from hell. Her dark arts and strange behavior scared everyone in town, and no one would go near her. And her son followed her every command. In his eyes, since his only child and dear wife were ripped away from his life, he had nothing left to live for. To him there was no God. He believed the only true justice would be to take the life of another child. At first his plan was to kidnap every kid who participated in sending Luke down into the well. It almost worked perfectly, the other children were taken away from their families, but my parents protected me and I was saved."

"Folks knew exactly who was to blame, although they didn't have any proof, and for days tried to reason with him peacefully to give them back up. When a fifth and sixth child went missing, the strain of waiting was too much on the patience of the families, so they formed a lynch mob and stormed over to the Smith house. He demanded that they return to their homes, that he had no knowledge of their children's whereabouts. But the frenzied crowd pressed against the door and smashed their way in, carrying shotguns, pitchforks, and knives. A large group of people, including my father and uncle, held Mr. Smith and his mother at bay, while the others searched throughout the remaining sections of the house. At first, the hunt yielded nothing. Men and women came back empty handed and frustrated. When the last of the search party came back into the living room, a scream from the basement sounded. Mr. Smith struggled violently from the hold of the farmers, while several people ran down to the basement to investigate."

"A man, who had followed and tracked down the source of the scream, came back upstairs and approached the group in tears. What he found that night in a small adjoining room in the basement would horrify and enrage the community for decades on end. Six tiny bodies were found dead and bludgeoned at the bottom of a four-foot tall, eight-foot deep, brick circular well. They were victims of some sort of weird satanic ritual involving a porcelain doll and the children's collected blood. It still gives me the creeps thinking about it."

Susan gasped and looked at him in amazement.

Harold summarized how the parents stormed the remaining parts of the house, screaming obscenities and tearing fixtures off the walls. When the massive crowd surrounded the sought-after man and his mother, they beat upon them mercilessly. Marshall law ensued, and before the suspects could be tried by a judge and jury, a radical father, who had lost his own son to the monsters, unloaded a shotgun shell into the chest of Mr. Smith and then a shell to the stomach of his mother. They fell dead instantly. Some folks wanted to torch the place and burn any evidence that such an atrocity took place. 'Burn the Devil and his witch,' they screamed. 'Burn 'em alive!' No arson took place, but they did loot and destroy everything inside. Harold sighed. "Some folks were later divided about whether it was inhumane to kill the Smiths in cold-blood as they had done, or if they should have been tried by a jury. My father never talked about that night, for as long as he lived. But my uncle did. He wanted me to know every detail, so that the atrocity would never be forgotten. It was a hellish experience that I wouldn't want my worst enemy to go through," Harold Snippet concluded.

He got up from his chair and went over to the sink and placed his cup in it.

"You know, I heard there were ghosts and strange behavior going on over there throughout the years. I never doubted it. Three other young boys died there, that I know of. In a way, they all resembled little Luke. I don't remember how they died, but you don't have to be a brain surgeon to see the connection. I've lived in fear of that house all my life. I always felt that Mr. Smith would eventually come back and get that seventh boy from the gang that took his son's life. I never moved away because I felt so guilty, and I wished that he had come back for me. I wanted to be released from all the pain that I've had to live with. That's why I never had children, too. Fear! I couldn't bear to lose my child like so many other folks had. My wife, bless her heart, understood. She kept me sane through all of it. When I met your daughter, I was afraid to let anything related to that house back into my life. Call me a hermit, but I've managed to survive this long," he said with a broad smile. "Please tell her that I'm sorry, and that I knew she wasn't hurt in my ditch. I knew she was a tough cookie by the way she gave me a good tongue lashing."

Susan smiled, "I'll be sure to tell her. I'm sure she'll like that."

"Susan. It's none of my business, but for the safety of you and your youngin', please move. Don't let this nightmare happen again. Please. I've seen this again and again."

"I will, Harold. In fact, we've already decided that. You could say we found out first-hand, the hard way."

Getting up from the table, she placed her coffee cup on the counter.

"Harold, you are a very charming and wonderful man. I'm so sorry that you've had to live with this guilt and suffering. I really do appreciate your honesty with me," she said, shaking his hand.

"Bless you, young lady. You sure do know how to make an old man feel good. If you and your family ever feel like visiting me and Pierre, we'd love to have ya over," he replied, showing her to the door.

As Susan waved goodbye from her car window, warmth and compassion fell over her. Here was a man running away from his past in hopes of a better future . . . how ironic.

*   *   *

The piercing wail of the dog echoed through the dark, damp confines of the basement. Its blood-curdling howl sent shivers down Kelly's spine.

He was walking through the small, concrete corridor towards the furnace room, when that familiar haze clouded his mind again; a recurring feeling of walking upon clouds, immune to the world around, spellbound and drawn to a place that he desperately wanted to run away from, yet was unable to.

The enclosed walls of the corridor sped and blurred past his eyes like a spaceship traveling at the speed of light. He felt unbalanced as the weight of his small body lifted into the air and approached the room with the well. The skin on his face contorted into awkward shapes, and the hair on his head stood on end as though he was standing in the path of a tornado.

By this point, Kelly's legs had stopped moving. He was being pulled and sucked into the awaiting room.

The cry of the dog burst forth in front of him again, this time longer and louder as if it was tortured by every step the boy took. Kelly winced at the sound, then screamed out to the animal that he was on his way to rescue it. His heartfelt voice died abruptly, stifled by a thick blanket of wind.

Kelly's body felt battered and beat as the maddening journey continued. The hallway was only another ten or fifteen feet longer, but he felt like he had already traveled miles.

Through the darkness of the corridor, he saw light inside the other room reflecting off the wall. Closer and closer, the illuminated room began to appear.

He tightened with fear.

With great acceleration, his body shot like a torpedo headfirst into the adjoining room and came to a complete stop, hovering five feet about the ground and face down inches above the well's rim.

Inside of the well was pitch black and not a sound resonated from within.

Kelly remained still, but his breathing was winded and strained. He felt the heat within his body rise steadier, until beads of sweat formed a solid pool upon his brow and then masked his face with perspiration.

While trying to remain calm to whatever dwelled in the rotted, stinking cylinder below, a small drop of sweat trickled slowly off the bridge of his nose and fell like a leaf aimlessly down into the stillness of the well. The single drop reverberated back up softly.

For one brief, shining moment, Kelly remained in peace and had hope. But the bloodied, rabid, foaming face of Sassy, lunging in mid-air from the sunken depths of the well, changed his outlook forever.

*   *   *

Kelly awoke with a start, and jumped off the couch.

The boy's scream from the living room took Davis by surprise, and he quickly dropped his pen. Before he could get into the next room to find out the problem, Kelly was upon him, sweaty and pale.

"Davis! Davis!"

"Kelly, what's wrong?" he asked in suspense.

"We've got to go back to the house. We have to!"

"Hold on, hold on. Did you have a bad dream?" Davis asked, trying to calm the frenzied child.

"It's not about me, it's about Sassy! We have to go back and get her," he implored.

In the mad rush to leave the house, the animal had been forgotten.

"Davis, let's go get her, okay? Before something bad happens."

"I don't think it would be smart if we just took off without waiting for someone to come back first," he reasoned. "Let's just wait until your mom or Samantha returns."

"We can't! Sassy can't stay there alone. I won't let her! It's my fault; I left her by herself. We just can't leave her. I had a bad dream that she was in trouble in the house. Pleeease, Davis, pleeease!" he begged, pulling on the man's shirt as his tears ran wildly down his cheeks.

A twinge snapped inside Davis' stomach. He knew it wasn't safe to go back to the house, especially with Kelly. Yet, compassion for Sassy and sympathy for the boy gnawed away at him. *If we could quickly retrieve the dog and get out safely, no one would get hurt,* he mulled.

"All right, get your jacket. Let's go get Sassy."

Kelly hugged her gratefully, and ran off to fetch his jacket. Davis pulled out a pad of paper and a pencil and began writing Susan a note.

BABE, WE WENT TO THE HOUSE TO GET SASSY. DON'T WORRY, I'LL BE CAREFUL! SEE YOU IN A BIT. LOVE U MUCH.

* * *

Susan drove down State Street with the radio off. Normally, she loved to listen to music whenever she ventured out, but tonight quietness was soothing. She reflected upon the wild chain of events the old man had described and how bizarre it was that he had lived in fear all of those wasted years, and how strange it was that she had found her house out of all the places in the world. It was over, though, and there was no need to dwell on it any longer. They would pack up needed belongings for the new house, wish the ghosts good luck and good riddance, and leave that awful nightmare behind. She thought about the young, beautiful mother Harold had mentioned, and how awful it would be to lose your only child to an innocent prank performed by cruel children. *Was her presence inside of the house along with the husband and the old woman?*

The car rumbled over the set of railroad tracks just before Mayfair apartments.

Susan smiled, recalling Samantha's exaggerated fear of Harold Snippet, when, in fact, it was Harold who was the frightened one. She was sure Sam would get a kick out of how amusing and fascinating he really was. He may have appeared to be an eccentric, old stick-in-the-mud, devoid of compassion, but he was really a sweet, kind soul. He wanted friendship, but he had lived alone for too long and was too skeptical to trust anyone.

Susan pulled the car into the parking lot in front of the apartment's entrance, slipped it into park and shut off the ignition.

Davis' car was missing. Something was wrong and she could sense it.

Suddenly, everything didn't seem quite so rosy. In fact, everything seemed dreadful, for that uneasy feeling of misfortune loomed overhead again.

Chapter 15

8:05 p.m.

The sky was chalky gray as a biting cold wind blew in from the Northeast. Davis and Kelly sat silently in the Taurus as the car crept down Denton. Although they smiled at one another and seemed in good spirits, both were weary about visiting the old brick house. Kelly, in particular, was nervous about showing his face to the always-watchful ghosts. But his love for Sassy far outweighed his fear of the unknown, and with courage, he continued on as planned.

The two-storey house appeared in the distance as the car edged closer. Its large structure was ominously silhouetted in a gloomy background of twilight, and every window from the top floor to the bottom revealed light; the house was alive and welcoming.

Davis knew that the task wasn't going to be easy, but he thought that by coming back unexpectedly they might gain an advantage of surprise over the spirits.

"Did you guys leave the lights on?" Kelly questioned.

Davis looked down at him and laid a hand upon his knee. "I guess we must have. Pretty dumb of us, huh?" he said, making light at his own expense.

"Naw. I do stuff like that all the time. Now I can make fun of Mom for forgetting too."

Get in and get out, Davis repeated in his mind.

"Kelly, I want you to wait here in the car when I go in, okay?"

The boy looked up, puzzled.

"How come? I won't be in the way. I promise! Sassy might not come to you, she might get scared," he said, offering insight.

"No, Kelly. You've got to promise me that you'll stay here. I won't be long. I'll get her and be quick about it."

"I'll stay here, but I'd feel better if I could help you out," Kelly said.

Davis' heart melted. The little boy couldn't have been any braver. He was willing to risk his own safety to ensure Davis'. The little guy was going to grow up to be quite a compassionate and responsible man.

"Kelly, I want you to know how proud your mom and I are of you. You've gone through something a boy of your age shouldn't have to. I know it hasn't been easy for you to talk to others about what you're feeling inside, but I want you to know that it's okay if you do. Don't ever be afraid to speak from your heart. It's not good to keep things bottled up. You're a special person, and you have so much to offer others."

Kelly gushed with modesty and embarrassment. He wasn't sure why Davis was paying so much attention to him. He was only trying to help and anyone would have done the same thing. Yet, hearing the man's compliments brought him inner satisfaction. He knew he wasn't a failure; he had finally done something right.

*　　*　　*

Susan fumbled clumsily with her keys while standing in front of the apartment door. The spare key that Davis had loaned her seemed to evade her on the key chain.

"Come on, come on," she muttered anxiously.

The gold door key finally appeared and she thrust it into the lock with one quick twisting motion and then burst into the apartment.

The room was empty. She hadn't really expected anyone, but all the same, it would have been nice to see a familiar face.

She found the note that Davis had left for her and read it anxiously.

"Oh, shit. Kelly."

Pacing like a wildcat in a cage, she contemplated out loud. "It's too dangerous, Davis. Why didn't you wait! Should I go out there? And then what?" *What am I going to do,* she thought. *I can't take off without waiting for Sam. She could be home at any time. She won't be able to get in. It's only a short drive from here. He'll pick up Sassy and come right back. I know it. I know he will!*

*　　*　　*

The car pulled into the sloped driveway, stopping short of the side door. Davis jumped out of the idling car and raced toward the screen door, thumbing through his coat pocket for the spare key that Susan had left at the apartment. Reaching for the lock, he instinctively attempted to unlock it, but to his surprise found the door already opened. He checked behind to ensure that Kelly remained in his seat, and continued forward through the doorway.

The house was brightly illuminated; every light fixture glowed radiantly. He was hoping for a dark and secretive entrance, but the spirits were wiser than he gave them credit for and foiled his plan for the sneak attack.

Davis stepped into the kitchen. Everything seemed exactly in place as they had left it, yet an aura of mischief seemed to lurk in the wings. Something was watching him at that very moment with invisible evil eyes.

A shiver ran down his spine. He felt like prey to a hunting beast.

Silence.

The quiet house bothered him. He had expected more—much more.

Where was the dog? Should he call for the animal to come? What if the sound of his voice brought on the wrath of the demons? He discarded that notion; if they refrained from attacking him upon entrance, then surely they wouldn't be prodded into it by his voice.

"Sassy! Here girl, come on! Sassy!"

A series of barks resonated from upstairs.

"Come on, girl! That's a good dog. Come here!"

Again the dog barked excessively, but remained out of sight.

"Wonderful," Davis said. He winced, realizing that he would have to go upstairs to retrieve the animal.

Burying his fear, he headed up. As his foot touched the first step, the lights above dimmed, then returned to normal.

He froze hesitantly, waiting and watching above, then moved forward.

The second floor was numbing cold. His breath transpired upon the air and he shook with chill rounding the top flight of stairs.

The doors to each room were closed, and not a noise crept from within their wooden frames. It was so silent, Davis could hear a maddening voice inside of his head screaming, *"Get out, you fool! Get out, now!"*

Blocking out the inner manic voice, he walked the hallway, listening attentively.

Sassy's sharp howl from within Kelly's bedroom made him spring backwards against the wall by the bathroom. His pulse quickened from the shock.

"Jeeze-louise!" he muttered, holding his heart.

He stood underneath the attic and in front of the bedroom door with focus.

Whatever's beyond this door is not going stop me. Nothing will. If this is what it's come down to, let's get it over with. Give me your best shot. I'm not afraid, you son of a bitch, I'm not afraid!

While standing in front of the door, his thoughts became distracted by a noise emanating from the attic. He couldn't make out what the sound was exactly, but it reminded him of a boat that was tied to a dock: the certain noise a rope made when it became stretched and strained trying to hold the weight.

He didn't want to know what was up there, no matter how intriguing the sound seemed.

He focused back on the bedroom door, disregarding the distraction. With an outstretched hand and sheer determination, he held the knob firmly and turned it.

As he began to open the door, he froze in horror realizing the nature of the unsettling noise above. Someone, or something, was hanging from a rope. It was obvious. He could hear rawhide twisting and rocking against wood in the rafters.

Davis envisioned a bloated, decomposing face of a lifeless, cold slab, swinging from side to side from the ceiling of the attic. Bile rose from his stomach to his mouth and he choked down the bitter taste, then leaned against the hallway wall to regroup.

"Jesus, sweet Jesus." *Just go in there, get the dog, and run like hell.*

Gritting his teeth, he flung the door open and stood gaping in awe.

Seated in a wooden rocking chair, facing the bedroom door was a white-haired elderly woman, with a grin so broad and wicked it implied something significant was about to happen.

*   *   *

8:15 p.m.

The front door to the apartment slammed shut.

Jumping off the couch, Susan ran into the kitchen and found Samantha slipping off her shoes.

"Hi, Mom. Why are you so excited to greet me?"

"Hi, honey. I thought you were Davis and Kelly."

"What's wrong? Is something going on?" Samantha asked, concerned.

"No, it's nothing. They just went to get Sassy. They'll be right back."

"You're worried about them, aren't you?"

"A little bit. But that's a mother's right. I know Davis is handling it. What did you and Stephen do?"

Samantha pulled a glass down from the cupboard and filled it with spring water from the refrigerator.

"We went clothes shopping, had a bite to eat, and then went over to see a girlfriend of mine. You know, normal stuff," she shrugged.

"Did you buy anything?"

"I wanted to buy him these really cute Marvin the Martian boxer shorts. Do you remember the little alien from Bugs Bunny who wore the helmet that looked like it had a brush on top of it? Bugs was always trying to stop him from blowing up the Earth."

"Yeah."

"I told Stephen that he'd look cute in them. He didn't think so, and told me he wasn't wearing a cartoon alien on his butt!'"

They both laughed and walked into the living room.

Susan looked up at the clock on the wall. 8:18. *Where on earth are they?*

*   *   *

Davis took a step into the room, unfazed by the cadaverous woman.

The panting dog sat beside the chair with its head draped low in anguish, while the specter held it firm by a leash.

The woman seemed so life-like. It was impossible, though, she was dead. She wasn't a transparent ghost, but appeared to be flesh and bone real.

A rotten odor penetrated the air, like a body that had just been dragged from a grave. Her appearance was frighteningly realistic. But even though the foul smell repulsed his senses and her intimidating over-sized murky white eyes fed upon his body, he continued towards her, determined not to show fear.

She would have to make the first move; he wasn't about to turn back and run just because her breath was horrid and her bluish face was bloated and rotted.

"Davis, such a pleasure to finally meet you," her frail, raspy voice announced. "We knew that you would come back," she hissed, as the corners of her mouth lifted.

"I want the dog!"

"I want the boy!" she snarled back, startling him. "Take the dog, please. Be my guest."

He wasn't sure if she was being sarcastic or sincere.

"What's the matter, Davis? Are you afraid?" she asked, leaning forward in the chair as her eye sockets began to fill with blood. "I won't stand in your way. We only want the boy. With or without your help, we will get him," her voice stated, dropping to an earthy bass tone.

Leaning back against the rocking chair, she smiled with satisfaction.

Davis remained firm and unrelenting just waiting for an opportune moment to grab the dog.

"I don't know why you want Kelly, but you're not getting him. I won't let you. I'm not here to make any deals. Understand?"

The old woman threw back her head in laughter, and in an uncontrollable fit slapped the armrest of the chair.

"You're going to stop me? You're going to stop us?"

She stopped laughing and regarded him adversely.

"How's Susan's brother Richard feeling these days? A little headache, perhaps? Pity, wouldn't you say? To go through life with your head on backwards, that is." Her tongue slipped out like a serpent's and traced the edge of her dried cracked lips.

Pleased with Davis' repulsion, she cackled with delight, causing the skin on her cheeks to split apart and release dark green and yellowish pus from within the slits.

Sickened, he recoiled from the sight and gagged.

"Take your bitch, Davis! Take your bitch and be gone," she shrieked, tossing the leash towards him.

"We will be seeing you all in Hell very soon," she said coldly, staring at him intensely.

With fleetness, he reached down and grabbed the chain, scooping up the dog in the process, and hustled out of the room.

As he ran and bounded each step, a voice shouted from behind, piercing his ears.

"The boy is ours! THE BOY IS OURS!"

*   *   *

Kelly sat in the passenger seat, agitated. The radio station he selected didn't do the trick of settling his preoccupied nerves, and every second Davis was gone only enticed him to look out of the side window to see if any thing was amiss.

Lights from the upstairs windows flickered off momentarily, then returned back on.

Kelly took his eyes off the radio and watched the illuminated windows with peaked interest. The car engine clanked to a sputtering halt and left him sitting in complete silence and darkness.

Realizing that something was wrong, he frantically scanned each window of the house looking for Davis and Sassy.

"Hurry, Davis! Hurry!"

*   *   *

Davis raced through the kitchen clutching the dog in his arms and leaned up against the wall by the side door. Sassy squirmed nervously as Davis tried to turn the doorknob. After a second and third attempt, the door finally unlatched and he exited through it.

Kelly pressed his face against the window with joy. He thought for sure that something bad had happened, and that they would never leave the haunted house.

The driver's door swung open and Davis placed the dog into the back seat.

"Sassy!" Kelly screamed enthusiastically.

The animal mopped his face with warm affectionate licks and Kelly hugged her back, delighted with the love and recognition.

"Kelly, what happened to the car? Why did you turn it off?"

"I didn't do it! It just shut off by itself."

Davis turned the key. Nothing. Again he tried, then again. The car refused to crank over.

"Damn it!" he yelled, drilling his fist into the steering wheel.

"Kelly, no matter what happens, stay here. You hear me? Stay here!"

"Okay."

"I'm going to look under the hood. When I motion to you, turn the key over once, just for a second, then turn it off."

"All right."

Davis opened the door and got out of the car, locking it in the process. Raising the hood, he attached the bar to prop it open.

He was caught in a serious dilemma. He didn't have a flashlight in the glove compartment, and there wasn't a working outdoor light by the side door. He only had the pale light of the moon to savor for sight.

Kelly tried to get a glimpse of Davis working on the engine, but a mere three-inch gap between the hood and the car's frame only allowed him to see the man's chest.

Readjusting the battery cables, just in case of a bad connection, he stepped away from the hood and went to the window and motioned to Kelly. The boy turned the key, and promptly shook his head no.

Frustrated, Davis went back under the hood and began feeling upon the engine block for a loose wire or a broken belt; lighting was extremely poor and he cursed, fumbling blindly.

He leaned in deeper, feeling his way over wires and hoses, hoping something would yield an answer. Resting his right hand against the starter, he clasped the part and inspected it. He wasn't a very good auto mechanic; in fact, he rarely considered getting greased up when car troubles occurred. Taking it to a garage where professionals have the know-how and proper tools was much simpler. But now, in this dire situation, he was willing to give anything a shot. There was always the chance that he could stumble upon the problem and solve it quickly and easily.

The metal rod constraining the hood began to shake back and forth slowly. Unaware of its movement, Davis continued to poke around in the dark.

The pole ripped out of its support with great velocity and force, collapsing the hood upon his back and sprawling him forward onto the engine block. Pain instantly shot through the upper region of his back and to his head, which was rammed against the steel block, leaving him dizzy and unbalanced.

Blood began to trickle from a gash on his forehead as he tried weakly to lift up the hood with his back. Light-headed, he lost his footing and dropped face first against the engine. His head pounded with pain, and his bones ached from the fall.

Gasping in cold air, he shook off the blow and began to gain his senses back. Suddenly a feeling of immediate danger overcame him. His gut was telling him to act quickly, before it was too late.

*   *   *

The sudden start of the engine startled Kelly and sent him into panic. Still uncertain whether Davis was hurt by the fallen weight of the hood, he was now very worried and scared. He never touched the key, yet, the car engine fired up on its own.

Tears rolled down his cheeks as he noticed blood splattered upon the windshield. He rushed from side to side of the car attempting to locate Davis. Unfortunately, his sight was distracted by crimson streaks beading down the glass in front of him.

*   *   *

Harold Snippet sat silently in the cluttered kitchen, preoccupied in thought. For the past two months dreams of Susan Adkins' young son had haunted him repeatedly. At first they were mere insignificant flashes, but then they began to grow into surreal detailed visions. He saw images of large, deformed creatures pursuing the child, never getting to him, but getting closer to him after every nightmare. He was also haunted in his sleep by the bearded Mr. Smith, who was wielding an ax that was raised to the sky as he chased from behind. Harold's dreams also revealed that Kelly had attempted to warn others about the danger within the house, but he was never believed. Kelly's life was in great peril, especially after the last dream Harold had seen. It was a frightening and vivid nightmare that woke him up and left him in a cold sweat: a hellish creature had crept into Kelly's bedroom during the night and sliced open the sleeping boy's jugular vein. Harold felt so horrified and helpless as he watched the monster from afar.

He knew that his dreams were prophetic, and that the boy needed some kind of outside help, besides his own family. He didn't know exactly what good an elderly man could do, but as long as he attempted, something good might come out of it.

He had a burning feeling in the pit of his stomach that something askew was going on at the Adkins' house right now. Susan told him that she had decided to move away, yet he deeply believed that their troubles were still ongoing at the house. If he went over there to confirm that they were okay, or at least to see if they were still living there, he could sleep a little better.

With his mind made up, he rose from the table and grabbed his jacket. Scratching Pierre upon the head, he set out towards the Adkins' house.

The last time that he went over to that house he was a rambunctious twelve-year-old kid. Now, he was ninety-two and reluctant to bring back the past. Fate was going to be played out tonight—it was inevitable; he was only a pawn in a diabolical chess game of life, and his presence was needed to fit the final pieces of the puzzle and end the curse, once and for all. The years he had spent locked away from the rest of the world, trying to forget a childhood trauma, were just a void of time; he was bound to return to the past. For as long as he lived, he knew that one horrible event would have to be rectified.

*　　*　　*

The fan blade quickly spun, catching and yanking Davis' coat sleeve. The metal sliced through his wrist and ripped into his skin and bone. Pain for the moment seemed nonexistent, but the sudden shock and realization that he had been severely wounded panicked him.

Blood from the open wound began to spray, and he desperately tried to loosen and free his coat from the fan blade.

Davis felt the weight of the car hood decrease and then raise off his back. For a brief moment he was unsure whether it was from his own exertion, or whether he was losing consciousness. The injury was more damaging than he realized, for his sight started to blur.

But no matter how grim the situation seemed, he still had hope. He was a fighter, and never gave up easily. He had faced adversity throughout his life, and this was just one more challenge to overcome. All that he needed to do was stay positive and focused. Someone would arrive soon to rescue him; there was still time to get to a hospital to save his life. They would just have to hurry.

The hood lifted slowly off of Davis' back and pointed to the stars. It stayed that way for five seconds, balancing in mid-air untouched, as though it was taunting him with false hope, until it slammed down onto his back with fierce power, smashing and ramming his head against the engine block, again and again and again.

Davis felt the cold, strong hand of death squeezing life out of him, and his muscles began to ease and embrace the process. He lay limp against the blood soaked engine and succumbed to darkness.

*　　*　　*

The car hood ceased its thrashing and remained down.

Wrapping Sassy's leash around his wrist, Kelly opened the driver's door and lifted the front seat forward to let the dog out. The dog paced with eagerness and pulled Kelly forward with its leash. As Kelly approached the front of the car, he noticed the hood was propped opened slightly. He knew Davis was underneath it because he had seen him working there. The sight of the stationary hood was disturbing, and he was afraid to take another step closer. Reluctantly, he continued walking until he was standing next to Davis' body.

Kelly twitched nervously, unsure of what to do or say. "Davis? Davis, are you okay?" he asked timidly.

A cold, winter wind roared and blew him off balance. Brushing hair away from his eyes, he called out again. "Davis, are you okay? Please answer me. I'm really scared," he cried, trembling.

Tears filled his baby blue eyes and he paced around the front of the car nervously.

Davis wasn't answering, and with the massive amount of blood spilled upon the car and ground, Kelly was afraid he never would again.

Sassy barked agitatedly at the car, and then returned next to Kelly. Bending down, Kelly hugged the dog around the neck affectionately, and then wiped away at his tear-streaked cheeks.

"Don't worry, girl. Davis will be okay, really. He's just knocked out, that's all. He'll get up and take care of us," he said, looking towards the body, and then quickly turning away with grief. But deep down in his heart, he knew differently.

Suddenly an idea flashed in his mind. If he called his Mom, she would come and rescue them. He began to recite a melody of Davis' phone number that she had taught him for emergency use.

"Two . . . four . . . two, two three, two three. Don't worry, Davis, I'll get help," he said, leading the dog towards the house.

*   *   *

Susan got up from the love seat and began pacing around the living room. Samantha, who was lying upon her stomach watching television, looked on sympathetically. She realized it was a typical reaction from her mother. Anytime she became stressed or worried, she tried to counter it by working or staying active. It probably made her feel like she was accomplishing something. Who knows, but if it helped her in any way, more power to her.

When the telephone rang, Susan was upon it before the second ring, seizing the receiver.

"Hello?"

"Mom? It's me," Kelly responded, happy to hear her voice. "I'm at the house."

"Kelly is everything all right? Where's Davis, let me speak to him."

"Mom, I don't know . . ." sobs started to overcome his voice, " . . . what's wrong with him. I think he's hurt really bad," his soft voice cracked with emotion.

"I want you to tell me exactly what's wrong with Davis. Where is he?"

"I don't want to be here, Mom. Please come get me."

"Kelly, I'll be right there. But you have to tell me . . ."

CLICK. The phone was disconnected.

Susan looked down at the phone in shock.

"Kelly? Kelly!" she cried desperately.

Slamming down the receiver, she raced to the closet and pulled her coat off the hanger.

"Sam, I've got to go back to the house. Stay right here," she said, fetching her keys.

"Mom, what's going on? I'm going with you."

"No, Samantha! I told you to stay right here and I mean it!" she snapped.

The girl cowered back against the couch.

"Okay, Mom."

Susan walked over to her and sighed. "Honey, I'm really sorry. I don't know why I barked at you like that. You're just as concerned about them as I am. I just don't want anything to happen to you, that's all. I know you'll be safe here."

She walked over to the door and gave her daughter a confident smile.

"Don't worry, I'll bring them right back."

"I know you will, Mom."

Susan opened the door.

"Mom?" Samantha yelled out. "Please, please, please be careful."

Susan smiled, nodded yes, and then turned away.

*   *   *

"Hello? Mom? Are you there?"

No answer.

Kelly placed the phone back into its base. For the first time in his life he felt truly alone, and doubt began to enter his mind about his chances for survival.

Now he had to rely on instincts. Should he wait outside for help to arrive, where the bad thing had killed Davis, or should he stay in the house, just in case his mother called back? As long as Sassy was at arms reach, he felt protected and safe. He liked his chances inside of the house with the dog.

"Come on, girl, let's wait upstairs in my bedroom and watch for Mom's car. If she calls, we can hear the phone from up there," he said, leading the dog by its chain up the stairs.

RRRRR. Kelly stopped midway up the stairs and listened keenly. Sassy, aware of the noise, held position, also.

RRRRR. That strange, awful, grinding, mechanical noise came from the basement level. His mom had called it a sump pump, but it sounded more like an evil robot with hands like saw blades, that slashed and cut apart children who neared it.

The BAD PLACE. Stay away from the basement, he reminded himself.

He crept upward cautiously, watching the next level suspiciously.

Sassy sniffed at the carpet then glanced ahead heedfully.

"It's all right, Sass. Nothing's gonna happen to us."

The dog offered a low supportive growl.

The hallway was quiet as Kelly approached his old room, the place where he had once sought immunity from daily problems.

Walking inside the room, he immediately noticed the rag doll seated upright upon the bed. Though he was used to the doll's antics and special unannounced visits, its ghost-like ceramic face, with red lips and piercing aqua blue eyes, paralyzed him like a deer frozen by car headlights.

His stomach tightened and churned with nausea, while his knees buckled as fear gripped and controlled him.

"What happened to Davis? Why did you do that!" he asked, approaching cautiously.

"He was in the way. He had to be stopped. I warned you, Kelly. If anyone tried to stop us, they would die. And they have, we've gotten rid of them. They were trouble."

"Why!" he screamed. "They never did anything to you! Why did you kill them!"

His cotton T-shirt began to stick upon his back from sweat.

"I know that your mother's coming," it responded coyly.

Kelly's eyes widened with shock. "No! Don't hurt her. Please don't hurt my momma."

The doll glanced away from Kelly, as if in deep thought, then returned its stare.

"You can save your mother from future harm."

"How? I'll do anything. Just leave her alone."

"The family wants to meet you. I want you to take me down to the basement where they are, and then your mother will be safe."

His heart crumbled as the words sank in. If he refused to abide by its demands, then his mother would fall prey to the same trap and fate Davis had. But if he lead the doll to the basement, and more precisely, the well, then he would die, as simple as that. Inside, he cried and trembled like a baby stranded by the wayside; on the outside, he showed no fear or emotion, and made the decision he knew was right.

Picking the doll up off the bed, he carried it out of the room. Behind him, the bedroom door closed violently, cracking the wood down its center.

From inside the bedroom, Sassy whimpered and scratched at the door.

*   *   *

8:25 p.m.

Harold Snippet crossed over Denton road and carefully proceeded over a small muddy ditch filled with crab grass. The cold air played havoc upon his straining lungs, one of which had collapsed ten years ago, and he stopped momentarily to rest. After regaining some oxygen and needed breath, he continued to tread through a knee-high grassy field, cautious not to lose his footing. After a few minutes of strenuous walking, he cleared the field and entered the Adkins' large open-spaced yard.

He stood on the lawn and looked at the house entranced.

In the waning moment, Harold Snippet reflected upon the vengeful Mr. Smith and recalled the evil man's promise to rid the town of every boy who had taken part in the death of his child. For a brief second, Harold thought about retreating back to his house to hide behind his locked door and never whisper or bring up the past again, and hope to God that he would be spared from the dead man's curse. But he quickly brushed aside the notion. It was only fear that was stopping him now, fear that had made him a prisoner most of his life.

With great conviction, he continued forward, unhampered by his inner childhood demons and determined to save the life of the young boy.

*   *   *

Susan fumbled with a packet of Marborlo lights, then drew out a single cigarette between her index and middle fingers. She placed the butt end to her lips and retrieved a Harley Davidson lighter, carefully watching oncoming traffic as she drove. As the paper burned and the warm mist crawled down her throat like a slithering snake, the tension weighted upon her neck and shoulders eased dramatically. She exhaled with delight. A good drag from a cigarette always did the trick and calmed her nerves. Ever since the days of rebelling against her parents, or what she thought was rebelling, a cigarette always helped to take stress away; not that this cigarette took away any pain of not knowing how Davis and Kelly were doing, but it did give her slight comfort.

The Blazer pulled up behind a gray Tempo stationed at a stop sign on the corner of Dix and Third. Susan tapped on the steering wheel nervously, watching the vehicle ahead.

The woman in the car fidgeted with belongings in her backseat, unaware of Susan behind.

A scowl emerged on Susan's face while she watched and waited as the oblivious person continued to dawdle. Angrily, Susan blasted the horn, holding on an extra measure to ensure the woman's attention.

Startled, the older driver looked in her rearview mirror, waved back at Susan, returned her focus back to the main road and quickly turned left onto Third.

Susan punched the gas and squealed off of Dix right behind her. The Blazer barely slipped past an oncoming speeding Mustang and took an outside position next to the Tempo.

Susan eyed the woman briefly with a bitchy look, then returned to a more pressing matter—getting to her house in record time.

What could Kelly have been talking about? How badly was Davis hurt? She thought about her brother's twisted neck and ghastly eyes and shuttered with revulsion. Tears dropped down her cheek and she rubbed them away, cursing to herself.

"Shit! Of all the times to lose your composure, you stupid bitch, now's not the time!" she said, controlling the wheel with one hand while dabbing her eyes with the back of her other hand.

The car roared along Third, then pulled to a halt at a red light on State Street. A sign directly in front of her warned "No Turn On Red."

She turned.

She floored the pedal and raced down the road, thankfully unseen, as the intersection was vacant.

Without any other obstacles it should take no more than ten minutes, she contemplated, staring down at the radio clock. Hopefully, ten minutes isn't too long.

*   *   *

The wooden floorboard creaked as Kelly slowly weighted his foot upon it. Decay from termite infestation and continual usage left the wood frail and vulnerable. He clutched the doll to his chest, holding it so the figure faced forward as he descended into the basement.

The air was damp and musty. He raised a sleeve to his nose, fending off the foul odor while his eyes darted back and forth inspecting the dark corners of the room.

A washer and dryer sat side by side against the furthest wall, and across from them was metal shelving occupied with canned goods. There was no trace of the so-called "family."

He had a feeling where they were waiting. It wasn't in the immediate part of the basement, it was beyond that, down the narrow corridor to the furnace room where the beast slept, where it dwelled in the brick well and licked its blood-soaked lips, just waiting for one more chance to get to him.

Kelly stepped off the last board and waited cautiously on the concrete floor.

"Should I stay here?" he asked the doll, perplexed.

"No. Walk through the hallway. They're waiting for us in there."

Kelly tightened his grip upon the doll.

It was the moment of reckoning. The moment the spirits had been waiting for ever since they beckoned him with a sweet, luring spell in Florida.

He moved forward entering the dark, narrow concrete corridor.

Water dripping echoed softly in the distance ahead.

Kelly's hands traced upon the cold concrete surface as he gauged his direction and obstacles. An extruded sharp chunk of brick in the wall, shoulder high, startled and frightened him and ceased his movement. When the object became recognizable, he proceeded again cautiously, shuffling his feet upon the concrete so that he wouldn't trip upon anything.

Light from within the furnace room reflected off the hallway wall and brightened his pathway. There were only yards between him and the awaiting spirits huddled by the well, but it felt like miles. His stomach rocked like an uncontrollable canoe descending down a steep waterfall. Every beat of his heart pounded with great volume within his ears.

Images of his mother and sister filled his mind. The last time they were together would be their last moment together. His mom had no idea what was about to happen to him and the thought was agonizing to him. They would never see each other again, ever.

If he had to protect her by giving up his own life, then so be it. He had no choice.

As much as he tried to reassure himself of that theory in order to toughen up and be brave, the scent of fear and doom still loomed large, and he wished to God she would show up and rescue him.

*   *   *

Pain gnawed at the bottom of Harold Snippet's feet. The soft-soled slippers that he had chose to wear were unworthy of a quarter mile jog, and every step he took caused his windblown, weather-beaten face to wince.

He tracked over the horseshoe-shaped dirt driveway and climbed up the steep, slanted front yard towards the front porch, deciding against entering the side door entrance.

Lights glowed through every window of the house, yet Susan Adkins' Blazer was missing. He remembered she had pulled up to his place in the blue vehicle, so instinctively he felt something was wrong. They wouldn't have left the place unattended with all of the lights on; maybe a few, but not all of them.

Harold noticed an older looking Taurus that was parked in the driveway near the front of the house. He wasn't familiar with who owned it, but it must have been out of commission and broke down because its front hood was partially propped open. *Maybe someone was working on it tonight?* He wasn't sure; it was far too dark to see, and his eyesight was poor.

He disregarded the disabled vehicle for the time being and stepped up onto the small porch and knocked forcefully upon the door, cautiously watching the surrounding area.

Something definitely smelled foul, that's for sure.

While waiting, his mind began drifting back in time. It didn't seem so long ago now. In fact, he felt like that same little boy standing at the front door waiting to meet his new neighbor.

It was all so similar—the house and yard. He felt a twinge of excitement course through his veins like he had felt that early morning when he first met Luke.

But the year was 2008, not 1928, and he became dejected, realizing that his bitter sentiments had clouded and interfered with his desire to get the boy.

He pounded again, this time with more vigor. With no answer still, he attempted again, harder yet, repeatedly striking his thin, bony fist against the wood.

No answer.

Something was wrong. Seriously wrong. Harold knew the boy was inside, he could feel his presence. Call it a premonition, or just call it a wise, old man's intuition—he knew the kid was here. It was a burning, unyielding feeling. If the boy was here alone, he could be in desperate trouble.

Without hesitation he burst into the house.

It was freezing cold, worse than the harsh temperature outdoors. So cold, that he buttoned up his hunting jacket and rubbed his arms to cause friction and generate heat.

He walked straight ahead, avoiding Susan's opened bedroom, listening intently along the way.

The stairway upstairs was illuminated.

Harold looked through the kitchen, to the bay windows of the sunroom, then back to the empty dining room. If the boy were anywhere, it would probably be upstairs.

Peering through the stairs' open doorway, he glanced up to the second level. A free-falling crystal lamp came spiraling down from over the top of the wooden divider. He dodged out of the way as the piece flew past his face and smashed into the wall, scattering shards of glass upon the steps.

That damn thing didn't just fall off the landing. That thing was hurled, he surmised, taking refuge in the kitchen.

"Hello, anybody here?" he yelled out. "Son, if you can hear me, let me know you're okay and where you're at."

*　　*　　*

Kelly heard the man's voice call out from upstairs. It was a stranger's voice. Even though it wasn't family, it was someone at least and he was glad for that. If it had been an evil person, like a demon, then they probably wouldn't be offering any support or help. They would be hunting him down. So, to have any unexpected guest in the house with him was comforting.

"I'm right here! Down in the basement!" he yelled elatedly.

Hope. There was hope after all. He wasn't going to die, he beamed.

Turning around in the corridor, he began to feel his way back, carefully placing his footing, remembering there were loose chunks of debris upon the floor.

Moving back into the laundry room, he dropped the doll to the concrete and walked toward the stairs with a relieved smile curled upon his lips.

His next step was thwarted, though, as a hard object struck him violently in the back of the head, eliciting a hallow crack, like the sound of a vase smashed by a rubber mallet.

Kelly fell groggily to his knees and then collapsed upon his back, crumbling like a coat thrown upon the floor. His eyelids fluttered, fighting back unconsciousness, and he searched the room for the source of the attack.

Lying next to him was the cracked open skull of the porcelain doll, with its decapitated body beside it.

*　　*　　*

The Blazer spun wildly onto Denton, fishtailing and throwing rocks into the air. Susan raced the speedometer needle past seventy miles per hour as trees whipped by.

The vehicle motored past a wave of aligned thick oak trees, which framed the sides of the road like a tunnel, and then slid around a corner of a sharp bend.

She flew past Mr. Snippet's house, barely paying any notice.

As the Blazer approached the house, Davis' Taurus stuck out like a bull in a china store. She was alarmed instantly by the illumination of the house; it screamed trouble, a whole lot of it.

Pulling up behind his car, she jumped out of the Blazer and ran for the side door. If it wasn't for the propped open hood in her peripheral vision, she probably would have dashed right past it in the hurry, but instead, she froze silently on the embankment by the side door, looking in horror. Simultaneously, she saw Davis' limp legs and fresh blood splattered upon the windshield.

Covering her lips with her hand, she tried to step forward towards him, but fell like rain from the sky and put her face into the frigid grass in denial.

She shook her head in disbelief, with mascara streaming under her eyes and down her cheekbones. Rising up, she walked forward, closer to the car. She was afraid to look under the hood. How could she? The sight would be too much to bear, if her fears proved true.

She had to know whether he was alive or dead.

Placing her fingers under the lip of the hood, she lifted the weight from his body. Although his face was down, the damage and carnage was indisputable.

Staring at his still body, she touched his throat gently.

No pulse.

She attempted again, uncertain of her accuracy.

Dead.

She quivered and turned away agonized, facing the house.

Everything about him she loved, and now it was all gone. Snatched away. *Why?*

Her lips trembled. With eyelids tightly closed, she shuddered, trying to refrain from crying.

KELLY. MY GOD, HE'S STILL IN THERE! The sobering thought awakened her. She bolted towards the house without another tear.

*　　*　　*

Harold Snippet stood between the dining room and kitchen just in front of the archway of the upstairs. He waited patiently for an answering voice and kept an eye open for movement upon the second level. He envisioned a maniacal killer, stained with blood, wielding an ax, running down the steps with crazed vengeance. Quivering, he moved backwards another step just in case, resting his body against the kitchen counter. At least nothing was creeping up from behind. If he were to be attacked, it would have to be from the other three directions.

Without any answer, he prepared to call out again. The boy's shout from below took him by surprise. It was the voice of fear and urgency.

The old man rose to the challenge, alert and attentive. "The basement. He's down in the basement."

Reacting to the voice, he stopped in mid-run. Two counter doors slid open, and from within three carving knives levitated into the air.

Harold Snippet could not believe his eyes. Never in his existence had anything so bizarre and unnatural occurred. *How were they floating? What was holding them in the air, magic?*

The knives swayed back and forth in front of his face, like alien space ships patrolling the sky and scanning the earth.

If he attempted to run past them to the basement stairs, they would surely dice him like a tomato. He had to think of something quickly. Something to bide time.

Slowly and methodically, he stepped back towards the living room. Gaining enough distance from the blades in the kitchen, he sprinted to the dining room table and withdrew a chair. Holding the seat outward, like a lion tamer would fending off a vicious cat, he charged full force into the kitchen and struck the first blow, slamming the chair downward upon all three knives.

The blades fell lifelessly in opposite directions upon the floor as he ran past towards the downstairs' landing.

The knives lifted off the ground in unison and shifted into attack positions, so that each shiny, stainless steel point faced directly at the back of the escapee.

Harold felt the glaring steel converge upon him, and ran quickly, gasping for breath without looking back.

He reached the mouth of the doorway when two dull thumps penetrated the wall beside his head. For a moment, he believed the third and final knife had landed aimlessly elsewhere, but when a sharp, burning pain tore at his back just below the shoulder blade, he knew he was hit.

Ignoring the pain, he slammed into the wall by the side door and stumbled clumsily down the steps to the basement. The burning became hotter and hotter as he tried unsuccessfully to dislodge the knife. In his angst to free the embedded blade, he tripped over his feet, lost his balance, tumbled down the remaining flight of stairs and landed hard on his belly upon the cold unforgiving floor; he howled in pain.

His lower back muscles tightened in a knot and ached; he was sure that his left arm was broken from the fall.

Coughing and gasping, he picked himself up and staggered across the concrete floor to the corridor. Blood trickled over his bottom lip, and the room began to spin drunkenly around and around and around in circles. His eyes felt like wildfire, burning out of control.

Harold stopped and collapsed against the rough concrete wall of the laundry room and closed his eyes. The pain was unbearable. Sweat fell from his face profusely as he grew drowsy.

"Oh Lord . . . sweet Lord. Give me the strength, please, give me the strength," he whispered.

A noise within the hallway emanated in the distance—a low repetitive noise.

The old man watched the pitch-black corridor carefully.

At first it sounded like a motor idling softly, but the level intensified. A muffled engine noise turned into voices. Different voices: a man and woman, small children—several small children. All of them calling out, "Harold."

Like bees buzzing upon a hive they filled the inside of the old man's mind, driving him insane with each different voice he detected. Raging with fury, he stormed ahead blindly into the darkness, screaming like a maddening warrior.

White trails of spiritual faces met him halfway. They soaked upon his skin, penetrating through pores and infesting his body. They burned within. Evil laughs and shrills circled his brain, taunting, tormenting, caressing his every sense. Faces of the old woman and her son, his wife, and several innocent children slithered up and down his body. Swollen, blue faces with empty glowing white eye sockets begged for mercy and help, pleading, "Harold, don't let us die! SAVE US! SAVE US!" Tiny winged, fragmented demon bodies darted about his eyes. He swung at them aimlessly as though they were droves of flies and mosquitoes nipping on his face and body.

If the beckoning call of death or the maddening sensation of a knife in his torso wasn't enough, this materialization of supernatural forces would surely test his resolve, or eat away at his mind and kill him with heart failure, he thought.

But through the torment he continued to run, waving his hands wildly through the air as faces of children, demons and insects passed through his sweaty body.

Within the other room ahead light shone brightly, and with it, Harold Snippet's belief in redemption.

As he stammered down the slope into the furnace room, a scuffling noise caught his attention. Kelly Adkins' body was dragging across the concrete floor upon his backside, with his arms limp and outstretched and his legs stiff and erect in the air, as though an invisible force was pulling them.

The boy was unconscious, unaware of his course towards the well and of the damage that was caused to his head after striking it upon the cement floor.

Harold Snippet froze at the ungodly sight, blinking as if a mirage had fallen over his eyes.

The little child of frail frame and peaked complexion came to a stop against the cylinder wall of the well as the soles of his shoes crossed over its rim.

The old man's sight became obstructed again as the swirling mass of translucent faces caught up with him from the corridor and came between him and the child. He covered his eyes as the swarm blinded and obscured the well and the boy.

Once again the voices beckoned him. "Save our souls, Harold."

His breathing became strained and haggard, causing him to cough up blood violently. He wheezed and gasped, clutching at his racing heart and fell back against the wall for support.

I've got to get to that kid. I've got to help him, he demanded of himself, wearily.

The hovering mass began to dissipate, its colors switching from white to red to green. Its shape contracted and expanded like silly putty, changing from an animal to a human, and then into other strangely contoured shapes.

The large form redefined, condensed and ascended toward the ceiling, sprouting arms, legs and then a head. It became the perfect transparent replica of old man Smith, standing larger than life.

Harold Snippet gasped with fear. Was he becoming delirious? Could this actually be the man who instilled fear in him and every townsfolk?

Kelly's legs lurched halfway over the well's edge.

The old man wiped at his brow, sweating in abundance.

"You're not real! I'm not afraid of you anymore. You killed my friends, I didn't kill your boy," he said in a pleading voice to the hovering apparition.

It watched with an amused broad grin.

The boy was going into the well; there wasn't time to waste.

Without fear and restraint, he charged through the wicked figure and caught the boy as his tiny body descended into the darkness of the well. By holding tightly onto the child's wrists and placing his own feet upon the base of the cylinder, Harold pulled with all of his might and plucked the boy from within. He cradled the boy and brought him to the side of the room, away from the tall, transparent figure.

Kelly remained unconscious.

"The boy belongs to us, old man. You should have never come back! You will DIE here along with him now," the specter bellowed.

"You were wrong, Smith! You're a cold-blooded murderer. You killed those poor, innocent children. They were people's babies, for God's sake. You of all people should know how it feels to lose a child! End this madness and leave him alone."

"SILENCE! You took the life of my child, my only son. Are you remorseful for that? No! So it is with great pleasure and satisfaction that I will bury you and this brat, along with all of the other poor, selfish bastards, into an icy grave of Hell where you all belong together," he sneered venomously.

*   *   *

Susan turned the doorknob on the side door and found it locked. She placed the key into the keyhole and unfastened the lock, only to find that the dead bolt had been set, and regrettably, she never had a key for it. Angrily, she shoved her shoulder into the door and bashed it repetitively, trying to break apart the old wooden frame. After several unsuccessful, painful attempts, she backed away from the house and searched for another entry.

The kitchen window. She could hoist herself up to it and climb inside.

Searching about the area for something to stand upon, she decided to go out to the tool shed and look for materials.

Thankfully the small shed was unlocked. Prying back the rusty hinged door, she entered the darkness, feeling her way around. Two quick steps inside, she tripped over an object on the floor and stumbled.

Reaching down she discovered it was a fuel canister. Pushing it aside with her foot, she moved forward while gasoline sloshed back and forth from inside of the metal can. Her hand groped against a shovel and a rake, knocking them both noisily to the ground. A stepladder was hung upon the wall in the corner of the barn, so she snatched it and headed for the door.

She realized that she needed something to break open the glass. Looking to her right she found a tool chest and opened it, rifling through pliers, wrenches, and screwdrivers until a hammer emerged from underneath the pile. Taking it in hand along with the ladder, she raced through the moonlight towards the house.

It was eerily silent outside. The cold, somber night sent shivers down her spine as she approached the window.

Unfolding and locking the ladder into place, she positioned it bedside the house under the window and began climbing up the four steps until she was standing on top. She peered into the kitchen. Everything seemed quiet and in order. Placing her ear to the glass pane, she listened. Not a sound.

Lifting up the claw hammer, she smashed the window and then cleared out the remaining fragments with short chops from side to side. Without wasting time, she planted her right leg on the window ledge and pulled herself in.

A wave of frigid air rushed out and hit her in the face. It was colder inside than outside.

Kelly might have hidden upstairs, but it was highly unlikely. It didn't feel right. She had a sinking feeling everything revolved around the basement, and that Kelly was there.

*   *   *

Harold Snippet shook the boy vigorously trying to awaken him from the coma, but the child's pale face remained oblivious as the apparition drew nearer to them.

"Wake up! Wake up, now!" he shouted desperately.

With an open hand, he slapped the boy's cheek repeatedly.

Kelly's eyes blinked and then came open. His vision was blurred and his head ached as though an anvil had been dropped on it from twelve stories up.

The old man's face drew in and out of focus. At first, Kelly couldn't recognize the man's features, but as he stared longer, he realized that it was the crazy, old man who lived down the road in the small house.

"What am . . . I . . . doing here?" he asked groggily.

"Don't worry, son, you're okay."

"Is my mom here?"

"No, boy. Not yet."

Kelly looked around the room disoriented, then gazed upon the floating, bearded specter. He stiffened with shock. "Ahhh! What's that?" He gasped as the figure got closer.

The old man held onto Kelly firmly by each shoulder.

"Son, can you stand on your own?"

"Yes . . . sir," he responded, scared, watching the spirit approach.

The apparition stood ominously just inches away from Kelly. With awesome agility it transfigured into a twelve-foot high two-headed dragon. Fire-red eyes scanned the boy the way a hungry wolf appraises raw meat. A long, yellow, mucus-coated tongue swayed through the air.

The beast heaved with convulsion, primed for attack. Crouched upon the floor, it spread its massive wingspan outward and dug its nails into the concrete. Slowly it drew in the claws, emitting a high-pitched screech and leaving deep gashes upon the cement floor.

The old man pulled the boy close to his chest and both trembled with fear.

The beast felt it, understood it. It was a look it had seen many times before, fear.

A diabolical grin curled upon its leathery face as it rose into striking position.

SMASH. The startling sound of breaking glass erupted over their heads near the kitchen.

All three looked up towards the noise with surprise.

SMASH. SMASH. SMASH.

The beast, shaken and distracted by the unwelcome visitor, shifted its gaze towards the hallway, listening intensely.

"Listen to me, Kelly. You have to get out of here right now," the old man whispered, holding Kelly close to him. "When I say go, I want you to run as fast as you can through that doorway to the stairs."

"But what about you?" he asked, frightened, "I'm not going to leave you here alone."

"I'll be all right, son. I've got to deal with this myself. Don't worry about ol' Harold. I'll be fine. You just make sure you go as fast as your little legs can run and I'll be right behind you, buddy."

Kelly nodded his head in agreement.

Alarmed, the beast lifted one of its heads into the air and sniffed.

With its attention diverted, Harold took advantage of the opportune moment.

"Now! Run, boy, run!"

Kelly darted past the beast to the corridor without looking back. As he ran, the old man jumped in front of the dragon.

The thing looked at Kelly's sprinting body with surprise and then intense rage. It had been tricked, something that had never occurred before.

A menacing growl from its belly shook the walls of the room and it stomped forward.

"Back off you ugly son of a bitch!" The old man sneered. "You might think you're scary to a kid, but to me you're just a piece of crap!"

The mouth of the creature widened, showing off rows of sharp fangs that glistened with saliva. It hissed with animosity, spraying hot, putrid breath upon the man's face and disrupting his vision.

Harold Snippet fell backwards gagging, holding onto his throat. It felt as though it was on fire. "You don't . . ." *cough cough* " . . . scare me."

The beast slammed its claws around the old man's throat and lifted him helplessly into the air.

Harold thrashed and kicked wildly, but it was useless; the demon's stranglehold was powerful and relentless.

With a final breath from his reddening face, Harold Snippet looked into the eyes of the man who had sought him for so many years and smiled smugly.

The beast crushed his neck like a grape, then heaved the old man's body down into the dark abyss of the well and waited silently for it to land. When a dull thud echoed from below, the beast flew like a bat out of Hell into the black corridor after the child.

*   *   *

Cold air stung Kelly's face as he hurried through the corridor. Losing his footing, he fell hard against the wall and collapsed to the ground. Lying upon the concrete, he listened for a moment to check if he was being pursued: he heard muffled, angry shouts, scuffling noises and then silence.

Frightened, he got back on his feet and ran, touching the sides of the walls as he passed.

Light from the utility room glowed ten yards ahead. From behind, beating wings closed in on him.

Kelly quickened his strides.

The noise grew louder. A cool breeze touched his back.

Don't look behind. Don't look behind! He warned himself.

He didn't, and continued running as fast as he could.

The passage at the end of the corridor grew larger and more welcoming with every step.

Suddenly he felt hot air, smelled the vile breath of the demonic beast upon his neck.

He wasn't going to make it out. It was too close and too fast, and would easily catch and kill him before he reached the first step of the stairs.

Shutting his eyes, gritting his teeth and furiously pumping his arms up and down, he made it out of the corridor.

*   *   *

Susan barely maintained her balance as she haphazardly rounded the small side door landing and descended down the basement stairs. Her foot caught awkwardly on the first step and she stumbled down the remaining flight.

She panned the laundry room for Kelly. Finding it deserted, she decided to go into the furnace room.

The trampling of oncoming feet stopped her abruptly.

Kelly raced through the opening of the corridor and ran directly into her. Before she could open her mouth, he pointed backwards frantically.

"It's coming! It's coming!" he yelled, out of breath.

Susan looked up and watched the opening. A raging wind slammed them backwards into the staircase and sent them sprawling upon it. Susan's back stiffened with pain as she attempted to sit up from the fall.

The wooden staircase began to shake and rock with extreme force. Susan jumped from the plank she was sitting on and leaned up against the wall just as four stair boards ripped out of their nailed position, flew into the air and were hurled into the corner of the room.

Above her, the side door opened up and then shut violently, ringing the glass window. It opened and slammed again, harder each time, until finally shattering the glass and spraying pieces down to the basement over and around them.

Susan shrieked and shielded Kelly from the sharp debris as it landed.

The doors on the washer and dryer opened and started slamming.

The stairway light switched on and off in quick spurts.

"Mama, I'm scared. Make it stop, please!"

"It's okay, Kelly. Everything will be okay. I'm not gonna let anything happen to you. I promise. Just hold on, sweetie, hold on."

Susan glanced up towards the darkened corridor. The wind had ceased.

A scuffling noise began in the darkness, an object dragging upon concrete.

She watched fearfully.

The first scaly, red head of the beast appeared around the corner. It stared at Susan, calculating her location. Then its next head appeared, and with it the remaining section of its large reptilian body.

Susan placed Kelly behind her upon the stairs and guarded him.

The beast slithered and writhed out of the opening and across the floor on its claws and belly like a gigantic lizard.

It approached slowly, snapping its jaws hungrily.

Susan cowered back against the wall as far as she could, but she was cornered.

With great agility it leapt through the air and landed firmly upon her.

The claw hammer that she clutched desperately slipped from her grip and bounded aimlessly to the floor.

Wriggling, she kicked and beat upon the callused skin of the hideous beast. It fought back viciously, prodding and slicing her with razor-sharp nails.

Screaming out in pain, she struggled under its massive weight.

Its lurid, green tongue stretched towards her face. Squirming, she reached out for the hammer. Her hand, only inches away, stretched, stretched further, trembled with exhaustion, and fell weakly to the concrete floor.

The creature's claws ripped across her stomach.

She screamed in agony.

The mass of weight lying upon her chest was crushing; air was fading from her lungs by the second. In another minute she would lose strength and succumb to death.

Realizing it was too late for her and that the only thing that mattered was getting her son out alive, she screamed, "Run, Kelly, run!"

He stared at her mute, with frightened eyes.

"Kelly, you've got to go on without me. Listen to me!"

He shook his head in denial.

"I won't leave you," he sobbed.

"Baby, please go now," she begged, wincing in pain.

Climbing up the stairs, he took one last look back down at her.

Her head was flailing up and down as the beast shook her angrily.

The door was open, yet Kelly couldn't continue towards it. He turned around, gathered speed and hurdled over the creature.

Grabbing the hammer off the floor as he landed, he swung the claw end deep into the throat of the beast and jumped back up on the stairs.

The dragon howled in agony and spun off of Susan's body, spurting blood out of its severed artery onto the wall. It tried unsuccessfully to dislodge the embedded hammer, but was unable to reach or pull it out.

"Come on, Mom! You can get away now!" Kelly yelled emphatically.

Susan rolled away from the wailing creature and looked up.

Kelly stood upon the top step motioning onward.

She rose to her knees and stood up wearily, then attempted to pull herself up onto the fourth step, since the other three had been ripped out.

The beast flailed and thrashed about, attempting to free the tool.

Exhausted and pained, she methodically climbed each step by propping her shoulder against the cold wall to maintain balance.

The thin, muscular arm of the demon reached out and latched on to her ankle.

Susan screamed from its crushing grip and attempted to kick loose with her free leg.

With a quick yank, it spun her around and pulled her off her feet. She landed upon her back with her head striking a plank of wood.

She was face to face to with it as it moved in closer. The hatred in its eyes was intense.

The beast leaned in closer, opening its mouth towards her face.

"You're not real! You won't hurt us. I won't let you hurt anyone again." A voice came from behind Susan.

As the creature looked up, Kelly jammed a shard of glass deep into its right eye socket. Blood spurted out of the wound, clouding its vision.

It screamed in agony and retreated towards the darkness of the corridor.

Kelly placed his arm around his mother's waist, helped steady her to her feet, and led the way upstairs to safety.

The cold night air brought life into her depleted, crushed lungs as she hobbled through the grass towards the car.

But she knew it wasn't over, not by a long shot. She wasn't naive.

"Kelly, I want you to go get in the car and lock the doors. Do not open the doors unless I come back."

"But why are you going back? Let's go! We can get out of here right now!" He had heard that same safety-conscious demand from Davis, and knew what the result turned out to be.

"Do what I say! For no one, you hear me! Don't open the door."

"You're gonna die trying to protect me just like Davis did!"

She looked into his troubled eyes. She hadn't thought about the trauma Kelly had gone through with Davis' death. She could feel a wave of tears coming over her, but she had to hold it together. She hugged him and held his hands tightly in hers. "Baby, listen. I know you've seen an awful lot of terrible, terrible things tonight. Davis did protect you. He kept you safe enough until I got here. But I have to go back. You might not understand now, but you will in time. I promise you, with all my heart, I will come back. Nothing will keep me away from you, Kelly. Now be brave for me, and wait in the car."

She waited for him to climb into the car and lock the door. When he had done so, she stumbled to the tool shed.

The cold wind penetrated through her torn shirt and burned on her open wounds. Four lacerations a half an inch wide and six inches long stretched across her stomach. Several minor cuts and scrapes were also upon her stomach, cheeks, and arms.

She lurched ahead on the dirt driveway towards the shed as unbearable pain flashed like lightning through every muscle in her body.

Clasping a hand over her stomach wounds, the warm sensation of blood soaked her fingertips. She drew the hand away and looked. During the adrenaline rush getting to the car, the wound seemed trivial. Now, she realized how severely cut and vulnerable she was, and the urgent need of medical attention became prominent.

She continued towards the shed, holding in the pain. Just one last thing to do, she repeated in her head.

The wooden door creaked open slowly. She entered, cautiously feeling the area ahead of her. Just inside the doorway, she found an opened box sitting atop a workbench, and inside the box were used towels and shirts.

She took a flannel shirt and tied it around her waist to slow down some of the bleeding. After a few steps further inside, she crouched down lower to the floor and felt from side to side until she found what she was looking for: the metal gas canister. She picked it up the by the steel handle and left the barn.

Why was she doing this? Just leave this nightmare behind and never look back. Take Kelly away and forget the past.

But she couldn't. She couldn't leave the problem for another family to learn from. She couldn't leave like all the others had before. Why should she turn her back and pass the tradition of evil and death to another generation, when she had a chance to do something now? *How many more innocent children had to die before someone stood up and became accountable?*

Pulling open the door, she ran into the house and went up the landing into the kitchen. She flicked on the light for the upstairs, headed up and rounded the corner like a bullet from a gun, forgetting her suffering body.

Running straight for Samantha's room, she loosened and removed the cap from the old kettle-shaped fuel can and doused the bedroom walls and floor.

As she headed towards the door to leave, the lights upstairs clicked off. The entire room was draped in darkness, with the exception of a patch of radiant white moonlight that was creeping in from the bedroom window.

No sound or light, just the devil inside of her mind whispering tonight.

Susan edged forward carefully. The floorboard squeaked harshly underfoot as she entered the hallway.

Something's moving ahead in the dark, she thought. *Something's coming towards me—I know it's there; it's so close. I can hear it. Oh God, what is it?*

Her heartbeat accelerated rapidly, and exhaled plumes of breath became visible in the air. Her face was hot and sweaty, though the house was freezing cold.

Gripping the handle of the can tightly, she prepared to throw it or run.

Woof!

Startled, she turned towards Kelly's room.

Woof! Woof!

"Sassy?"

Scratching persisted from inside the bedroom door.

Susan braced herself against the wall and scooted towards the bedroom. Gripping her hand around the doorknob, she opened the door.

The dog raced past, knocking her off to the side. Her paws scampered down the stairs and into the kitchen.

Susan followed her cue and hustled behind.

The attic ladder swung down with precise timing and hit her upon the forehead, leveling her. She landed in front of the bathroom door dazed and confused.

Charging back upstairs, Sassy sniffed the air, then prodded her on with enthusiastic barks.

She lay motionless upon the carpet for a brief moment, and then rolled to her feet. Thankfully, the metal can landed upright and still contained the fuel.

A gust of wind descended from the attic and slammed her body into the wall with tremendous force. Her vision swirled as though she was on a tilt-o-wheel at an amusement park. Her body felt depleted of energy and drained of hope.

What more could she do? The invisible force was too powerful to fight against. There was no defeating it. Look what happened to Davis: he lost his life trying to combat it. How could she fight such a powerful entity, if he couldn't?

She loved him so much; it pained her immensely to think about him. *Why did he have to come back tonight? Why couldn't he just stay away? Why, God, did she have to lose such a special love in her life after only a brief period of time together?* It wasn't fair.

Kelly's face appeared in her mind as the wooziness in her head began to subside. He must be frightened being left alone in the car. She imagined hearing his fragile voice calling to her through the car window, begging for her to come back.

I can't give up now, she thought. *I've got to fight. I've got to make it out of here alive. My children need me. I can do it, I know I can.*

Hurrying upright, she grabbed the can and took off down the stairs, with Sassy leading the way. As she ran, she left a trail of gas upon the carpet.

As Sassy turned left into the kitchen towards the side door, Susan turned right into the dining room, and doused a curtain, carpet and table with gasoline.

Chairs levitated into the air and began rotating clock-wise around her, like leaves caught up in a windstorm. She attempted to move past a flying chair but was struck against the head. Cowering down, she protected herself and scuttled on her hands and knees into the living room.

The television set slid out from against the wall, snapping the plug from its socket, and bee-lined towards her. She jumped away from its homing path just in the nick of time, and landed on the couch as the set crashed against a corner wall and fell over on its side.

The couch began to shake spastically with her on top of it, like a bull bucking a young broncobuster attempting his first ride. She held on momentarily, but was catapulted into a crystal lamp upon the coffee table.

The can of fuel flew from her hand and landed against the wall. As the can settled upon its side, gasoline spilled upon the floor and filled the air with fumes; the smell burned inside of her nose and she gagged, sickened.

Sassy ran back into the dining room and barked repetitively towards the living room, instinctively sensing danger.

Susan lifted the can off the floor, entered her bedroom and proceeded to soak the bedroom furniture.

Ceramic knickknacks flew from a hutch in the living room and sprayed against the opposite wall. She shielded her face from scattering shards and ran for cover in the dining room, where she quickly found the dining room table spinning around in circles, first slowly, and then exceedingly faster. Sliding effortlessly across the carpet, it headed straight for her.

Unable to run from its collision course, she became pinned against the wall at her mid-section.

The wooden table pressed harder into her stomach, determined to slice her in half.

Placing her fingers underneath its bottom, she flipped the table over and ran towards the kitchen, where she fetched a packet of matches from the junk drawer.

All at once every glass, dish, pot, pan and utensil sprang from within its storage and cluttered the kitchen area.

"Sassy! Come on, girl, get out of there!" she called, slapping her legs to entice the dog from the living room.

The animal moved without hesitation and ran to her.

"Good girl."

The house shook within like an earthquake as debris littered the air in a swirling, turbulent motion. A drinking glass smashed against the side of her head and bloodied her face. Recoiling from the blow, she staggered towards the back door. Again she was struck, this time from a stainless steel pot upon her back. Again and again and again, utensils hurled forth relentlessly and bounced off her body.

With resilience, she fought through the onslaught, dousing the walls and carpet along the way.

She opened the side door and Sassy bolted out first, quickly heading straight for the Blazer.

Blood was dried up on the bridge and sides of her nose and her lip was swollen and cracked.

A howling, blood-curdling scream beckoned from deep in the basement.

She froze in horror, and turned around to face the basement stairs.

Clattering resounded, growing louder and obviously approaching.

Closer it came from within the darkness: an animalistic noise screaming.

Susan's jaw clenched. Her hands began to shake with fear, and she tightened them into tight fists. She kept her sight locked, though, peering down into the blackness of the basement to see anything.

A flying demon emerged through the black veil: the head of Mr. Smith on one side, the withered and grinning face of his mother on the other.

Claws were extended outward through the air and its bloodthirsty fangs snapped like a rabid dog as it ascended up the stairs.

Susan stood undaunted. Cut and bleeding, she eyed the beast all the way up.

"You son of a bitch, have a nice trip back to Hell!" she screamed, whipping the can of gasoline into its head. The demon flipped over backward from the blow and landed upon the concrete floor.

Drawing a match, she looked straight into its glaring red eyes and struck the match. Lighting the remaining sticks in the matchbook, she tossed it down upon the beast.

A ball of flames rocketed upward in an explosion of heat.

Jumping out of the door onto the lawn, she felt the searing heat against her back as she rolled out of the way. Satisfied that no flames were burning upon her clothing, she scampered to her feet and raced to the car.

Watching her approach, Kelly quickly unlocked the driver's door.

Susan opened the car door and watched as Sassy jumped inside and landed happily onto Kelly's lap, licking him with sloppy kisses in the process. She got in after the dog, slammed the door, started the engine, floored the car in reverse and spun out of the driveway onto Denton.

They parked on the side of the road far away from harm and watched the old house start to burn. Susan knew that she was in dire need of hospitalization, but she wasn't about to budge until she was satisfied the house was on fire.

Kelly looked to her and noticed the blood and cuts. He was worried for her, but not afraid. She was alive and with him, and that's all that mattered.

After a few minutes, the house erupted into flames. Smoke billowed out of the windows behind long tongues of red and yellow flames. The crackling of charring wood echoed in the calm night as the building became engulfed with fire and lit the sky with light.

Kelly was sure that he heard tortured cries and screams released forth from the flames, and as they did a pleasant finality filled his heart.

Susan placed her hand upon his knee. They both smiled.

For the fist time they both felt truly free of an unbearable pain and guilt, and finally had inner peace. It was rejuvenating, refreshing, as though the world seemed like a whole new place.

"Mom, it's all over, right?"

"Yes, honey," she promised. "It's all over."

*   *   *

TWO MONTHS LATER.

Sunday morning beamed of promise: a cloudless, sunny day in the low seventies was welcome news for March weather.

The weather channel ensured a clear and warm day for travelers, and Susan was glad to hear that.

After packing a few personal belongings into a suitcase, she went into the spare bedroom of her good friend, Ida Allison, and fetched Kelly.

He sat on the bed reading a novel.

Surprised to see him awake, she sat down next to him. "You ready to go, sport?"

"Yeah, I've been up for about an hour," he smiled.

"Really? I thought you would have been sleeping soundly still. I had to wake Sam up, you know."

"That figures. She's always sleeping. Not me, though."

She ruffled his hair and sat up from the bed.

"We'll be taking off in about ten minutes. Make sure you've got all your books and toys."

"Okay, Mom."

Samantha sipped some coffee and then went back to folding up the sheets Ida had loaned her to sleep on during the night. Instead of sleeping in bed with Kelly, she opted to let her mom keep him company during the night, in case he was restless. It was more her idea than her mother's. She cared for her brother deeply, even though at times it seemed as though she didn't. From what details her mom had told her about the tragedy at the house, he needed as much loving and understating as she could give.

"Ida, I don't know how I could ever repay you for letting us stay here with you. I just couldn't stay at Davis' place with him being gone and all." Susan said.

"You're my friend, of course I'm going to let you stay here. Your family has been through such a horrible time. It's the least that I could do. Where are you going to move to?"

"It's on the south side of the county. I can still keep the kids in the Caseville school district. I don't want to pull them away from their friends. Kelly has a best friend, and Sam's got a boyfriend. Plus, it wouldn't be beneficial for them to move during classes. And how could I ever go anywhere without talking to you all the time!"

"You've got that right!"

"Listen, Ida, after we get situated, I'll give you a call."

Susan hugged her and picked up the suitcase off the floor.

"All right kids! Let's move it.'

Samantha and Kelly appeared with suitcase in hand, and then gave their hostess a peck upon the cheek.

"You be sure to call me, Susan."

"No problem," she replied as they filed out the door.

After stopping to eat fast food, Susan took the interstate highway towards the end of town.

Kelly buried his nose into his book in the back of the car, while Samantha entertained herself by changing the radio from station to station in the front passenger seat.

The old brick house had burned completely to the ground. No foul play was associated in the matter. Alcohol was found in Richard's blood system, and his death was brushed aside as a drunken mishap; Susan knew better, though.

Harold's disappearance became a mystery to the community. Although he was considered peculiar and reclusive, no one understood why the old man left his house unlocked and all of his belongings untouched. For weeks, they searched the town for him, but, of course, came up unsuccessful. No criminal investigation was started in the matter of Susan's house, and no remains were ever discovered inside. Davis' death was ruled accidental, caused by a fatal fan blade induced injury and from head trauma sustained from his car hood and severe high winds. His body was cremated, which only fueled community speculation that his death was somehow related to the house fire and disappearance of Harold Snippet. The day after the fire, Ida went over to Mr. Snippet's house, rescued Pierre and dropped him off at the Humane Society.

Susan thought about Davis with every beat of her heart. At first, she wanted to blame herself for his death. But as time healed the sore wound, she understood that he gave his life for them, and she loved him even more for the kind act.

She rolled down her window and a gentle morning breeze glided upon her skin. It was cool and satisfying. The sun continued to lift skyward, brightening the world more and more as it rose.

A new day was upon them—warm, pleasant and full of promise. She had to look onward to a new horizon. Whatever card life was about to deal her, she had to look at it with eagerness and anticipation. Though loved ones have passed on, they are always present in spirit and in heart, and it's there that they will always remain.

Chapter 16

THE REVIVAL

The headlights of the car spliced through the night around two-thirty in the morning.

Ida Allison felt tired and drained after working a double shift at the hospital. The night before she had spoken to Susan about how she and the kids were enjoying their new house, and that they made plans to get together soon. Susan had refused to set eyes upon the old house in its ruins, even after eight months time. According to her, as long as the place was in ashes, she was happy.

Ida's car continued to travel down State Street as Denton Road approached on the right.

Though she could take State to Lexington to Chandler—all paved roads—to get home, she could cut across on Denton and come out upon Chandler and save time.

Changing her route, she slowed down and got off on Denton.

The car shimmied upon the rough ground.

"Shit! I knew there was a reason I don't take this stupid road."

The car rocked and rolled slowly past the Snippet farmhouse and then approached Susan's old house.

Gone, burnt to a crisp, she marveled.

The little tool shed stood off in back of the house, alone and still intact like a tombstone or memorial monument.

Too bad she didn't torch that little thing, too.

She eyed the charred wreckage while drifting by it; a cold sensation tingled upon her skin, causing the hair on her arms to rise.

Shaking off the chill, she concentrated back on her driving.

A man appeared standing on the side of the road across the street from the house.

He was tall, bearded, with a ghastly-white complexion, and wore a large, black coat.

Her mouth gaped open in surprise and she couldn't move a muscle if she tried.

He watched her, consumed.

She passed by him slowly, staring all the way, unable to pull away her glance.

He met her stare and followed it as the car passed.

Trails of sweat dripped down her forehead. She gripped the steering wheel tighter with clammy hands and wiped the sweat away.

For her ensuing trip home, the vision of the haunting figure replayed over and over inside of her mind like a bad dream, and with it followed the disturbing hold of the silence.

LaVergne, TN USA
17 August 2009
155088LV00010B/115/P